THE CALABAR HOARD
A PICTISH TREASURE

THE CALABAR HOARD
A PICTISH TREASURE

JAMES C. RANKINE

The Book is a Work of Fiction, Names, Characters, Places and Incidents are either products of the author's imagination or are used fictitiously. Any resemblance to actual events or locales or persons, living or dead is entirely coincidental.

Copyright © 2009 by James C Rankine

ISBN 978-0-9537466-3-7

To my wife, Margaret, for her patience, support and forbearance.

Acknowledgements

For Godfrey and Jean Fairbairn and Bill Duthie who checked the manuscript and made valuable suggestions.

For Steve Johnstone for his assistance.

THE CALABAR HOARD : A PICTISH TREASURE

HISTORICAL NOTE

THE PICTS

During the early medieval period from the third to the tenth centuries part of what is now Scotland was inhabited by a people called the Picts. They predominated in the area north of the River Forth for long periods before disappearing from history, leaving little trace of their language and culture. No written records, a few names from King lists, some place names recognisable as being of Pictish origin, constitute most of what is known about them, apart from meagre archaeological material, unearthed in recent times. The most significant relics of that little known people are the large numbers of sculptured standing stones that are scattered over their presumed territory. Most such stones are weathered, broken, half buried, cannibalised for building material, or are yet to be discovered.

List of Characters

RUTH, BARONESS MCFRANKLIN, aged 79 years, educationist, antiquarian, and a national heroine; lives in Allanford

BELLE RAMSAY, aged 45 years, Deputy Principal of a Further Education College; lives in Queenstown

RODDY NEILSON, aged 44 years, Member of the Scottish Parliament, partner of Belle Ramsay; lives in Queenstown

DUNCAN MCNAUGHTON (Rangi), aged 31 years, part Burmese, Information Technology graduate, divorced and living with his mother in the village of Naughtonwood

CHEONG YU (Jade), aged 33 years, Singaporean Chinese research scientist working in a research facility in Aberbrothy; lives in Milltown-on Devon

SIR RAB BRUCE, aged 55 years, billionaire owner of Drumannan Holdings, a multi-national conglomerate with interests across the world in oil and engineering; lives in Drumannan.

NATASHA BRUCE, aged 46 years, widow of a Russian oil tycoon, married to Sir Rab Bruce; lives in Drumannan.

MURDO MACLEAN McMANNAN, aged 35 years, world renowned pop star, creator of the group Triple M.; lives in Queenstown.

CATRIONA McMANNAN, aged 34 years, famous film star, married to Murdo MacLean McMannan; lives in Queenstown.

ANGELA BULL, aged 50 years, Professor of Archaeology at St. Regulus University; lives in Crail

THE CALABAR HOARD : A PICTISH TREASURE

CHAPTER ONE.

RUTH, NAUGHTONWOOD, 2009

The trapdoor creaked, and fell open with a solid thump on the flagstone floor. The old woman tentatively shone her torch to reveal a short flight of wooden stairs into a kind of cellar. Gingerly she edged her way down and turned to face the darkness. The beam of light illuminated a recumbent stone slab of reddish sandstone some eight feet in length. On the upturned face was sculpted a collection of symbols with the outline of a fish predominant. Two other symbols were abstract designs. Below them a hunting scene was depicted. Towards the bottom of the stone appeared lines of script. Only the words Regnum Nechtani in Latin were decipherable.

The woman gasped with excitement. A Pictish Sculptured Stone! And with writing on it! And unweathered! It must have been protected here for centuries. Ruth McFranklin subsided on the cellar steps, contemplating with delight the unexpected archaeological find.

The previous week Ruth, Baroness McFranklin, had received a letter from a firm of solicitors informing her that she had been bequeathed the holiday cottage of a former lover from her youth, the student leader of a university group called the Pict Hunters, the expeditions of which had generated a lifelong enthusiasm for that lost people who had lived in Scotland in the so-called Dark Ages.

A life-long conspiracy drove Ruth and her lover apart. Both had married and pursued very different careers. After the violent death of his wife, her lover had become a virtual recluse until his recent death in Edinburgh. Now, 60 years after their love affair Ruth now sat in a cellar below the garage of a cottage in the village of Naughtonwood, Drumannanshire, a few miles from her own home. The cottage was hers for her lifetime. On her death it would revert to her lover's children. The letter had intimated that the reason for the legacy was the possible archaeological importance of the house and its surroundings. Ruth was enjoined to investigate the cellar below the garage in memory of "our old Pict hunting days". Clearly her lover had never forgotten those innocent boisterous times at St Regulus University.

Consumed with curiosity by the bequest and its intriguing letter, Ruth had made the short journey round the shoulder of the Ochil Hills along the hillfoots to the village of Naughtonwood.

With mounting excitement Ruth slowly crouched and sidled almost reverently round the huge stone, examining the sculptures in detail. She identified the abstract symbols as two of most common seen on similar stones. Would there be anything on the reverse side? Impossible to see! She waved the torch beam around. The cellar contained no other artifacts but seemed to curve round beyond the boundary wall of the building. Huge stones formed the walls overlapping inwards until the final stones made the low roof. Ruth crowed with delight. She was in a weem or earth house. It was clear that archaeologists would have to be called in to verify what she had uncovered and to record every detail.

Obviously her lover, Weelum, had discovered the stone, choosing to keep it a secret until she fell heir to the little house and its garage with the hidden treasure below.

His house was situated in the village of Naughtonwood, nicknamed Calabar, the Gaelic for "haven on the hill" of generations of highland cattle drovers. Weelum had lived in it as a boy with his aunt who left it to him when she died. He had retained it as a holiday home when his career progressed and he moved to Edinburgh and London.

Ruth climbed the steps out of the cellar, her head filled with ideas about how best to have the find investigated. Her unrestrained whoop as the trapdoor thudded shut startled a passer by in the Stinking Wynd outside.

With renewed interest Ruth explored the nondescript ex-mining village that was Naughtonwood. (Nechtans wood) The very name suggested Picts loud and clear. Its situation at the top of the steep southern ridge of the Devon Valley, flanked by a burn to the east and west, with its southern aspect guarded by a sparsely inhabited hinterland, formerly the northern edge of the great forest of Drumannan, made it a good defensive position. The Nechtan of old, whoever he was, had chosen wisely. The address of Weelum's house was similarly intriguing. Number 2 The Castle was situated halfway up a steep unsurfaced lane at the junction with another narrower lane called The Stinking Wynd. It had previously been a smallholding with a small field behind. Ruth remembered Weelum say that his grandparents had kept a cow in the byre attached to the house. Would there be any other remains in the neighbourhood? Did the street name Castle have any significance? The village had expanded in size with the advent of mining. Much had been destroyed and rebuilt over the years. There was however enough evidence for an archaeological evaluation of the site with a possible "dig". Her mind made up, Ruth determined to contact Weelum's children. She knew his daughter Belle. Flipping open her mobile phone she dialed the number.

CHAPTER TWO

NECHTAN AND ANGUS, AT COILLE NECHTAN: MID EIGHTH CENTURY

Angus, nephew of King Nechtan (or Naughton), High King of the Pictish Tribes, bowed to the imposing figure of his uncle.

"Your treasure is stored safely in the weem," he reported. Angus had led an advance party of the King's retinue to his southern bastion on the edge of Coille Nechtan (Nechtans Wood), stretching from the Ochil Hills in the north, to the River Forth in the west and south, and far into Fife in the east. The area was a favourite hunting ground of the King and his nobles. Largely uninhabited, it was a mixture of forest, heath and bog. The title the Picts held to the area was an uneasy one. It was the debatable land, fought over by the Angles, the British of Strathclyde, and the Picts. Raiders from the other side of the North Sea often ravaged its shores, Friesians and others from further afield. Now the Picts were in ascendancy and Nechtan was trying to strengthen his grip on the territory by spending more time south of the Ochils. He had begun to build a fortification, and was encouraging settlers to establish farms and settlements in the area. Already a number of garths were occupied- Garto, Gartmorn, Gartenkeir, Gartary, Gartwhinzean. King Nechtan's place was the only stone building in his base on a commanding ridge to the south of the River Devon. Cunningly he had built it over the site of an old weem or earth house used by earlier inhabitants of the area. The entrance to the weem was concealed under his own bedchamber. It was to there that Angus and his trusted lieutenants had brought the treasure that accompanied the King on his peregrinations throughout his Kingdom.

"The fewer people who know where the treasure is the better, Angus," he said sharply to his nephew.

"You brought it here under the cover of darkness as I ordered?"

"Yes, sir. Only my most loyal men know of its whereabouts."

Nechtan grunted. "Good! When we've settled in I want you to organise a boar hunt but first I have an important mission for you. I have intelligence from the King of Fife that there is a raiding party of Friesians somewhere in the River Forth and activity by the Angles south of the River. There may be nothing to the report but, as you know I am suspicious of my traitorous son, Taloran. He has almost certainly taken refuge with the Angles and he might try to gain their support to usurp my throne. We have only a small force of sixty warriors with us, not enough to defend this area against a big attack. I've sent for reinforcements but they will take time to muster during harvest time. I want you to contact the Gillieserfs in the forest. They are my eyes and ears. If there is any untoward activity they will know of it. Take half a dozen of your best men and report back by nightfall".

Cursing inwardly Angus quickly organised the scouting party. He had hoped for some respite after the long trip through the hills. There was a girl at Garto….. She would have to wait. He thought of his arrogant cousin, Taloran. He had suffered insults from the older man when, as a boy, he had visited the court. He hoped the rumours were true. Now that he was a full grown warrior he felt he would be a match for the sneering Taloran.

Angus tensed. The forest remained silent. A leaf quivered. He knew they were there, the watchers. How often they had surrounded intruders, unseen until they revealed themselves. Angus feared the Gillieserfs, the so-called followers of St. Serf, the Christian missionary from nearby Culross who had lived there centuries before. Small dark men, they lived like ghosts in the depths of the great forest, an expanse of dense oak, open heath, bog and deep gorges. Most people avoided the forest, fearful of the savagery of the mysterious Gillieserfs, nominally Christian but practising pagan rituals, headhunting, and, so the story went, able to call on the spirits of the forest to bewitch men who crossed them. They had few fixed settlements, preferring to hunt and forage for berries and roots, taking deer and wild boar with the tacit permission of King Nechtan. He maintained an uneasy relationship with them. Technically under his suzerainty, the people of the forest retained memories of other overlords who had attempted to wipe them out, and were grateful for his tolerance of their way of life. In return they gave advance warning of raiders.

Reining in his pony, Angus held up his hand to halt his escort. The ten long-haired, mustachioed warriors unsheathed their long swords, dropping easily from their stirrupless saddles. Protectively they closed round the King's nephew, peering cautiously into the oak grove. They had journeyed south beyond Gartmorn, one of the few Pictish farms near the edge of the forest. Now they were on a bluff high above the River Dubh Devon, rumbling in a ravine far below. It was a favourite meeting place for receiving intelligence from the Gillieserfs.

Noiselessly a dozen naked tribesmen materialised from the screen of foliage, tattooed all over, bows at the ready. Angus lowered the blade of his sword, signalling to the others to do likewise. Hesitantly they obeyed, eyeing the leader of the savages, a wizened shaman-cum-headman with a necklace of bones and a couple of human skulls hanging from his belt. Incongruously he was leaning on a staff with a Christian cross atop it. Angus gazed arrogantly at the group. He knew better than to show uneasiness or indecision.

"I am Lord Angus. You have news for King Nechtan?"

The shaman eyed him rheumily, half stifling a bronchial cough.

"We have not met before, young man. Do you have the ear of the King?"

Angus had some difficulty in understanding the dialect the old man was speaking. It sounded outlandish to his northern ears but it was just comprehensible.

"Yes, you insolent savage! The King sent me as his emissary."

Ignoring Angus's harsh tone, the shaman enquired about the health of Nechtan, the latest number of his offspring, and his success in hunting. Containing his youthful impatience, Angus replied in kind, drawing a sardonic toothless grimace from the shaman.

"We have noticed the game animals are restless, moving steadily north. We have sighted smoke in the east. Our kinsfolk to the south have passed on disturbing news. The Friesians are here. They are looting and burning. Aberdour and Inverkeithing are in flames. They are approaching Kincardine."

"As close as that," Angus whistled. "We will need to send a counterforce to repel them."

"I think not, my Lord. Our scouts have seen a fleet of a hundred ships in the River Forth. Our old enemies, the Angles have returned, this time in overwhelming force. I fear my tribe will be exterminated."

Angus was thunderstruck.

"Are you certain? This isn't just exaggeration?"

The old man pushed forward a lean sinewy figure.

"My son saw them himself."

Thinking rapidly, Angus calculated. A hundred ships meant at least a thousand men, a staggering force. There was no way King Nechtan's small band could withstand such superiority in numbers. The King must be informed with all possible haste.

"Keep us informed of any movement north," Angus ordered the shaman. "They are less than a day's march away."

"We'll keep watch but what about my folk?" the old man asked, for the first time showing anxiety.

"Retreat before them. Screen us as we fall back over the Ochils, or hide in the forest as you have done in the past," shouted Angus as he wheeled his horse and whipped it into a gallop.

***

Thin trails of smoke drifted over the huddle of wattle and daub huts surrounding a stone building situated on top of an eminence in their midst. The standard of King Nechtan drooped lazily above. Some warriors lounging around the fort straightened sharply as they sensed the urgency of the rapidly approaching horsemen. A carnyx blared the alarm, its harsh note rousing the warriors, women and children into a frenzy of activity, grabbing spears, drawing barriers across the entrances to the village and rounding up horses and livestock. Halfway up the slope to the fort a large workshop spilled forth workmen carrying tools. The fire in the forge inside was smothered. King Nechtan appeared, his hunting dogs snarling around him.

Angus and his troop pulled up in a lather of sweat and spume. Angus flung himself off his pony and knelt in front of his King, pouring out his story. Nechtan questioned him closely, brow furrowed.

"Are you certain about that?" he thundered. "I need facts. Rumours abound."

Angus flushed.

"I spoke with the shaman's son who himself counted the number of boats in the River. I myself saw the pyres of smoke to the south."

"Hm! It seems there's no doubt. Our main host has not even mustered at Forteviot. It will take two or three weeks at least before it could form up south of the Ochils. We have sent most of our pack animals back north to help. With our small force here we are in mortal danger.

I'll wager that traitorous dog Taloran is behind this invasion. To think of it! My only son seeking the help of the Angles to usurp my throne."

Spitting in disgust, Nechtan called his captains and issued the kind of decisive orders that had made him such an effective leader.

"We can't defend this area against numbers like that. We must withdraw and regroup north of the Ochil Hills. There is no time to lose. Angus, load up the most valuable pieces of my treasure, only as much as one pack horse can carry. Collapse the fort in on itself, destroying everything else. Fire the village; let other settlements know if possible. You yourself take six men back south to act as a screen and warn us of the enemy's approach. Don't fight. Report back with numbers, positions, and the amount of time we have."

"Sir, what about the monument we have nearly finished carving? It is the finest work I have ever done, and it is for your glorification." The sculptor was in tears.

"Hide it as best you can. Put it in the weem beside your workshop if there's time.. Angus and his men will help your workmen to move it," shouted the King fiercely.

Soon a straggle of women, children and slaves, escorted by warriors, was wending its way down into the mosses and hags of the valley of the River Devon, across the ford, and into the hills at Dollar before the trek through Glen Quey to Auchterarder and Forteviot.

Angus sent two men to the east, two to the west, while he and the remaining two rode cautiously south, the likeliest line of approach. Breasting a rise at the top of a clay brae they were amazed to sight a long column of warriors advancing through the Gartmorn valley with mounted men in the van. They would reach the fort in half an hour. Wheeling their ponies the three men galloped back the way they had come. They had been spotted. With whooping cries the Anglian scouts gave chase. Thundering down the reverse slope to the smoking village Angus bellowed to the others to go on.

"I have business at Garto."

"You are foolish, sir. The girl's not worth it," his principal lieutenant threw back over his shoulder as he whipped his pony to greater efforts.

"I'll be fine," called Angus fiercely. "You warn the King. I'll be with you shortly."

Heading for the little farm at Garto he was suddenly confronted by a mounted figure, accoutred as a Pictish warrior. Angus pulled up, astonished at the sight. There should be no warrior so far south.

A mocking shout provided the explanation.

"Cousin Angus, we meet again. Hand over your sword. I need you as a hostage."

Angus recoiled in shock. The King's son, Taloran, had received the help of the Angles with a vengeance. Mounted on a sixteen hand horse he presented a formidable presence, arrogantly pointing his long sword at his lightly mounted cousin.

"Don't resist. You may be my father's favourite and heir to his throne but that is about to change, you miserable stripling. I will be the new King when my friends the Angles defeat King Nechtan. Now be my prisoner or lose your life."

Angus estimated his chances. Taloran had not realised that his cousin was no longer a mere boy. He had filled out, practising the martial arts with dedication, and had proved himself fighting the Scots. Taloran was alone, having out-distanced his escort in his desperation to capture Angus. It looked as though he wanted to fight on horseback although the Pictish tradition was to dismount to fight on foot.

Angus roared defiance.

"You betrayed your father. You are an outlaw. Surrender to me and the King might treat you leniently."

Taloran sneered, urging his warhorse into a charge.

"You young fool. You've lost your chance to be a hostage. I'll kill you instead".

Angus's nimble-footed pony skittered aside, avoiding the heavy warhorse as it thundered past along the peaty edge of the sacred Garto pool. The horse skidded as it was wrenched round by a furious Taloran, canting him sideways out of his stirrupless saddle. Cursing he tried to right himself.

Angus thrust his pony against the flank of the heavier horse and simultaneously slashed the exposed throat of his opponent. Taloran's body pitched sideways off his horse into the peaty edge of the pool, sinking slowly out of sight in the murky water. His horse bolted.

Angus, disbelieving, peered into the water, fully expecting him to surface. The lucky slashing sword stroke must have mortally wounded him. Breathing heavily in shock at the sudden end to the fight, Angus gazed anxiously around, fearful of other approaching foes. A surge of movement on the crest of the rise to the south revealed a troop of mounted men in full cry after him. Whirling his pony he galloped headlong towards the village. His luck was in. Local knowledge of tracks through the scrub allowed him to gain on his pursuers until he rejoined his troop on the outskirts of the burning village. Without pause he led them down the steep slope to the River Devon, catching up with the stragglers of the retreating Picts. Soon he was informing King Nechtan of the extent of the invasion of the Angles and the proximity of their leading elements. He did not mention the fight with Taloran or its outcome. After all Taloran was the son of the King.

CHAPTER THREE

BELLE RAMSAY: QUEENSTOWN, 2009

Belle woke, frightened and choking. Roddy clutched her to him, soothing her trembling body.

"Another nightmare," he quizzed.

Belle nodded violently, fearful, sobbing and unable to speak.

"I'll get you a cup-----"

"No! Just don't leave me".

The nightmare was the worst of her recurring dreams. She usually awoke feeling that she was drowning in a maelstrom of blood, fountaining in an impossible stream from her mother's throat. The nightmare began with a vision of her mother lying, face mottled with blood, in the smouldering ruins of her home with Belle trying to stem the blood flowing from her wounds, and screaming away her girlish innocence into the stickiness in her hands, in her hair, on her face, and in her mouth. Then the enormous jetting spout engulfed her, awaking her howling in the darkness of the bedroom.

Tonight had been the worst yet after all these years since her mother had been fatally injured in an I.R.A. bomb attack.

Belle had not been there when it happened. A hushed Head teacher had uncomfortably broken the news to her at school. No one had ever described the scene. The nightmare was fantasy and horror born of the shock to her adolescent mind. The dreams will fade a doctor had said. But they had not. This was a really bad one. It would be followed by an intense migraine lasting two days at least, leaving her drawn and depressed.

The bomb dream was one of a series that tormented her, all connected to her mother and father. The dreams were very often triggered by political events. Both parents had been active politicians, their home always overflowing with ideas, theories, and gossip. As a young girl Belle enjoyed the excitement, the arguments, and the merriment. Her parents lived life to the full and transmitted their joy to their children.

The tragedy all these years ago had scarred Belle. Although she retained her mother's Hungarian insouciance, her gypsy looks and fiery temper, there was something in the core of her being that faced the world sometimes with a coldness and hardness that frightened her. It made close acquaintances and colleagues wary of her. Only very close friends appreciated the sudden moods and made allowances.

Qualified as a lawyer Belle had switched to education as a matter of social conscience which was rapidly deserting her. In her present position, Deputy Principal of St. Bernard's Further Education College, she was becoming disillusioned with the politics of education and with politics in general. It was an irony that her present partner was an active politician himself.

Belle hugged her knees. Sometimes she felt that Roddy was drifting away from her, or rather she was becoming more distant from him. The tea appeared. He knew better than to make some hearty remark, merely placing it on the bedside table. A quick look at the tightly closed eyes gave him all the warning he needed. He hunched his thickset body round his hot chocolate wishing it were a single malt whisky. An incipient ulcer made him careful of his alcohol intake, much to Belle's disgust. She thoroughly enjoyed her alcohol, especially red wine. Roddy resembled her father, both in looks and temperament although his commitment to socialist principles was suspect. Belle sometimes thought that her advocate partner saw the Labour Party as the best means of advancement in Scottish politics. Chiding herself for such disloyal thoughts she reached out and squeezed his hand. Roddy was charming and attentive, and an inventive lover. He responded to her wan smile with a grin of relief.

"Leave the curtains closed tomorrow morning, Roddy. The migraine you know."

Nodding his understanding he backed out of the room closing the door on her misery.

***

Grey light filtered into the room. Belle blinked awake. No migraine! Cautiously she lifted her head. Still no funny head! She fell back with a sigh of relief. Nearly midday. She had slept for twelve hours. Saturday. They had planned to go hill walking, one of their shared interests, second only to golf and fishing. Pict hunting on the other hand left Roddy curiously uninterested. He scoffed at her enthusiasm for heaps of old stones. There was still time to reach the Ochils from their Queenstown home in the afternoon if she hurried.

Belle groaned as the phone rang. Delay!

"Ruth, how are you? You sound a lot more cheerful than you were when we last met."

Belle regarded Ruth with some affection and not a little awe. A wary meeting about her father's will had started a growing friendship. Belle was intrigued by Ruth's tales of the young lovers, scarcely believing the portrait of Weelum as a harum-scarum student, giggling at the thought of a government minister-to-be shyly introducing his middle class girl into a mining village society.

"I have some amazing news for you Belle, dear. It concerns your father's house. I'm not going to tell you any more. I would like you to join me there this afternoon, please."

I would love to, Ruth, but I have something planned. We're going to do the Dollar-Glendevon walk."

"Naughtonwood is on the way. If I mention the word "Picts" will that tempt you to break your journey?"

Belle did not demur.

"We'll be there at two o'clock," she laughed.

Belle was euphoric, infecting Ruth with her excitement.

"This is the first time I've been involved in a discovery," she crowed. I'll bet you were like this as well when you found the Fish Cross. Good old Dad! What a wonderful thing to do! He must have loved you as much as he loved Mum. What are you going to do about further investigation, Ruth?"

"You mean, what are we going to do," replied Ruth, winking at Roddy, "We are in this together if you can collect yourself together sufficiently to think rationally." Roddy watched the two women indulgently

"I can hardly believe what I'm seeing. Two no nonsense professional women behaving like teenage girls at a pop concert are worth a photograph."

He produced a digital camera.

"That's a thought, Roddy. You can be our cameraman."

Suddenly Ruth was all business.

"We need a sponsor if we want a dig established. Unfortunately the top of the Castle Lane has been mostly built over with modern housing but Weelum had the good sense to retain the little field to the north-east of the house. That has possibilities for further discoveries. We must send or take photos of the stone, the weem, and the surroundings to Archaeology Departments of selected Universities. They'll be falling over themselves to get their hands on the stone at least. A dig is another matter. Money is involved, local authorities, government departments, university budgets, museums. Come on, Roddy. I'll show you the camera angles. Belle, you stay out of the way and drool."

CHAPTER FOUR

THE MCNAUGHTONS
JOHN MCNAUGHTON: BURMA, 1947

The boy whimpered. Savagely the man pressed him to his bare chest, his knobbly hand covering mouth and nose. Shocked into silence the two year old burrowed into his father's chest, quivering with fright. Tomb like, the darkness was complete. The clanging boom of wood on metal caused reverberations to travel through the massive empty boiler. The boy's little body arched in terror. The father stilled him with a hiss. A fusillade of shots caromed off the tank to the accompaniment of hoarse shouts of command. Gradually the sounds faded and after a while ceased.

The man waited, sweltering in the confined space, trying to soothe the child. Two hours later, the boy asleep on his shoulder, he eased open the inspection trap on the tank. Cautiously he surveyed the immediate area, straining to pick up the slightest sound. Satisfied he wriggled free and lifted the boy to the ground. The plantation buildings were wrecked and smouldering. Corpses lay around some slashed with dahs, others with bullet wounds.

"Good boy, Peter," he muttered, as the child rubbed his eyes, half awake. Humping him on his back he ghosted through the debris, constantly admonishing him to keep quiet. The bungalow was gutted by fire with all his possessions inside.

"We'll have to get out of here fast, Peter. These terrorists will be back," Jock McNaughton murmured, "We'll make for the Sittang. There are British troops in Toungoo."

Peter sniffed, knitting his fingers into his father's hair.

"Juice," he coughed.

"Later, Peter," Jock whispered.

He was now the ex-manager of the plantation. He realised he could never return. Burma was in chaos. His Karen wife was dead. The British were pulling out fast. Grimly he trudged through the regimented rows of the rubber plantation and into the jungle beyond, squelching along a muddy track to the river bank.

He was ill equipped for the trek, having been in bed when the attack came. He was clad in trousers and sandals only and carrying a snatched prepared haversack, while Peter had a nappy and a scrap of favourite blanket. Both were vulnerable to the perils of the wilderness. Plagued by mosquitoes McNaughton struggled on. A shot went off to his right. He knew what it was. He had stumbled into a trip wire. Ahead was a village, silent, aware of intruders. From the far side of the clearing came seemingly random fire, followed by the deeper yammer of a Bren gun. A British gun! Crouching, he slipped along a bund at the side of a small paddy field, reaching a deep chaung. Cursing under his breath he cast about for a boat. There, a canoe with a few inches of freeboard! Sliding silently over the sleek black water he manoeuvred the craft to the far shore, sweating as Peter shifted, nearly tipping them into the water.

"Stay still, son, for God's sake. You'll have us over."

Horrendously close, the Bren hammered again. A British voice called on him to halt. Relief flooded him. An army patrol!

Burma 1947. The last days of the Raj! Half a dozen warring factions trying to seize control of the country when the last British battalion sailed down the Rangoon River. The Burmese Prime Minister and his Cabinet gunned down in their office. Burma was on the brink of anarchy. And here he was a British Army deserter with no future in the country.

Jock Mc Naughton stood up.

"Don't shoot. I'm a British soldier.

***

"I don't know what to do with you, McNaughton."

The Commandant of the transit camp in Rangoon picked at his sweat stained shirt, frowning as he examined the A.B. 64, Jock's tattered pay book.

"Royal Engineer, absent without leave since 1945; unit back in the U.K. You claim this child is yours, and has no other family. We are pulling out. The last troop ship leaves next week. You'll be court-martialled of course when you arrive there. Meantime you remain under arrest.. I've no idea about the status of the child, and I have no time to sort it out legally. Have you anyone in the U.K. who could look after the child?"

"Yes, Sir. My sister will take care of Peter." stammered the sweating deserter, tripping over his words as hope rose within him. He had been fearful that they would jail him, leaving Peter behind.

"It's all highly irregular. I'll have to seek advice. I've no sympathy for a deserter but the child……….."

"Please Sir, Peter means everything to me. You can't leave him in this shit hole."

"You should have thought of that when you got yourself involved with the girl," said the Colonel dryly.

"Look, there's a medical unit on board the S.S. Devonshire. We'll put the boy with the nurses.""

Liverpool docks a month later.

"Helen, this is my son, Peter. Please look after the little chap. It'll be at least two years."

CHAPTER FIVE

PETER MCNAUGHTON: NAUGHTONWOOD 1985

A dull rumble and a cloud of smoke was the signal for Peter (Chinky) McNaughton to begin his "brushing "shift, extending the main tunnel of the coal mine. The explosive charge had brought down a large heap of sodden grey lumps of solid stone and sticky rubble. Chinky's job was to clear it on to hutches to be wheeled to the mine head, and to erect a new set of roof girders to support the heading of the tunnel.

To what purpose he thought as he strained to move the heavy sludgy muck with his wide shovel. This mine will shut in a matter of weeks. We've lost the coal seam and they tell me it will cost millions of pounds to develop a new one. Maybe tomorrows strike will change Thatcher's mines closure policy. Bloody woman!

Chinky McNaughton was half Burmese, a small wiry man with raven black straight hair, an olive skin and eyes with a slight slant. A Scot in every other way, he was nevertheless set aside by these physical characteristics, for ever an outsider, an object of curiosity to the children of the mining village of Naughtonwood. Most fellow workers and neighbours joked good naturedly about his appearance although there had been a few ugly incidents- catcalls in the streets, sneers directed at his wife Janet for marrying a foreigner, and on occasion a stone through his council house window.

Chinky's reputation as a hard man and the fact that both he and Janet had grown up in the village prevented more extreme harassment He was quick to take offence, quarrelling readily and making up just as readily. The pair had three children. This generation showed fewer signs of their mixed ancestry. The oldest, Duncan, (nicknamed Rangi, short for Rangoon) had little trace of his unknown Burmese grandmother. Chinky was reticent about his father and the mother who was only a wisp of memory. His father had disappeared when he was young, to make his fortune in America he boasted. He would come back for his son. He never did. Brought up by his aunt Chinky was a typical product of his mining background, socialist to the core, loyal to his trade union.

Strangely Chinky was scornful of higher education. Most miners wanted their sons out of the mines. He and Janet quarrelled about their bright young son, Rangi, who, Janet was determined, should go to university.

"Ye'll go to uni and get a collar and tie job."

Aye, and who's gaun' tae pey for it?" mocked Chinky, "He'll be lucky if he doesn't finish up on the dole-like me if we lose this strike."

"I thought you said the miners would win, Peter," said Janet anxiously.

The strike had started off violently as Scargill faced up to the Thatcher Government

"This demonstration in London tomorrow is our best chance to make our case"

"Well, be careful. You've already had a hammering from the polis. Watch that temper of yours."

"Aye, aye!"

Chinky winked at Rangy.

"Your mammy's an auld fusspot. If you were big enough you would come with me, would ye no?"

Eight-year old Rangy stared at his father solemnly. The coal dust impregnated hands were shaking. His dad was scared.

***

The police line buckled, broke. Howls of triumph exploded from contorted faces as stubble faced miners surged through. Chinky kept low, swinging his steel capped boots into the ribs of a fallen police sergeant. Too late he saw the police horse rear over him. His scream was cut short as a hoof caught him on the side of his head, fracturing his skull and slicing off his left ear. Sent reeling, he was smashed to the ground by the crush of shouting men. The press moved on, leaving groggy stragglers in its wake, some sitting hunched elbows on knees, head in hands, or limping away from the melee. One body lay motionless. The sergeant Chinky had kicked winced as he crawled over to attend to the silent figure.

"Not much we can do for this one," he snarled to the approaching ambulance man, "What's a Chinaman doing here anyhow?"

CHAPTER SIX

DUNCAN (RANGI) MCNAUGHTON: WALLACETOWN, 2007

"Let's see now, McNaughton, you've been with us a couple of years now. The reports I get show that you are a bright young man with lots of ideas, just the kind of fellow we need here at Californian Computers. So what's all this I hear about unionisation? You know we won't have unions in this company."

The squat American took off his rimless glasses and rubbed his watery eyes.

"You knew that when you joined us. What's your game, buster?"

"Mr. Sikorski, the recent Act states that if a majority of the work force wishes to join a union then the Company has to acquiesce. Of the 300 workers at this Company 194 have indicated that they want to join the Union of Technological Workers. I have been appointed their representative and am here to establish an agreement with the management about future negotiations over pay and conditions. Here is a draft of our demands."

Sikorsky's tongue flicked over his blubber lips as he considered Rangy through bushy eyebrows. He reached over and painstakingly tore the document into precise little pieces.

"Demands is it? Well let me tell you Mr. Union Man, that no employee makes demands in this Company. I told that dam fool Board back in L.A. that it was a big mistake to invest in this tin pot little country. You Brits are all too uppity. This interview is terminated."

Rangy blinked nervously. He had been flattered when people had urged him to be their representative. A keen member of the local branch of the Labour Party, he felt strongly about unions and thought that the new Act would ensure the success of his case. The contemptuous dismissal of his carefully worded paper dismayed him, and the arrogance of Sikorsky's attitude towards his country angered him.

But Mr. Sikorsky, The Act has to be obeyed. You can't......."

"Don't say can't to me, boy. Bugger the Act."

Heaving himself upright to his 5 feet 3 inches in height, he lowered at Rangy.

"You're fired. Get out of the premises by the end of the day."

Crestfallen, Rangy reported back to his informal committee.

"We would like to support you, Rangy, but we can't afford to lose our jobs."

Later, even Moira Falkland, a buxom programmer who had encouraged him to approach the management, was cool. Miserably he retreated to the male toilets feeling sick. Seething, he overheard from his cubicle a conversation among a group of activists as they relieved themselves.

"A real innocent, that Rangi! The idealism shines out of his eyes."

"Aye, a sacrificial lamb, if ever there was one. We were able to keep our heads under the parapet while he took the flak. New Labour will be discredited now in the eyes of the workers. We'll persuade them that leftist policies are their best hope. I can't stand these wogs anyway. He's half Chinese isn't he?"

"No, Burmese. He should go back to the jungle where he belongs. I'll bet he didn't realise Moira was one of us, and was flirting with him for the sake of the party."

"Sssh! Don't say party. We're a debating group."

To general laughter they departed.

Long after they had gone Rangy sat in the cubicle, sick at heart. His fellow workers! His socialist ideals were crumbling round him. Stony faced he walked to his work station passing averted eyes. To complete his humiliation two security men watched closely as he collected his possessions and stumbled from his collision with capitalist reality.

"Yeah, Jake, it looks as though this Scottish operation is a bust. We're going to bump up against union power and that, combined with the market down turn, makes a removal to Eastern Europe a sensible idea."

Sikorsky listened to the voice on the phone as it issued terse instructions.

"O.K. I'll do that. Yeah, within a few days"

A week later Californian Computers closed down their Scottish operation.

***

Rangy stared at the badly creased sheet of paper, carefully flattening the fraying folds. The cheap stationery was yellowed with age and ingrained dirt and sweat. It had obviously lain in the mildewed wallet for years.

"Your father said that this should be given to you. I forgot all about it. I could never bring myself to clear out his stuff."

Janet McNaughton pawed aimlessly through the heap of insurance documents, birth certificates, old income tax forms, a building society pass book, a Miners' Union card, a broken pipe, a Royal Engineers cap badge, a ten rupee note, and a faded photograph of a laughing girl dressed in 1920s fashion. The photo was in such poor condition that the facial features could not easily be discerned. The hair style and the dress dated it. Blurry ink made the inscription on the back indecipherable save for the name Margaret Ramsay. A scuffed sealed envelope addressed to Mr. Duncan McNaughton completed the collection.

"Why have you left all this so long, Mammy? There's money involved here."

"The compensation paid for the funeral. I left everything else, his clothes, his ain wee box of private things, even his favourite chair. The others aren't interested. Your father wanted you to get all this."

Janet McNaughton looked bleakly at her oldest son.

"Your father thought you were the pick of the bunch. He certainly didn't show it, always belittling you, but he said you would puzzle out what to do with what he referred to as his big secret. There's a family mystery for you to unravel. So the least you can do is look through this stuff. Do it to please me, Duncan. I loved your father, thrawn though he was."

Janet broke suddenly. During all these years since the tragic death of Chinky she had maintained a silent composure only breaking it to rail at the Government, the Miners Union, and anyone else connected with her husband's murder, as she termed the incident. Now her shoulders slumped, a wail started in her throat and the loss stared from her eyes.

All Rangy could do was hold and rock her, the sound of her grief lost in his shoulder.

Most of the contents of the box were straightforward. A whole life insurance policy for £500, a few pounds in the building society account, a marriage certificate and the birth certificates of the family. There was however no birth certificate for his father and no explanation for the Royal Engineers cap badge, the rupee note, or the photograph. Janet was vague about the material.

"Every family has a collection of mementos like this. Your father never discussed his family. Your Grandfather disappeared leaving poor Peter to be brought up by his auntie."

Rangy had always been aware that he belonged to a lopsided family. With a plethora of uncles, aunties and cousins on one side and a blank on the other he soon learned not to question his father about the imbalance after encountering the famous scowl and being told to bugger off.

He eased open the old envelope. The yellowing sheet of paper, smudged and fragile, contained some typescript. One line jumped out before his puzzled eyes.

Dishonourable discharge from His Majesty's Armed Forces. 1947.

Rangy leaned back, flicking the document over so that his mother would not see the writing.

"You are right, Mammy. I'll have to research the family history."

CHAPTER SEVEN

SIR RAB BRUCE AND MURDO MCLEAN MCMANNAN: PERTHSHIRE, 2008

The gillie sounded anxious.

"The water's gey rough: the winds getting up to gale force. We'll catch nothing the day, sir."

The Gore-Tex clad figure in the bow of the broad beamed rowing boat half-turned.

"I think you're right………..Wow! I'm into one," he bellowed as his rod snapped down and the line screamed from the reel. "It feels like a good fish," he added excitedly, scrambling to his feet.

The boat lurched, throwing him to the side. A hurricane force gust did the rest. Tipping over, the boat deposited both men into the loch and capsized. Glad in their bulky fishing gear the men floundered, saved by their life jackets from going under. The gillie, Tam Stoddard, grabbed hold of the upturned boat and pulled his client alongside him. Sir Rab Bruce grimaced fiercely.

"I've kept hold of the rod. It's still on," he laughed.

"That's the least of our worries," muttered Tam, "we're far out in the loch and there isn't another boat out. Visibility is nil. We'll just have to drift and hope the wind drives us ashore. Break your line and forget the damned fish. We're in serious trouble, sir. It's early May. The water's freezing. Think hypothermia".

"As bad as that." Sir Rab sensed the fear in his gillie's voice.

"So, where are we likely to make landfall?

"This westerly gale will take us to the shore below Ben Ghobar. There's no habitation along that side of the loch except the odd isolated cottage or shooting lodge. It'll be a matter of luck if we land near one."

The pair relapsed into silence as the gale slapped three foot waves into their faces, forcing them to hang on with all their strength. Tam thought it was just as well the fifty-five-year old beside him was reasonably fit. Many of his clients, fat and puffing, would have lasted no time at all in these appalling conditions. The boat lurched from wave to wave as the wind continued unabated. Both men were now suffering badly. Tam began to think the worst. He heaved himself up on the hull and managed to pull the older man up to spread-eagle himself over the widest part of the boat. This manoeuvre gave them some respite. After ten minutes an indistinct shoreline appeared through the sheeting rain. The boat grated on shingle. Stumbling, they staggered up the little beach, collapsing on slate grey pebbles, sodden and shivering.

Tam tried to orientate himself. He thought he recognised the little beach as a place where he sometimes picnicked with his fishermen.

"There's a holiday lodge up the hill a bit. It'll probably be empty but at least we'll get some protection from this storm there."

The two bedraggled figures set off through a larch plantation, reaching a substantial house of grey stone huddled in the lee of a steep bluff.

"Good for you, Tam. A haven in the storm! I do believe it's occupied. I can see a couple of S.U.V. s outside."

They thundered on the door, thankful to see a light appear in the gathering gloom.

■ ■

"So you are Sir Rab Bruce. I've read about you and seen you on television sometimes but our paths have never crossed unfortunately. Welcome to my home, albeit a rented lodge."

"And you are Murdo McLean McMannan. I've certainly seen you on television and heard your voice constantly from my daughter's room at home."

Sir Rab and Tam, after a hot bath, a quick bite to eat and a comforting whisky in hand, were lounging in deep cushions on cosy armchairs.

"It is most kind of you to open up your home to two stranded fishermen. I don't know what we would have done without your wonderful hospitality," Sir Rab spoke with genuine gratitude, to Murdo's delight.

"Think nothing of it. You brought some excitement into what was becoming a fruitless week for me. I've rented this place as a retreat to give me peace to start on a new album. The muse has been totally absent I'm afraid. I'm about to give up and go home."

The mainspring of the internationally acclaimed pop group, Triple M, Murdo McLean McMannan, six feet two inches with a thatch of auburn hair had a handsome sculpted face with high cheek bones and lips that seemed to smile confidentially at everyone in his orbit. No wonder my daughter swoons thought Sir Rab sardonically. Even Tam's initial suspicion had thawed perceptibly under his charm.

Murdo studied the multimillionaire opposite him. Sir Rab was a legendary figure in Scotland, the epitome of the kind of entrepreneurial skill for which Scottish people used to be famed. Capitalising on the potential of North Sea oil, he had cornered the market to supply equipment and maintenance before entering the field of oil exploration and development, becoming a major player. Intriguingly he had married for the second time the widow of a Russian oil tycoon who had invested her massive fortune mainly in the west. Knighted for services to industry, he was a fervent Scot, scorning the opportunity to protect his interests by living overseas, unlike many of his rich contemporaries. Darkly jowled, his swarthy skin gave him a black Irish look, not uncommon among the people of the industrial lowlands of Scotland. His thinning grey hair topped a high brow, a heavy black eyebrow bar and grey, considering eyes. A slightly bulbous nose and wide expressive mouth with a ready shark's grin, which often confused people in the boardroom, not sure if there was humour behind it, made for a strong rather than handsome face. A man accustomed to power, to making decisions, with the leadership skills to ensure that these were acted on. It would be foolish to cross him, thought Murdo.

"You'll stay the night of course," Murdo offered, "This is more of a shooting lodge than a cottage. There's plenty of space and I'd enjoy the company."

Sir Rab demurred but without conviction. The ordeal had taken a lot out of him and he was enjoying the comfort of this house.

"We couldn't impose on………"

"You're not causing me any trouble. Please stay," Murdo interrupted.

Well, what about you, Tam? Have you any problem with that?"

"No sir. I'll phone the wife."

"That's settled then. The housekeeper will prepare your rooms."

So there's a housekeeper Sir Rab mused to himself. Murdo did not believe in roughing it. Tam disappeared with the housekeeper, leaving the host and his guest to settle down comfortably with their drinks. Soon they were deep in discussion, deploring the state of the country in general and the inadequacies of politicians in particular.

The United Kingdom was at an all time low. The economic down turn, the chaos in the Middle East causing a steep rise in oil prices, government incompetence, and the seeming disintegration of the Union, together with problems over immigration and race had resulted in disturbances in different parts of the country. A semi-fascist grouping, the Sons of St. George, had attracted a large following. In Scotland a minority S.N.P. government was so impotent that it could not get legislation enacted. People were disillusioned with politicians as never before. The country was in a dangerous mood.

Sir Rab found that Murdo was no bar room ranter. He cared deeply about the plight of Scotland and was desperate to do something constructive to remedy matters. Sir Rab, who had fully matured plans to rescue the situation, began to see how he could be helped by the younger man and his reputation. The pragmatic business man and the consummate musician were an unlikely pairing but within a year they had formed a bond.

CHAPTER EIGHT

SIR RAB BRUCE

The village of Drumannan straggles down the long slope from the old tower which dominates the landscape. The glory days of the tower as a hunting seat of kings had long gone. Now the heart of Drumannan was where the High Street, the Main Street, Port Street and Kirk Wynd converged at the remains of the old Tollbooth and, raised on a plinth, an ancient stone, reputed to be connected to the old sea god, Mannan. A rash of council housing surrounded the core of the village with its church, school, town hall and Cooperative Store.

It was in this mining village that Rab Bruce spent his early years, absorbing the atmosphere and skills of his father's engineering workshop. Jeemsie Bruce ran a precarious business repairing agricultural machinery and acting as a sub-contractor for minor jobs for surrounding industry. Rab was a quick learner and was soon adept at anything from using a lathe to tuning a car engine.

At the grim fortress-like school he was conscientious but dour. His teachers appreciated his attentiveness and his achievements were solid if not spectacular. Known for his fiery temper, he was a loner who made other boys wary. Uninterested in sport, he spent his spare time in or around the workshop, annoying the workmen with his curiosity.

At a time of segregation in secondary education Rab easily passed the so-called "Control" examination, graduating to Aberbrothy Academy where he excelled in Maths and Physics.

His father's decision to up sticks and establish an engineering business in Aberdeen astonished his wife, family and the community. Various comments, from risky, foolish, or just plain daft did not deter him. The North Sea Oil Industry is booming and I intend to be part of it was his response to the sneerers. Rab fully supported his father. Even aged thirteen he could see the possibilities.

Ten years later Bruce Engineering was well established and Rab had entered the firm with degrees in engineering and management. When his father died of a heart attack caused by overwork a year or so later Rab fell heir to an expanding business supplying the needs of the oil industry.

Rab moved into the oil business proper, acquiring the rights to minor fields. He took over a firm providing helicopters for the North Sea oil rigs. His career was in full flow. He had a penchant for taking over moribund and failing businesses, turning them into profitable concerns. He acquired a substantial property portfolio and expanded his interests overseas. Rab Bruce by the age of forty was a multi-millionaire. In the by-going he bought an engineering factory in Aberbrothy, transforming it into the hub of his manufacturing concerns, and thus beginning the rehabilitation of a once proud industrial tradition in Drumannanshire.

Intensely proud of his name, his native village and the royal Bruce connections with Drumannan, he spent much time patiently negotiating the purchase of the ruinous Bruce

Tower and planning permission to build a house alongside. He agreed to make the Tower a local history museum and conference centre.

He acquired a reputation as a ruthless dealer in business and a manipulative chairman of boards of directors of the organizations in which he was involved. He had learned to control his temper and had cultivated a smooth charm most of the time. Only occasionally did the mask slip and then strong men quailed before his wrath.

The abrupt departure of his first wife shocked him. Absorbed in his business interests, he had neglected his family life. His wife exchanged him for a lover who was home every night at five o'clock and never worked weekends, albeit that he earned only a modest salary. Their daughter accompanied her mother.

Rab determined to avoid further family commitments, embarking on the lifestyle of a very rich unattached man with a string of mistresses and high living. Its attractions, however, soon palled and he threw himself into making himself a billionaire, basing himself on the mansion called Bruce Tower House. His ambition received a huge boost on a business trip to India

***

"All helicopter flights are grounded. This monsoon weather is the worst I've experienced, and it looks as though it will continue for the next few days."

Sir Rab Bruce cursed. He had flown to Calcutta intending to continue his journey to the far north-east of the country by helicopter. He was investigating the possibility of opening up a major new oil field in the Ledo region of Assam. His team of geologists had been working there for some time with the permission of the Indian Government. Reports were extremely favourable and he was making the trip to confirm that the operation was logistically feasible.. Other players in the oil industry were equally interested and it was a race to clinch a deal for the exploitation of the field.

The helicopter pilot was adamant. He would not risk flying.

"You could always take the train," he suggested.

Sir Rab assessed the possibilities. It would take at least two days, the latter part on a ramshackle local railway. He decided to opt for the uncomfortable journey, secure in the knowledge that that any rivals would be in the same position.

A day later he stood on the west bank of the River Brahmaputra, watching in dismay the immense swollen flood surging balefully, brown and turgid, south from the Himalayas to the Bay of Bengal. Tree trunks, foliage, and animal carcasses jostled and tumbled in the swirling eddies and sullen waves. The railway line on the east bank had been washed out in several places further up the line.

Sir Rab double cursed. It seemed he was to be thwarted again. Turning to his young aide, Charles Seton, he growled,

"What about that river boat?" He pointed to a large rust –streaked craft moored to the near bank. Boats such as that plied up and down the river, carrying hundreds of passengers and cargo. This one was packed to overflowing, families camping on the steel deck, cooking fires lit, all sorts of domestic animals around, and bulky bales and containers being loaded.

"See the shipping agent and book a cabin for us."

"But, sir, it looks overloaded already. It could be dangerous".

"Just do it. Bribe the agent or the captain if necessary. I need to be in Ledo tomorrow."

Half an hour later Sir Rab's party was ensconced in the Captain's quarters aboard the now throbbing boat as the engine fired up. The other two cabins had already been taken. The Captain was not sanguine about the prospects of making it upriver as far as Dibrugarh. "This flood is one of the worst I've seen. In places the River is like a lake, a sea even. The notorious Brahmaputra sandbanks will have shifted, making navigation all but impossible. I'll do my best but I can't promise anything".

The Captain's betel-stained teeth flashed in a wolfish grin.

"It'll be a challenge. It might take three or four days though."

Sitting in what passed for a lounge- dining area, Sir Rab gloomily looked forward to a period of discomfort and inedible food. He hoped the oil discovery would be worth it.

"Who's in the other cabins?" he asked idly.

Charles Seton grinned.

"You'll never believe it. There's a European woman, striking-looking, in one of them: the other has two Russian-speaking men".

Sir Rab was immediately suspicious.

"I wonder if they are the opposition. I don't know about the woman though. Maybe she's a travel writer. The world's full of them".

"You are quite right and wrong, Sir Rab," a female voice with a strong Russian accent whispered behind his right shoulder. He swung round, incredulous..

"Yes, Rab. It's me, Natasha Molotov. The last time we met was in Vienna at an OPEC meeting, remember?"

Rab jumped to his feet.

"Natasha! Of course I remember. What a surprise!"

"It shouldn't be, Rab. I suspect we are both here for the same reasons."

Rab had mixed feelings about this development. Natasha Molotov was the widow of a Russian oil tycoon who had died in an air crash three years before. He had prudently siphoned off most of his wealth to the West and Natasha had fallen heir to it. Instead of sunning herself in the Riviera to enjoy her riches, Natasha had emerged as a formidable force in the oil industry, expanding the Molotov empire considerably. Now she was heading for this remote corner of India. Clearly she was intent on acquiring the Ledo oil field.

Charles Seaton was correct in his estimate of Natasha as a striking-looking woman. Five feet nine in height, with a full figure, and a mass of unruly auburn hair, she was a commanding presence with her hawk like slightly crooked nose, high cheek bones and flashing teeth, white except for an incongruous gold one. Her full lips were slashed with orange lipstick, a trade mark. Workmanlike jeans and tee-shirt, with scuffed suede boots surmounted by a khaki bush hat did not detract from her head-turning glamour. Rab had encountered her in conferences but had been only one of a busy press of admirers who continually surrounded her. Only once, wearing a kilt, Rab had secured her undivided attention. She was in love with things Scottish she laughed before being swept off to meet an Arab prince. In her early forties, childless and mega-rich, Natasha was one of the most sought after women in the world.

"I can confirm your suspicions, Sir Rab," she smiled. This new find should be worth exploiting. The Indians must be rubbing their hands at the prospect of the potential tax revenue. I've come to run the rule over the viability of the project. I expect I shall outbid you. You Scots are so cautious", she joked.

Rab laughed in response. She obviously did not know him as well as she ought. He was as capable of taking risks as the best of them, as many rivals had found to their cost. Meanwhile, however, he determined to make the most of the experience of being, for the next few days, in the company of this beautiful woman who had attracted him from their first encounter.

"You'll join us for a meal, Natasha. There's no point in isolating ourselves even if we are business rivals."

"I'd like that. It will give me an opportunity to learn more about your wonderful country. I studied the poetry of Robert Burns at school and I have always longed to visit and explore the places I have read about. You must tell me about kilts and tartans. Rab had not the heart to disillusion her. Instead he launched into the story of the Picts, the Scots, the Angles, the Britons and the Norsemen and the formation of Scotland, his genuine Indian curry half-forgotten as he enthused over the mysterious Picts. Natasha listened, enthralled.

"You were a savage lot, you Scots, almost as bad as my ancestors.

Two days later they were still deep in conversation as they stood on deck watching the Captain trying to dislodge the boat from another submerged sandbank.

***

The oil discovery was a substantial one, worth developing in spite of its remote location. Drumannan Holdings and Molotov Oil formed a consortium to develop the field.

Natasha eagerly accepted Rab's offer to stay at Bruce Tower House as a base while she explored Scotland. He accepted her invitation to cruise the Mediterranean on her superbly appointed yacht. Eighteen months later they were married in Drumannan, Rab resplendent in full highland dress. The joint assets of the pair made them two of the richest people in the world.

"At least they didn't marry each other for the money," observed Charles Seaton sardonically.

Nevertheless a pre-nuptial agreement was made. Natasha and Rab formed a brilliant partnership in business, in their social circle, and in their desire to make Scotland a better place.

Fiercely patriotic, the state of Scotland dismayed Sir Rab. The old virtues of hard work, fair reward for labour, thriftiness, and respect for law and order seemed to him to have been eroded so far that drastic action was needed. The ongoing crisis in Britain dismayed him. His low regard for politicians in general was confirmed by politically correct policies introduced by successive Labour, Conservative and Scottish National Party Governments. The United Kingdom was at an all-time low. The country had entered a period of recession following a banking crisis. The Labour Government collapsed after the sudden resignation of the Prime Minister and the Conservatives had swept to power with a large majority. Difficulties over oil and gas supplies compounded the problems faced by the new Government. The promised referendum over the European Constitution produced a resounding NO vote, and an ultimatum from France and Germany telling Britain to fully commit to the European Union or be expelled.

In Scotland the minority S.N.P. government, after a honeymoon spell with the voters, soon ran into trouble over its failure to take effective measures on law and order and the defeat of its proposals on local income tax by the combined opposition parties. The usual broken promises, the same old politicians' excuses went the refrain from frustrated voters. The stern attitude of the new Conservative administration towards what it considered the unduly generous U.K. Government support for Scotland together with its over representation in Parliament soured further relations between Westminster and Holyrood.

The increase in racial tension fomented by nationalist organisations such as the Sons of St. George in England and the Bannockburn Boys in Scotland was erupting into violence across the country.

Sir Rab Bruce was certain that a different type of government, freed from professional politicians, would make a much better fist of coping with the besetting problems of Scotland. A government with direct links to all sections of the community should be given the chance to avert what he was sure was the impending collapse of society.

He had prepared an action plan for a Scottish Peoples Alliance, as he named it. He was prepared to spend millions on publicising the idea. The popular appeal of Murdo McLean McMannan and his Triple M pop group together with the charisma of his film actress wife, Catriona, would give an extra impetus to a nationwide campaign to gain wide support for his ideas.

CHAPTER NINE

MURDO AND CATRIONA: QUEENSTOWN, 2009

Murdo and Catriona occupied a house called The Knock on the slope of a hill overlooking Queenstown. Both had been born and raised in the town. Strangely they had not met until Murdo was seventeen and Catriona sixteen.

Murdo's family owned a large farm to the west of Queenstown and Murdo attended the local schools, in contrast to Catriona who commuted daily to a fee paying school in Edinburgh. Their paths had not crossed until both were playing in a mixed pairs junior golf tournament at the local club.

Murdo stared at his girl opponent in open admiration. He had heard rumours about the stunningly beautiful haughty Catriona Hamilton from friends, but the reality surpassed all the inadequate descriptions he had heard. Her perfect oval of a face, bow-shaped lips, slightly retrousse nose and enormous corn flower blue eyes, were framed by jet black hair, escaping in rebellious ringlets from her forward-tilted visored hat Her slim figure, teenage –gawky, was clad in a royal blue shirt and red shorts, displaying shapely legs above her white ankle socks and scruffy golf shoes. She blushed under his gaze, sensing male interest.

She had seen this strapping handsome red head about the town from her High Street window above the confectioners business her mother ran, and learned of his prowess at golf, his musical talent and his consuming interest in girls from several of her friends. She determined to be cool and aloof, wary of his reputation.

Murdo tried to flirt with her as the golf round progressed. He and his burly girl partner were 3 holes up by the turn at the 9th hole. Catriona gritted her teeth, lost her rhythm on the next hole attempting to smash a shot to the green on the short 10th in an attempt to cut Murdo's lead. The inevitable happened. The ball hooked savagely, hitting Murdo, unwisely standing in front of and a little to the left of the tee – the better to appreciate her elegant swing he had smirked. The ball hit him on his t-shirted chest, keeling him over.

The other three players, a little apprehensive, waited for him to get to his feet, Catriona uttering a half-stifled sorry. When he lay motionless his partner screeched,

"Is he breathing?"

Catriona panicked, rushing forward and throwing herself on the prone figure, trying to administer the kiss of life as she had been taught in the Girl Guides.

Suddenly she felt arms around her, eager lips responding with vigour to her life-saving efforts. Shocked, she tore herself free from the laughing Murdo, spitting fury at him before storming off in high dudgeon, the game abandoned. She felt totally humiliated.

Later when he appeared at her flat to apologise she refused point blank to see him. He had made a laughing stock of her in the town. The story even percolated through to her school, she wept to her mother who was sympathetic but secretly amused.

Murdo, as the oldest son of his farmer father, was expected to follow the tradition and become a farmer himself. He had, however, a precocious musical talent, fostered by his mother whose family had a musical background. A brilliant pianist, he composed music and wrote lyrics for the school group he led. It was with some difficulty that his mother persuaded him to enroll at the Glasgow college of Music and Drama in preference to a pop group career.

Catriona's banker father had died when she was very young, leaving her mother "in reduced circumstances" as she put it. As a single mother she had to struggle on the precarious income from her sweetie shop as the unkind called her confectionery business in Queenstown High Street. Determined to do her best for her daughter she scrimped and saved to send her to a fee-paying school in Edinburgh which she herself had attended.

A natural actress, Catriona displayed her talent in school productions. Disappointed that her daughter opted for Drama as a career rather than a respectable academic discipline Mrs. Hamilton nevertheless fully supported Catriona's enrolment at the Glasgow College of Music and Drama.

For a year at the College Catriona studiously cut Murdo dead when their paths happened to cross. The Ice Maiden Murdo called her after one embarrassing encounter. He was still greatly attracted to her and rued his silly prank on the golf course. It came as a relief to Catriona when she heard that he had dropped out of College to return to his all-consuming interests in popular music, forming his own group.

For two years he and his group tried to obtain gigs in discos and clubs throughout Scotland, using the initials of his full name, Murdo McLean McMannan, as the title of the group. Triple-M developed a unique mixture of what is known as glam rock and Scottish folk music. His mother's family, keen traditionalists had given him an early enthusiasm for his native culture.

Like most groups, Triple-M led a hand-to-mouth existence, the small intermittent income from gigs barely enough to sustain them. Often Murdo's family had to help out. His music, however, developed a distinctive sound backed by powerful lyrics. He had the knack of producing melodies that people could whistle in the street. Rave notices in the Scottish press popular music columns attracted the attention of London record companies.

Soon Triple-M migrated to the Capital, obtained a record deal with a major player in the business. A single from their first album was given sustained air time on radio and reached the top ten in the charts. The album sold thousands of copies. Triple-M's gigs attracted huge audiences. Their first tour was a resounding success. Within eighteen months Murdo and his group were rich and famous, about to try to break into the American market.

Catriona spent three years at college before graduating and moving to London to find work in the cut-throat world of the stage. She obtained bit parts in various productions, eking out a precarious existence, living in friends' flats and bed-sits when on tour. Resolutely refusing the casting couch route to bigger roles she despaired, almost giving up and returning home. It was in this mood that she sat in an underground train heading for Kings Road and a shopping trip more longing than buying.

The thunderclap of an enormous explosion momentarily stunned her as she was tossed from her seat to batter against the stanchion of the one in front, showered with shattered glass, debris and gritty dust. A searing pain in her shoulder made her scream, her cries lost in the hubbub of shouts for help, other screams and sobs of hurt and broken people. The lights had been extinguished and dense, swirling smoke made her gag. Her terror grew. Weakly she called for help as the grinding and screeching of tortured metal died away. The only sounds were those of humans in agony.

Catriona moaned softly. She could feel a trickle of blood on her leg. Her shoulder throbbed. She could feel a body, motionless beside her.

"Is anyone there?" she croaked.

A male voice answered her groggily.

"Hold on. I'm crawling over to you."

Catriona sobbed with relief.

I'm here but it's so dark and I'm frightened."

A hand grasped her reaching, clutching fingers, and a deep voice uttered reassurance.

"Rescuers will be here soon. Try to keep calm. Stick close to me."

Catriona moved towards the man, clinging to him, shuddering with fright.

What happened? I can't see anything. I'm so scared."

He put a comforting arm around her

"Take it easy. We'll just have to wait it out. There should be lights soon. What's your name?"

"Catriona," she stuttered.

There was a quick intake of breath.

"That's Scottish. I'm Scottish too. Where are you from?

"Queenstown, near Edinburgh," she replied.

"I was sure I recognized the voice. You are Catriona Hamilton. Thank goodness I found you. I'm Murdo McMannan. Remember me. The one you hate."

Catriona was sobbing and laughing at the same time.

"I don't care. I'm so pleased there's someone with me, even if I was angry with you long ago. Are we going to be rescued or will we die here?"

Murdo squeezed her closer, suppressing his own fears as he confidently asserted that the London rescue services were so efficient that they would reach them soon. The moans and the crying of other similarly trapped people died away. There seemed to be no one conscious in their immediate vicinity.

The darkness was stygian; the smoke swirling unseen but choking. Time passed. Catriona was still fearful. Were they going to die here? She had so much to live for. She had just been offered a leading role in a B.B.C. costume drama.

Shyly she whispered her news to Murdo who sensed her despair. He began to talk about his latest concert tour to take her mind off their predicament but inwardly he was concerned about the air quality. They were beginning to have difficulty in breathing and it was becoming unbearably hot.

"Why don't we team up and make a D.V.D. together. I have this idea for a rock opera with a Scottish theme and I need a Narrator to provide a linking background. You would be ideal for the part. What do you think?"

In spite of her state of mind, Catriona was intrigued Here were two people in mortal danger and here was this man planning a scenario for a future that seemed unlikely, given their present plight.

"I don't think we are going to be rescued, Murdo," she quavered, "I think we are going to die."

Nonsense" Come on. Let's get down to the detailed planning of how we will make this opera."

Another fifteen minutes passed during which Murdo jollied Catriona along, forcing her to think about the putative opera.

"Do you think I could wear a tartan dress?" she almost giggled at one point.

Good for you, Catriona! I'll opt for trews and a Glengarry hat."

Their foolishness was interrupted by a battery of powerful lights and a stentorian voice asking them to respond.

Catriona flung her arms round Murdo, kissing him wildly.

"We're saved, Murdo. Thank goodness!"

He cuddled her reassuringly.

"I was beginning to get really worried."

Twelve hours later Murdo visited Catriona in the hospital to which the injured from the latest terrorist attack in London had been taken. Propped up in bed she was feeling much better. The shoulder was not broken, only badly bruised and the cut on her leg was not serious.

"How are you?" he asked cautiously.

Catriona responded timidly, her usual poise gone.

"Thank you for helping me. I don't think I would have coped without you. I was so scared."

"So was I, but I wasn't going to tell you that."

There was an awkward silence before they both tried to talk at once.

"Murdo, you……"

"Am I at last forgiven for my silly prank on the golf course?"

"Of course you are. You are my hero." Catriona grinned at him mockingly.

"Seriously you were wonderful in that hellhole. By the way, it was a tremendous coincidence that both of us were on that train."

Murdo looked sheepish.

"I have a confession to make. I spotted you going into the station and followed you. I was going to try again to apologise but you looked so aloof and haughty in that carriage that my courage failed me. I really would like us to be friends".

"Don't be soppy, Murdo. Of course we are friends. You want to take me out, don't you? Shall I tell you a secret? I still dream about that first kiss of ours."

Murdo heaved a sigh of relief.

"Well, Ms. Hamilton, have you considered my offer of a joint venture?"

Mr. McMannan, it will take several meetings before I finally make up my mind."

Murdo and Catriona quickly became a familiar sight in celebrity circles in London, constant companions at functions, in clubs and trendy restaurants. A year later they were married – one of the show business events of 2006.

Now, three years later, celebrities in their own right, they had made their base in Queenstown in the house they had bought overlooking the town.

Murdo's chance meeting with Sir Rab Bruce and their shared concern for the future of Scotland resulted in the beginning of a joint campaign to publicise the ideas behind the Scottish Peoples Alliance. The timing was just right. The public seized on the S.P.A. as a new hope for society in the midst of a collapsing old order.

CHAPTER TEN

BELLE AND RODDY: The Ochil Hills

Belle Ramsay gazed in fascinated horror at the scene before her. She lay prone at the top of a tussocky bluff, peering through a spiky gorse bush at whorls of woolly smoke shot through with flame. The fire was swamping a ten foot tall wicker construction with a human figure in it, supine against the struts. The shifting pall revealed an irregular circle of savage figures, plaid clad, with rough leggings, long unkempt hair and luxuriant beards. Helmeted, they brandished upraised long swords and crude spears as the fire began to consume the wickerwork and the person inside.

By her side, Roddy gasped in disbelief.
"It must be some sort of cult………"
As Belle half rose to shriek in protest, he gripped her wrist pulling her down with his other hand over her mouth.
"Quiet!" he hissed, "We have to get out of here before we are seen. We must call the police."
The painful tightness of his fingers and the urgency of his voice changed her outrage to alarm and fear. Releasing her he placed a finger to his lips and began to edge back from the crest, Belle following. They slithered down the gentle reverse slope in a state of shock before stumbling into the shelter of a small depression in the hillside, the source of an Ochils burn. In her tumbledown haste Belle had lacerated her hand and cursed softly as she tried to staunch the flow of blood.
"Here, tie this hanky………"
"Bugger the cuts, Roddy. Get your Mobile out and phone the police."
Fumbling with his rucksack he searched for the phone.
"I don't think we were seen," he muttered, "What on earth was going on up there? Some sort of obscene ceremony?"
What ever it was it was criminally wrong. That poor man, burned alive!"
"No signal! Damn! We'll have to run for……"
Roddy's voice tailed away. Belle shot him an alarmed look. Silently he gestured. Behind her stood a row of two men and two women, wearing full Barbour gear and green wellies, armed with exaggeratedly long shepherd crooks. The oldest of the group, a thick set man in his fifties, his graying hair bed-headed in the wind, called down to them in an educated Scottish accent.
"Hello there. Did we scare you? We were staging a rehearsal for a film we are making – an ancient Celtic ceremony. The figure in the wicker contraption was a stuntman. It was clearly realistic enough to take you in."

The others laughed. Belle exploded.

"Idiots! You scared the living daylights out of us with your stupid film. You should have had warning notices up. I'm going to let the police know. Look what you've done to my hand. I could cheerfully throttle whoever's responsible."

Glaring at the now discomfited green wellies she made to stalk off.

"Hold on, please, madam. I apologise sincerely. I agree it was stupid of us not to warn people. It won't happen again. Can I make amends by inviting you to join us? We're having an alfresco lunch close by, and we have a first aid person on the set who'll attend to your hand."

Dropping down into the gully, grey hair extended a mollifying grip, taken reluctantly by Roddy.

"Please say you'll come." The two women fluttered over Belle, uttering sympathetic noises

Recognition dawned on the faces of Belle and Roddy.

"Rab Bruce!"

Belle gasped in astonishment.

"And I'm Murdo McLean Mannan," beamed the burly, auburn haired giant of a man who appeared at the side of his companion. "And this is my wife, Catriona."

"And my wife, Natasha," announced the first man proudly.

"It can't be," stammered Belle.

"But it is," the foursome chorused, smiling.

Roddy came to her rescue.

"May I introduce Belle Ramsay? I am Roderick Neilson. We are pleased to accept your invitation."

Winking imperceptibly, he urged Belle to follow the group to the picnic area over the hill.

"Didn't you recognize them," hissed Belle.

"Of course I did," whispered her partner, "This is too intriguing to miss."

The grey haired man was billionaire leader of The Scottish Peoples Alliance. The red head was the star of the internationally acclaimed pop group, Triple M and his wife, a famous film star.

The ragged slash of a bulldozed track scarred the rounded heather clad hill, angling down to the bowl where the narrow glen opened out to form a natural amphitheatre. A burn trickled through, summer shrunk. Clustered on the banks were the erstwhile makers of the human sacrifice, now laughing and joking as they wolfed down their picnic lunch, complemented by copious amounts of tea and coffee and beer. Film making was clearly thirsty work. People made way respectfully to the newcomers as they bellied up to the long trestle table that had been set up for the food.

"Help yourselves, folks. Have some champagne." Murdo waved the bottle genially splashing the wine into flutes.

"The film is set in the Dark Ages and partly in modern times. Catriona takes a leading role as a Celtic princess and as the Curator of the Terence McCool Foundation. We were testing to see if we could reproduce a Wicker man effectively. It worked," he added with a chuckle.

"It surely did," said Belle dryly.

Roddy started. A short, stout woman looked equally startled before recovering herself.

"Why hello, Roddy. I didn't think you were one of the converts like me. What a surprise! And you Deputy Chair of the Assembly Labour group."

Roddy responded stiffly.

"I'm here by accident, Anne Marie. I can assure you I have not changed my allegiance."

The woman smiled, unabashed. The Labour M.S.P. for a constituency in deepest Lanarkshire, she had a reputation as a left wing firebrand.

"Times change, Roddy. We must move with them." With a cool nod she moved off, leaving Roddy bemused.

***

Belle drove, listening while Roddy used his mobile phone, explaining, expostulating, raging and eventually thumping the dash board in exasperation. Finally he snapped shut the phone and stared blankly ahead.

"Well, tell me Roddy. What's happening?" Belle turned her head irritably.

"Eh? Sorry, I was thinking."

"Roddy will you snap out of it and bring me up to date," ground out Belle with a snarl.

"Twenty-four Labour M.S.P. s have expressed their support for The Scottish Peoples Alliance, a truly national movement out with party politics. Their number includes three ex-ministers."

"And you knew nothing of this?"

"Well, there have been rumours, the usual tittle-tattle, but I was kept out of the loop obviously."

The wheel shook as Belle's shock registered. She coasted to a stop at a convenient lay-by. A protracted silence ensued. At last Roddy murmured,

"Maybe they are taking the correct course of action, considering the mess the country's in. We need a Government of all the talents."

"Roddy! Where are your principles? I don't believe what I'm hearing. ….."

Her partner made no reply, hunching uncomfortably, hands clasping and unclasping between his knees. Belle exploded. Furiously she gunned the engine.

Bloody politics!

CHAPTER ELEVEN

SIR RAB BRUCE: SECURITY CONCERNS

In a moment of weakness Sir Rab had employed the son of an old school mate as a member of his security staff. The man, Jack Drummond, had done twenty years service in the Royal Corps of Military Police, overcoming the shame of a months custodial sentence for theft when he was a youth. His career as a security officer had been exemplary and he had gained promotion to Head of Security for Bruce Engineering at Aberbrothy. Sir Rab had asked him to provide security for the filming operation in the Ochil Hills.

Lately, however, there had been signs of a slipshod approach to security, and Sir Rab was paranoid about the protection of the research facilities at Aberbrothy. He determined to use the incident at the film set as a warning to Drummond to raise his game.

"Why didn't your men spot these hill walkers before they stumbled on the wicker man scene? demanded Sir Rab.

"There is only one track from the south leading to our film set and I had a man posted there. I also had a man at the other end of our operation to warn anyone coming from the north. A third man was covering the open hill but he missed those two."

Jack Drummond was on the defensive. To cross Sir Rab was unwise in the extreme.

"What have you done about the man keeping watch on the hill," he asked quietly.

"I've reprimanded him," responded Drummond uneasily.

"Sack him." barked Sir Rab, suddenly angry. "I want the work of your security team to be of the highest standard. You are aware of the need for the utmost vigilance at the research complex. Pull your socks up, Drummond. I want no more lapses."

CHAPTER TWELVE

BELLE AND RANGI: ABERBROTHY RIOT

Belle Ramsay bit her lip in frustration as the procession approached, led by a swashbuckling piper skirling a march. A street wide banner had The Scottish Peoples Alliance scrawled in a splatter of blue paint across its full extent. Four scowling men strove to support its bulging weight against the gusting wind, their kilts moulded into their fleshy thighs. Behind them pressed a motley column of kilted men, tartan sashed women, and capering children. Supposed clan tartans were many and varied with green and red predominating. The accoutrements were bizarre: training shoes, green wellies, and hiking boots easily outnumbered brogues. Balmoral bonnets, glengarries and baseball caps vied with sober tweed caps, deer stalkers and head scarves. Many of the men were hirsute; others shaven headed. The less successful wispy beards adorned youths striving to appear macho. Women wore ankle length dresses, tight jeans showing bare midriffs, sensible tweeds, and every conceivable fashion in between. Shirts and T- shirts emblazoned with The Scottish Peoples Alliance. Triple M or Brave Heart Bruce completed a picture that was colourful and flamboyant if not sartorially elegant.

There must have been upwards of a thousand people straggling down the High Street of Aberbrothy watched and encouraged by clapping and cheering shoppers

Halfway down the broad gently sloping avenue an uneasy line of police shuffled across at a convenient choke point created by an ancient Mercat Cross and Tollbooth.

Belle turned impatiently to her partner, Roddy Neilson who was eyeing the procession with curiosity and puzzlement

"For God's sake, Roddy, don't encourage them. Let's get out of here. People power of this kind is anathema to me."

Roddy grinned, "It's interesting to encounter the opposition in the raw like this."

Roddy smiled fondly at the fiery eyes of the petite, raven haired woman beside him. Belle, with her high cheekbones, and vivid colouring, showed her Hungarian ancestry. Slightly crooked teeth and a jutting chin made her attractive rather than conventionally pretty. Her slim figure was somewhat spoiled by heavy ankles, an imperfection she had at last accepted after many tears in her teens. Roddy bent to whisper in her ear.

"Your eyes go all sparkly when you are angry Belle. It turns me on."

Her head upturned to match his confidential stoop, expecting a serious political point, Belle's rage evaporated in pleased laughter. Her eyes shone as she cuffed him about the head.

"You're impossible, Roddy. Come on. We should be well on our way to Queenstown by now."

A shared interest in old pottery had brought Belle and Roddy to Aberbrothy where a large scale Victorian pottery had disappeared almost without trace. Successive redevelopments had obliterated in turn most of the medieval town, early industrial works and street layouts. Recent de-industrialisation had left the new framework of a by-pass, one way streets and open spaces without a working heart. The decline of Aberbrothy was evident in the empty shops, charity shops and cut price stores. A typical central Scotland town of the early 21st century, except for one thing, Aberbrothy was the main base of The Scottish Peoples Alliance. Sir Rab Bruce had acquired Bruce Tower, an ancient hunting lodge of the royal Bruce family, extending and transforming it into an opulent home and administration headquarters of his business empire. Two miles from Aberbrothy town centre it was beginning to rejuvenate the whole area, providing jobs and investment and a new hope for the community.

The compelling boom of a big drum from the bottom of the street creating a discordant ostinata to the bagpipes, and the thin whistles of a flute band began to be heard. A confident phalanx of shaven-headed men swung into sight at the T-junction of the High Street and Mill Street, turning uphill to face the advancing Scottish Peoples Alliance procession, makeshift banners emblazoned with the words Bannockburn Boys, Wallace Warriors, Bravehearts and S.N.P. After a faltering moment a great cheer erupted from the crowd. The march became a helter-skelter rush as they charged. The dozen policemen were quickly engulfed by a hooting, shrieking mob of men and women and older children. Younger ones began to be herded to the uncertain safety of the pavement but onlookers, caught up in the excitement, surged forward. Some little ones were knocked to the ground to the despairing cries of their carers. Other more circumspect of the spectators drifted away, anxious to distance themselves from any trouble.

The Nationalists were vastly outnumbered. No more than a hundred strong, their parade were reinforced only by another musical accompaniment, The Star of Sauchen Accordion Band. The shock of the Alliance charge splintered the ordered lines, and soon the street was a mass of brawling, swearing people.

Belle cowered in the entrance to a pend, terrified of being caught up in the melee. Roddy seemed to have been swept up by the onrushing crowd. From her low viewpoint she could only see a confusion of legs, passing in squeals of tortured rubber and the clatter of heavier soles, unheedingly trampling a fallen figure. Wisely he had cradled his head in his hands, curled up and cursing weakly. The rush lessened. A few stragglers swerved past him, eager to catch up with the throng. Belle risked a glance up and down the street. A few injured lay prone; more were getting to their feet, dizzied and bleeding; a young boy was being entreated to waken by a sobbing mother. Some householders peered at the scene in shock. A dazed policeman was desperately trying to get his radio to work.

The man near her on the ground groaned. She edged over to him, trying to remember her rudimentary first aid training.

"Oh God! It's happened again. My father died in a situation like this." He was white and shaken, holding his ribs. "I'm going to die too."

"Nonsense," Belle Said briskly, nurse fashion, "You don't look all that bad, apart from a bleeding nose."

She tried to stanch it with tissues but it bled copiously over both of them. This was the sight that confronted Roddy, searching for Belle.

"Belle," he screamed," are you badly hurt?"

"It's not my blood, Roddy. It's this man's."

With bloody nose, split lips, jet hair matted with more blood, and one grubby trainer shoe half of, he pulled himself up. A Chinese thought Belle, rapidly proffering more tissues. His slanting eyes and olive skin were vaguely oriental in spite of the gore and snot.

"We'll better get him out of here to a hospital for a check up," muttered Roddy,"there might be more trouble. What's your name?"

"Duncan McNaughton. People call me Rangi, you know, after Rangoon."

CHAPTER THIRTEEN

RODDY NEILSON: EDINBURGH

The Labour Member of Scottish Parliament for the Queenstown Constituency, Roderick Neilson, felt rudderless. As he journeyed by rail from Queenstown to Edinburgh to meet the leader of the Labour opposition he found himself querying his beliefs.

Brought up in the Giffnock area of Glasgow to parents who were both medical practitioners, he had enjoyed an uneventful childhood, attending the fee-paying Hutcheson's Grammar School before going to Glasgow University and qualifying in Law. He was a typical product of Glasgow's middle class. With parents who had a strong social conscience and participation in the Dewar/Smith tradition of university debating, he was drawn into Labour politics at an early age. It was no surprise to his contemporaries when he graduated from his apprenticeship as a local councillor to become an MSP, escaping from the west of Scotland old Labour politics to find a constituency in the east at Queenstown. He quickly made his mark in the Assembly, acquiring junior minister status in a recent Labour administration.

Roddy's main strength was his engaging manner and powerful oratory, linked to a considerable intellect. The political pundits marked him out as a coming man, the best of a mediocre bunch, some averred. With his dark regular features and ready smile and instinctive mollifying language Roddy could defuse sharp differences with disarming ease. Evan his opponents admired his negotiating skills although a few of his more hard bitten colleagues muttered darkly that he gave too much away in his eagerness to reach agreement.

Until recently, Roddy's career had been an orderly progression towards high office. Political chaos and lack of competent leadership had changed all that. The defeat of the once mighty Scottish Labour Party machine in an election for the Assembly jolted him out of his complacency and had been the start of his uncertainty and indecision. The defeat of a Labour Government in London exacerbated the situation. Long scornful of the west of Scotland Labour mafia he was now questioning some of the basic beliefs of his liberal New Labour colleagues. It horrified him to discover that many of his misgivings were echoed in the concerns expressed by the Scottish Peoples Alliance.

His relationship with Belle too was crumbling. He sensed that her inner demons were affecting their hitherto comfortable partnership. She was becoming more and more disillusioned with politics in general and politicians in particular. She was impatient with his colleagues, avoiding necessary attendance at functions and scathing about the duplicity of the movers and shakers of all parties. He in turn found her views about independent thought and individual freedom together with sheer bloody-mindedness somewhat eccentric. Her frequent nightmares and migraines were wearing away his sympathy and understanding. They were still physically attracted to one another. He could charm her by making laugh and she could rouse him by a flick of her hair or a flashing smile. Irritations and little tiffs, however, were happening too often. The fact that they were childless did not help. Belle had put her career first. Her biological cloak had ticked past midnight. Roddy, a modern man, had gone along with her feminism and now regretted it, as did she, although she never admitted it.

Now, as he strode into the office of Seamus O'Hare, he frowned at the thought at what awaited him. Corpulent, ailing, heavily jowled, O'Hare was an elder statesman who had been dragooned into service when sleaze and scandal had overwhelmed the Party. He was not coping well.

Indignantly, Roddy told of his encounter in the Ochils with their colleague, Anne Marie Westwood.

"Did you know anything of that?" he demanded.

"I have heard rumours, Roddy, as you have. But as you would expect, we are the last to know about desertions and treachery."

Roddy glowered at him.

"So what are we going to do about the situation?" he bit out.

"Well my informants tell me that about half of our colleagues are joining the new movement – and here's the interesting part – they claim they are not leaving the Party, merely adding membership of the SPA to their membership of the Labour Party".

The leader chuckled sardonically.

"Have you ever heard anything so daft?"

Roddy nodded thoughtfully, reprising what he knew of the Alliance.

The brainchild of Sir Rab Bruce and the Triple M pop star, Murdo McLean McMannan, the announcement of its formation had been greeted with derision by politicians of all parties in Scotland. It would prove to be a damp squid, just like other movements started by cranks, rich business man or semi-fascist establishment figures. It had all been tried before went the refrain

The pundits were wrong. The movement caught the public mood. A slick public relations exercise and a promise to take radical action to change the way the country was governed, ignoring the political parties and introducing a team truly of all the talents, offered a solution to the chaotic state of the country.

"Did you hear the speeches at the S.P.A. rally last night? queried Seamus.

"No, I was out for a meal." replied Roddy, "Did I miss much?"

"Well, listen to this recording."

Pensively Roddy listened, first to Sir Rab Bruce and then to McMannan.

"The traditional virtues of hard work and a fair days wage for a fair days work have been eroded over the years. We all must strive to make sure they return.

Scotland used to be famed for business enterprise and inventiveness. Let us resurrect this spirit of adventure and risk-taking, and reward those who benefit themselves and the whole country by their efforts.

To ensure that our children and grandchildren can take full advantage of opportunity we must re-invigorate our educational institutions, once the pride of the nation. For too long trendy educational ideas have short-changed our children. A more structured and rigorous approach is necessary to provide children with the skills and attitudes they will need in a global economy.

It is beyond belief that successive administrations have broken so many promises about law and order. Every one of us knows that we need more and better police, and we will accept that less will be available for other things if only action is taken to secure full and effective protection for all citizens against lawbreakers.

Lawbreakers must be punished severely. Those who make our laws and judges who administer them must accept that the public are no longer prepared to put up with the apparent leniency shown to many criminals. If a change in policy means more jails, then so be it.

The National Health Service is completely the wrong model. It is clear that it cannot cope with the demands of an aging population and the advances made in medicine which require more and heavier expenditure. A new model is needed that should draw on best practice in other developed countries.

The dependency culture of state handouts must be eradicated by tough measures to ensure that people earn a living.

Government at national and local levels must become much smaller - less regulation, and fewer people employed by the state.

"I say to the London and Edinburgh Governments, these are the imperative demands of the Scottish people. Politicians have ignored them or fudged the issues. They will now pay the price.

May I now introduce my colleague, Murray McLean McMannan?"

"Thank you, Sir Rab.

We are all too aware of the lamentable state of the country. After the collapse of the Labour Government in a confusion of sleaze, incompetence and bereft of vision, the new minority Conservative administration has proved unequal to the task of coping with the challenges of rising oil prices, worldwide economic recession and seemingly unstoppable immigration. The humiliating withdrawal from Afghanistan after the Iraq fiasco has irreparably damaged not only our standing in the world but also the morale of the armed forces. The policy of gradual withdrawal from the European Union has been scornfully scuppered by the ultimatum from France and Germany to commit or be cast completely adrift.

In Scotland the minority S.N.P. Government is impotent against the intransigence of the other parties. A failed referendum on independence further eroded their position The Labour Party in Scotland has been exposed in all its inglorious venality.

The rising tide of resentment in England against the favoured treatment given to Scotland in terms of U.K.Government financial grants is leading the Conservative administration to cut the amount by 25%. Scottish M.P.s can no longer vote on English matters: the number of Scottish M.P.s has been reduced by seven. The emergence of English nationalism led to the terrible events at the European Cup match between Celtic and Chelsea. Foolish Scottish nationalists exacerbate the situation by their "white settlers go home" campaign which has led to ugly scenes and house burnings. The latest stunt of stealing the Woolsack from underneath the Speaker's Chair in the Houses of Parliament and displaying it at Bannockburn would have been an amusing students' jape in more settled times. That stupid act is likely to provoke violent reaction. Threats of breaking up the Union or even of civil war are being bandied about.

We must stop this descent into anarchy. We can no longer trust politicians to do so. We, the ordinary people, must take matters into our own hands. What the Scottish Peoples Alliance propose is a government truly of all the talents drawn from the best leaders from all sections of the community, people willing to be seconded from their usual jobs for a limited period of say three years to serve their country would fill responsible positions as local councillors and M.S.P.s. The forthcoming elections will give us the opportunity to demonstrate that the people can take control of their destiny."

"Switch that rubbish off, Roddy. It's pure saloon bar "putting the world to rights" stuff you hear in pubs all over Britain." Sean burrowed the heels of his hands wearily into his eye sockets. What do you make of it? It's not by any stretch of the imagination a viable proposition."

"It is certainly far fetched but it has caught the imagination of the public," Roddy muttered thoughtfully. "It's a typical grassroots thing like Solidarity in Poland all these years ago."

"Nonsense! You can't possibly compare the two movements," Sean grunted," Anyway, I've had enough. I'm resigning immediately. I'm old and tired and I cannae cope with…………" Helplessly he flung his arm in an arc which seemed to encompass the Assembly building, the warring factions, the economic thunderbolts, the whole sorry mess.

Roddy sympathised. He was wondering himself how to come to terms with this fast moving situation.

"We should send a delegation to meet the Scottish Peoples Alliance and find out what lies behind the rhetoric."

Roddy was thinking aloud, trying to feel his way into unknown territory.

"You do that, Roddy. Best of luck!"

Heavily Sean hoisted himself up, supporting his corpulent figure with a silver headed cane.

"I won't be back." So saying he limped out of the office without a backward glance.

"So much for leadership," Roddy grimaced.

CHAPTER FOURTEEN

BELLE RAMSAY: EDINBURGH

Incandescent, Belle glared at the uneasy figure of Thomas Torrance.

"The Workers Council wants financial assistance from the Tourist Board! I don't believe I'm hearing this," she spluttered in her rage, "The proposition is ludicrous. "Why should our firm have any more right than any other company to what amounts to a subsidy. You assured me last year that the loss we made then would be overturned this year by the measures you had taken to remedy matters. What has gone wrong? You have some hard questions to answer, Tommy."

"Trade is slack, Belle, and we failed to renew a big contract. We were undercut," muttered Torrance. He was a heavy man, florid faced and running to seed. The stolid confidence of the glad early years of the workers cooperative he managed had evaporated to be replaced by a shifty blustering style. It was absent today, however. Torrance cut a poor figure as he attempted to justify himself. He was clearly not on top of his job running Bartok Publications.

Belle chaired the Board of Trustees which was supposed to supervise the activities of the Company, begun and developed into a thriving publishing concern by her mother. Specialising in guide books and associated publications for the tourist industry. Bartok Publications had gained a solid reputation in that niche market. Her father, Weelum Ramsay, in a generous memorial to his dead wife, had transferred ownership to the workers in the company, with the proviso that trustees should oversee the business. As a mark of respect Belle had been appointed to chair the trustees. The actual running of the company fell to a workers council with Torrance as the executive head.

This sorry tale was the result. A successful company on the rocks after a steady decline! So much for workers cooperation thought Belle savagely.

"I want a detailed report on absenteeism, overtime payments, leave of absence records, manning levels, and rates of pay for different pay grades on my desk next Monday morning," she snarled.

She sensed that a subdued Torrance was relieved that she was involving herself.

"I'll do my best. I should warn you however that you should be careful in dealing with the Workers Council. Most of the old members have retired or have been replaced by younger men with a different outlook. I find it difficult to………." His voice tailed away as she withered him with a look.

After Torrance had gone Belle slumped in her chair. She knew in herself that she had neglected Bartock Publications, hoping the firm would recover from a bad patch. It was such a well-doing company. How wrong she had been. The warning signs were plain now.

Was it too late to retrieve the situation? She had been too sanguine. Angrily she looked at the photograph of her mother on her desk, Hungarian eyes flashing as she was caught in a parody of a gypsy dance. She remembered that evening well. Eva, bringing a rather staid party alive through the sheer force of her personality, had always been a catalyst for her father, causing him in turn to reveal a sparkling wit often damped down by the weight of Labour Party politics. Another photograph showed the two of them with a ten year old Belle between them, triumphant on the summit of Ben Lomond.

Belle could feel another migraine beginning. Whenever she dwelt on that time before the explosion that left her mother in a coma and indirectly caused the death of her father she succumbed to another painful episode. One side of her head seemed to swell to an excruciating climax of pain, her sight fractured into silvery lightning flashes. A deadly nausea left her cringing and exhausted. Weakly she pulled the Venetian blinds closed and lay supine. And another crisis in her professional life loomed in two days time.

CHAPTER FIFTEEN

BELLE RAMSAY

The Deputy Principal of St. Bernard's College of Further Education swung away from her computer screen and surveyed her visitor sourly.

"Advance warning, you say. This merger has been signalled for months. All you are doing is confirming what spin doctors have been briefing to the media."

The languid figure of the Under Secretary poised fastidiously over the desk, his elbow nudging the stacked files to find space for a slim black notebook. Hugo Forrester smiled thinly as he swept back a lock of his silver hair, worn a little longer than was usual among senior civil servants.

"Ms. Ramsay, my department cannot be held responsible for rumour and speculation in the media. I have outlined to you the contents of a paper that is being distributed for consultation. Until that process is completed, as you know, no final decision will be taken."

Belle snorted,

"Consultation! You know perfectly well that the Minister has made up his mind."

Forrester shrugged.

"Perhaps St. Bernard's College would like to submit a counter proposal. We would be prepared to listen. "

"We certainly will," snapped Belle, "What you told me sounds not only ill-considered but quite unworkable."

What they were discussing was the possible merger of her college with two other colleges, one five miles away on the other side of the Capital and the other thirty miles away in Wallacetown. The abandonment of the Barnet formula with its special dispensation for Scottish government finances had resulted in massive cutbacks in its spending plans. The Scottish Assembly was impotent in the face of rising English resentment at supposed Scottish preferential treatment. The forthcoming exclusion of Scottish M.P.s from essentially English Parliamentary business would create similar outrage in Scotland.

"Always moaning, always on the take," the blunt Tyneside M.P. averred, "We in the north east demand a level playing field."

The intransigent stance of a minority Scottish National Party administration had exacerbated an already deteriorating situation.

The disparity between the amounts spent on Education in England compared with Scotland demanded a substantial redistribution in favour of England. Hence the reason for the major reviews of spending on Further Education generally and a reduction in the number of colleges in particular. The problem was that two of the threatened colleges were situated in marginal Labour constituencies. If these two were reprieved it would result in a skewed distribution of provision across the central belt of the country. As the largest and most successful college St. Bernard's should have been immune from any closures policy decision. Now it was in mortal danger. Belle wished her Principal were present to confront the problem. He was a heavy weight more than capable of handling this mess. Belle owed a lot to his clarity of thought, compassion and vision. Unfortunately he was on long term sick leave.

"If St. Bernard's were to be sacrificed it would make for a politically acceptable solution," the Under-Secretary said silkily.

At last the gloves were off. Belle had a fight on her hands.

CHAPTER SIXTEEN

RUTH AND BELLE: ALLANFORD

"I'm hitting a brick wall every time I make an approach for funding for the dig, Belle. Neither the Local Authority nor the universities are remotely interested. There are no funds available for their basic services far less archaeological projects with scant evidence to support further investigation. They are willing enough to examine the stone but that's as far as it goes." Ruth McFranklin spoke dejectedly on the telephone to Belle.

"No more problems, Ruth," muttered Belle, "I'm up to my neck in trouble as it is."

"Oh, I'm sorry about that, Belle. I won't add to your stress. Don't worry about it. I'll just ferret away at finding finance. There's bound to be some Archaeology Department somewhere with the means to tackle what will be a preliminary search.

"Well, if you, with all your experience and contacts in the field, can't get the money perhaps we'll have to wait for better times when funds will be more easily obtained."

Belle, though disappointed, was a realist.

"Ruth chuckled wryly.

"I may not have a year or two, Belle. I'm nearly eighty years of age. I must find out if there are any more secrets up the Stinking Wynd."

"Good for you, old timer," laughed Belle, "Have you thought of approaching some rich person who might be interested in sponsoring a dig? It's just a thought. It's unlikely that you would find such a benefactor but it's worth considering."

"Belle, you might have come up with a winning idea. Your suggestion isn't so fanciful. As it happens I'm a trustee of the Terence McCool Foundation and, wait for it, so is Sir Rab Bruce. It's conceivable he might be interested. I'll sound him out."

"What a coincidence! I ran into the man only last week."

Belle described the circumstances of her encounter at the film shoot.

"If he's interested enough to make a film about the Picts, surely he would be willing to uncover more knowledge about them."

"He seems to be fully occupied with The Scottish Peoples Alliance just now. There's no harm in asking though. Shall we make it a joint approach?"

Belle pondered. Would her background and the circumstances of their unfortunate meeting be a drawback? On balance she thought not.

"Let's do it Ruth," she affirmed, her other problems forgotten.

***

Sir Rab Bruce listened impassively. Ruth's presentation was professional, forceful and persuasive. He questioned her about planning permission, where the archaeological team would come from, what costs were involved, and what was the legal position about finds. Ruth was able to satisfy him on all the points he raised.

An uncomfortable silence ensued. Ruth and Belle exchanged rueful glances. At last he excused himself, suavely indicating that there were a few points he wanted to check on. After he left the room Belle turned her thumbs down but Ruth remained hopeful.

"He's a cautious man. I've noticed that in meetings before. He takes time to make up his mind."

Bruce returned, still impassive. He scribbled a few figures on a pad before apologising for the delay.

"I've considered your proposal and I am willing to sponsor the dig with a strictly limited budget initially until we are clearer about the evidence for further investigation," he announced, a smile at last breaking over his face as he saw their reaction.

"That's wonderful news," Ruth enthused, "We wont let you down. I'm positive there's much more to be found on the site."

Belle was ecstatic.

"Sir Rab, I owe it to my parent's memory to carry out this investigation. Thank you for making it possible."

"It's a gamble," Bruce declared, "but it's one I'm willing to take. We must gain more knowledge about the Picts. As you know I'm keenly interested in our Scottish heritage. Ruth's friend, Terence McCool, left a treasure house of paintings, artifacts, stories and Scottish culture generally to the nation. We must add to it."

He beamed at the two women.

"There are five provisions:

1) We wait until my people run the rule over the figures, the legal position, etc.
2) You keep within your budget.
3) I reserve right to be present at any significant find.
4) My partner Murdo McLean Mannan shares the sponsorship
5) I take care of publicity and media interest.

"I have some reservations about the last proviso," Ruth demurred, "We don't want a media scrum crawling all over the site."

"Don't worry about that," Bruce assured her. "There will be full consultation with the archaeologists on the spot. Now let's drink to our joint venture."

CHAPTER SEVENTEEN

BELLE AND FAMILY: QUEENSTOWN

Jamie was adamant.

"We're not going to mess about with father's property on the off chance of finding some old bones or arrowheads or whatever," he expostulated, "We could get a good price for it. God knows, I need the money."

Belle regarded her brother sourly. She had not expected support from the younger of her two brothers. Jamie Ramsay was a Public Relations executive between jobs at the moment, a frequent occurrence given the precarious state of industry in recent years. Resignedly she offered to buy out Jamie's share, explaining that the archaeological project was dear to her father's heart, and that she was determined to carry out his wishes as passed on to Ruth. Jamie, however, still demurred.

"He didn't even leave the property directly to us. He gave it to that old dearie for her lifetime. My mother must be turning in his grave. Imagine! After all these years of marriage and family he still hankered for Ruth McFranklin whom he hadn't seen for donkey's years. He must have been senile to do that to us."

Belle was amused.

"I think it's very romantic, Jamie. The old man was faithful to his women unto death."

"One doesn't associate one's parents with that sort of thing," he retorted stiffly.

Belle laughed unkindly.

"You're very immature for a forty plus, Jamie. I don't think you've outgrown your adolescence. Come on! Let's not have a family row about this. I'm deeply committed to the investigation. Go along with it to please me. The property will still be there after it's all completed."

Jamie respected his big sister. She had rescued him from scrapes many times. Still somewhat petulant, he acknowledged to himself that she was deadly serious about the project. Sighing inwardly he gave way to her brisk authority. Belle smiled fondly. The same old Jamie, weak as water!

The telephone interrupted their agreement. She listened intently, her eyes glistening.

"You'll be home soon?" And you like the idea of a dig. Oh! Thank you, Johnny. If you are on leave you can help us. You will? Excellent! Bye!"

Triumphant, she replaced the receiver and swung Jamie round.

"You heard that. That was brother Johnnie. We're in business."

In spite of himself Jamie was caught up in her excitement.

"You will ensure I get my entitlement eventually," he flung at her even as he joined in the impromptu dance she led him round the room.

"I promise, Jamie," cried Belle gaily, "You can help too. It'll get some of that flab off. By the way, Sir Rab Bruce is one of the sponsors of the dig. Do you know him?"

Know him! The industrialist was remote from a mere P.R. man but his participation in the project put a different complexion on the affair. The chance to impress a tycoon of his magnitude was the opportunity of a lifetime.

"I'm in, Belle," he practically shouted.

Belle phoned Ruth later.

"The decks are cleared, Ruth. Over to you to set up an archaeological team."

CHAPTER EIGHTEEN

RANGI MCNAUGHTON: Naughtonwood

Rangi McNaughton fingered the faded army pay book, A.B. 64, and again turned to the last entry. Dishonourable Discharge, 1949. What had his grandfather done to deserve the disgrace of being dismissed from the army in that fashion?

After undertaking a search on the internet he accessed British Army Records for the period. Focussing on the Royal Engineers, he eventually found the name, Sapper John McNaughton. Switching to Court Martial Records he trawled those for 1945 onwards. There it was. Sapper McNaughton was sentenced to two years imprisonment in a military detention centre for desertion in Burma in 1945. He gave himself up in 1947. There was no record of the reason for his desertion.

He deserted in July 1945. Rangi investigated further, accessing the records of the Burma campaign of the 14th Army. By July Burma had been cleared of Japanese so it was not desertion in the face of the enemy.

It was more likely he had become involved with a Burmese girl who had become pregnant when he was due to return to the U.K. and he had opted to remain with her. Pure conjecture of course Rangi mused. Whatever the truth of the matter John McNaughton had returned to the U.K. under arrest and with a small half Burmese child. The story handed down was that his father's mother had died, leaving John to care for the child. So that was why that child, Rangi's father, was brought up by an aunt. Grandfather McNaughton was in jail. When he did appear, according to the family story, he stayed one night before departing, saying he was going to America to make his fortune. He was to come back for his son. He had not been heard of since.

Rangi turned to the Scottish and English Records Offices but could find no trace of his death. He decided to go back to records of births to try to find out about his origins. The Pay Book gave his date of birth as 1908, making him about 31 years old when World War 2 started. He tried births in Drumannanshire for that year and immediately struck gold.

John McNaughton, born 7-1-1908

Father, William McNaughton

Mother, Helen Cook

Both of Naughtonwood

So he was a local boy. Did he perhaps marry? After all he was in his thirties when he met the Burmese girl. The Register of Marriages for 1928 showed

John McNaughton married Margaret Ramsay on 26-7-1928 in the parish of Milltown- on-Devon

Did they have any children? Rangi was becoming more and more intrigued by the strange history of his errant grandfather. The register of births for 1928 showed

William Ramsay McNaughton, born on 7-12-1928

Margaret Ramsay must have been pregnant when she married. Was it a forced marriage? It was common place in those times for the man or boy to "do the decent thing" and marry the girl. Margaret Ramsay died on 8-12-1928. She must have died as a consequence of child birth. What became of William McNaughton? Rangi could find no record of a marriage or a death. It looked as though he had reached a dead end. There was one possibility. William could have taken his mother's name. He looked up William Ramsay under the registry of Marriages. There was nothing in Drumannanshire, but in Scotland as a whole twenty six William Ramsays were married in the 1950s when William Ramsay would have been of marriageable age. Gritting his teeth Rangi ploughed his way through the list. After nineteen searches he turned up the name he was looking for.

William Ramsay married Eva Bartok in 1957 in Edinburgh. This William was born in the parish of Milltown –on-Devon in 1928, birth name McNaughton. Bingo! Rangi congratulated himself on his detective work. Perhaps he should set up as a genealogist he grinned inwardly.

There was still work to be done however. He checked to see if the pair had any children. Three children were recorded as having been born in Edinburgh.

Isabelle, 1959; John, 1961; Jamie, 1965

Eva Bartok died in 1975.
William Ramsay died in 2008

Rangi sat back, staring at the family tree he had drawn as he worked.

John McNaughton	
Married Margaret Ramsay, 1928	Partner of Burmese girl, 1945(?)
Son, William McNaughton	Son, Peter McNaughton
	Married Eva Bartok, 1957	Married Janet Condie, 1965
Daughter, Isabelle Ramsay	Son, Duncan McNaughton
Son, John Ramsay	Son John McNaughton
Son, Jamie Ramsay	Daughter, Jean McNaughton

It seemed that he had relatives he had never dreamed existed. Why had he been kept in ignorance? Was the stain on the family's reputation so grave that nobody would talk about it? Or was he the first to find out the full story of John McNaughton and his two families? On reflection that seemed to be the case. His old great aunt, dead long ago, had never revealed the family secrets to anyone.

Rangi determined to find out more about his new found half cousins. The Census records might help. Sure enough! He unearthed an Edinburgh address for the family. It would probably be out-of-date but it was a starting point.

A few days later Rangi stood looking at a small block of flats in Morningside. They were no more than twenty years old but they stood on the site of the house address he had researched. William Ramsay must have been reasonably well off to have lived in this area. Had he sold the property to a developer? Rangi repaired to a newsagent's shop where the avenue of large houses joined the busy shopping area.

The shopkeeper was informative.

"Number 21? There's no number 21. Flats have been built on the site. It's now Mount Pleasant."

"I know that. I was wondering about the house that was there previously," Rangy questioned.

"Oh! Dae ye no ken? That's the hoose that was bombed. The I.R.A. did it." With that he bustled off to deal with another customer.

Rangy was stunned. He had heard of the atrocity. Quickly he accessed the Scotsman newspaper archive on the computer to refresh his memory.

TERROR COMES TO SCOTLAND. March 1975

Slowly he read the news story and the follow up articles over the next days. What he saw he at first disbelieved. He was dumbfounded. Hurriedly he checked his computer trail. There was no doubt. His facts were accurate. It would take time to digest the monumental significance of the information his researches had revealed. Meantime he had a Scottish Peoples Alliance march to attend in Aberbrothy.

CHAPTER NINETEEN

SIR RAB BRUCE AND MURDO MCLEAN MCMANNAN: DRUMANNAN

Rab Bruce turned away from the panoramic view framed in the floor to ceiling window overlooking the spread of the strath of the River Forth. The window wrapped round the new tower from south-east to north-west encompassing the Forth bridges, Wallacetown Castle and the distant Trossach Mountains.

"I tried to have this window installed in the old tower," he chuckled as he handed his friend Murdo McLean McMannan a glass of whisky. "I can't understand how you can pollute your whisky with ginger ale," he continued with an amused snort.

"Surely you're not one of those whisky buffs who discuss malts interminably." smiled Murdo.

They both laughed.

"I can see I'll have to educate you. Come though, you must inspect Drumannan Tower House. The women are already half way through the tour.

The old Tower dates back to the fourteenth century. Later, when the country settled down, a mansion, since demolished, was built next to it. I've completely refurbished the old building, which was ruinous, and erected a new house on the site of the mansion. It was difficult getting permission to tamper with an ancient monument but when I pointed out to them that it would collapse completely if nothing was done, they reluctantly agreed. Mind you they interfered every step of the way when the plans were being prepared. I won out in the end, however, as you see.

The old tower has been rebuilt to retain the historical detail of the original purpose, a typical Scottish tower house of mediaeval times. The interior however contains all the modern conveniences and comforts missing from the lives of people long ago.

It houses a conference centre. I and my executives hold staff meetings and give presentations to clients here. The local community can also use it for small functions. One of the rooms has the beginnings of a museum I'm trying to establish."

"Is there no conflict of interest?" Murdo enquired.

"As a matter of fact there is very little," Rab replied, "When Historic Scotland made the stipulation that there should be community involvement I demurred but it has turned out quite well. Of course I have first call on all the facilities."

"It's surprising how the mediaeval atmosphere is still felt."

"Yes, the interior designers worked with the architects to achieve the correct ambience. For instance the tables and chairs are of heavy oak and tapestries, albeit modern, adorn the walls. I've eschewed things like suits of armour although Natasha was keen to make a kind of film set of banqueting hall, pipers, hounds, tartan carpets, the lot."

Murdo laughed, accustomed to the foibles of rich wives.

"The house is some way removed from the Tower because I am developing the immediate environs into a courtyard and gardens to try to copy the original layout.

Now for the house itself! As you see, it is L-shaped like the Tower. The short leg contains my personal office: the main part of the house boasts its own three storey tower where we started off. With four public rooms, six bedrooms, a gym and a music room, it is a substantial house. We need servants to run it and it goes against the grain given my humble background." Sir Rab shrugged.

"I'm interested to hear that you have a music room. Is it you or your wife who is the music buff? Murdo was intrigued. He had not associated cultural interests with Rab's hard-bitten business persona.

His host grimaced. "That's a sore point. The whole family-me, Natasha, my daughter Anna when she visits, vie for possession of the studio. Unfortunately we all have different tastes."

"And you, Rab? What are your particular interests in music? Murdo asked slyly.

Rab looked at him quizzically. "Not your stuff, Murdo, I'm afraid, if you are fishing for compliments. I am no highbrow though. Puccini, Lehar, Novello and the like are what I prefer. I confess to having a sneaking admiration for a Scottish Eighties group called The Associates but don't tell the family.

Let's repair to the tower room and get down to business."

The meeting was the culmination of a series of discussions the two millionaires had held over a period of months. The meetings had been acrimonious sometimes. Both men were accustomed to negotiation with business associates but nevertheless expected to reach outcomes favourable to themselves. Rab occasionally showed flashes of temper easily controlled after years of experience in boardrooms. The younger man tended to petulance when things were not going his way. The fact that there was so much common ground between them however made agreement relatively straightforward. Murdo produced a draft he had prepared.

1) We are a grassroots organisation.
2) The aim of the organisation is to rescue Scotland from the political and economic mess it is in.
3) The method of doing so will be to supersede the professional politicians at national and local level in government.
4) The forthcoming elections will provide the opportunity to take over the reins of government.
5) Our movement will provide candidates from all walks of life.

6) These candidates will be people who volunteer their services to the country for a limited period of say three years before returning to their own careers.
7) They will be drawn from as wide a spectrum of the population as possible.
8) A Manifesto of reform will be drawn up after the widest possible consultation.
9) The provisional name of the organisation will be The Scottish Peoples Alliance.

"That's an excellent summary of our previous discussions, Murdo. We should get our public relations people to come up with ideas for a continuing publicity campaign. I've had a website prepared. T.V. radio, internet and the press should all be involved.

The men were interrupted by the entrance of their wives.

Both were excitedly discussing the décor of the guest bedrooms.

"I'm going to totally redecorate and refurnish," she announced to a bemused Rab.

"We've only just finished ...."

Tanya brushed him aside with an airy flourish

"Oh, Rab! You know we agreed I would look after the interior of the house. You're merely the outside man. Don't be tiresome." Her Russian accent thickened in amused exasperation.

Catriona backed her.

"Rab, I think the old Tower and your new house are fabulous but Natasha wants perfection. I agree with her that the décor of the guest bedrooms was a mistake."

Rab held his hands up in surrender.

"What's more important is what the two of you have to say about the launch of the S.P.A. Murdo will ask for your approval of this action plan shortly.

Catriona outlined the conclusions of the two women.

"It mustn't be seen as an all-male operation, that's for sure," She stated with a warning glance at Murdo, "Natasha and I want to ensure that a substantial number of women volunteers come forward. To that end we envisage being on platforms beside you and on our own, giving T.V. interviews and participating in the activities on our websites. Selection committees for candidates should comprise equal numbers of men and women. Oh! And we want to start a competition to design a new tartan for S.P.A. Finally the future of the nation's children and grandchildren should be given more emphasis."

The two women sat down together in a display of unity ready to argue their case.

"Let's not get into a feminist propaganda exercise," protested Murdo, "You could overemphasise the female rights bit. Let's keep things in perspective."

Rab intervened,

"I agree with Murdo. We should just take it for granted that men and women will take part without making an issue of it. The only quibble I have is about the selection of candidates. They must be chosen on merit only."

He thought to himself that Catriona must have worked on Natasha, whose country of origin was remarkable for the paucity of women in the higher echelons of government. That lady will have to be watched he mused.

"We are all agreed, then," cried Natasha grandly, "Let's eat. We're having Italian tonight."

As the women led the way to the dining room, Murdo muttered to Rab,

"We'll have to watch these two. If we're not careful they shoot off on wild schemes."

"Don't worry, Murdo," he whispered, "I've got plans that will keep them out of mischief."

CHAPTER TWENTY

MURDO MCLEAN MCMANNAN AND SIR RAB BRUCE: QUEENSTOWN

Triple M and his wife lived in a sprawling house on the south-facing slope of a hill overlooking Queenstown and the loch of the same name. The patchwork quilt of fields folded down to the valley below where the gaunt outline of the ruined palace on its promontory on the loch dominated the landscape. The incongruous union of mediaeval church architecture and a modernistic silver aluminium cross sat uneasily beside the palace. Queenstown , with its long straggling High Street and rash of new housing creeping up the opposing hill behind the town, was still a transport choke point - road, railway and canal squeezed between loch and hill - although a controversial motorway route by-passed the town. The southern hills, low and rolling, completed a pleasing prospect viewed from the picture windows of The Knock as the house was named.

The elegance of the eighteenth century main part of the house had been spoiled by ugly Victorian period additions. In an attempt to redress the balance Triple M's architects had made alterations that restored some of its former symmetry. The result was a handsome blend of architectural features of which Murdo and Catriona were inordinately proud. Separate from the mansion on a wooded spur of the hill squatted a recording studio and guest accommodation for visiting artists. The extensive grounds backed on to a private 9-hole golf course owned by a consortium of Triple M and like-minded colleagues. Golfing fanatics Murdo and Catriona revelled in the game, playing regularly on the reverse slope of the hill which offered panoramic views of the Forth valley and estuary. The house and golf course nicely complemented the similar mansion and public golf course to the west on the hill.

Sir Rab Bruce, a competent golfer, but with only a lukewarm interest in the game, played mainly for business reasons. Nevertheless he enthused over the views. He could even see his own beloved Drumannan Tower in the distance.

He was disbelieving.

"You have completed negotiations to re-roof Queenstown Palace!

Murdo laughed.

"It's a joint venture with Historic Scotland, with the addition of Lottery money. The costs are not as prohibitive as you would imagine. It's a way of preventing further deterioration of the building, and it will enable some parts to be used as a museum, lecture rooms and function rooms etc.

"You'll encounter a lot of local opposition. I know I did at Drumannan. It sounds like a magnificent idea though." Rab responded, considering the possibilities.

"We carried out a survey of local opinion to gauge reaction. So long as there was to be no burden on Council Tax people were mainly enthusiastic. I'm a Queenstown boy. The Palace has been woven into the framework of my childhood memories. I want to put something back into the town I love. I can afford to contribute to the cost - to the tune of four million pounds I might add." Murdo confessed.

Not trying to impress Rab he nevertheless waited for the reaction. Rab was noncommittal, merely warning against the probable cost overrun if Government departments were involved.

"I was wondering about your involvement as a trustee of The Terence McCool Foundation. I know you are having difficulties with your Glasgow premises, and I thought the Palace would be an ideal replacement. The Collection would enhance the other features of the enterprise.

Teeing up on the short fifth hole he said,

"Perhaps you and your fellow trustees might think about the idea."

Rab considered the proposal. The whole project seemed bristling with difficulties. If, however, it were brought to fruition he could see advantages in having the Collection in such an attractive site. Ever cautious, he merely remarked,

An interesting idea, Murdo! I'll certainly discuss it with the others."

So saying he concentrated on his selection of club for the tricky little hole.

"What do you recommend here?" he queried.

Murdo smiled inwardly. Rab was nibbling at the bait.

A low handicap player, Murdo shouted,

As an 18 handicap player you'll probably need a 5 iron, and a bit of luck."

Rab clenched his teeth. Golf Club badinage was all very well but he hated losing.

"I think I'll take a bisque here," he announced.

"You'll need it," Murdo grinned.

Later, back at The Knock the pair resumed their discussions about the progress of the Scottish Peoples Alliance.

"It was unfortunate that the Aberbrothy rally finished in violence," Rab mused, "The resulting publicity did us no good."

"Yes, that event was a disappointment. I'll make sure that my forthcoming musical spectacular at Kinross will be better stewarded. There's no lack of volunteers."

Murdo was staging a rock concert of his own group and other leading Scottish bands that supported the S.P.A.

"There's huge interest among young people," he smiled, "It'll be a sell out. We might even play an Associates number," he added slyly.

Rab laughed.

"You'd better, or I'll be very disappointed."

"Why will you be disappointed?" Catriona asked, joining them in the bow window seat of the lounge.

"Oh! It's Rab and his Associates. He thinks we should perform a whole album of their songs."

Catriona grimaced.

"I could never understand most of their stuff. Anyway, how is Natasha enjoying her trip to Russia? She was seeing her parents, wasn't she?

"I phoned her yesterday. She sounded a bit fraught. Her parents are refusing to join us here." Rab sounded frustrated.

"Oh, dear! Mind you I can understand that. I would hate to leave Scotland permanently." said Catriona pensively, "By the way, we have a problem. Some women candidates for election are worried about child care if they are elected. We don't want to deny a whole category of people the chance of participating in government because they think their families will suffer."

"Yes, most firms and organisations have agreed to offer temporary leave of absence for their staff if they are elected but housewives……….That's a tricky one," Murdo mused, "Funds are rolling in but are they sufficient to subsidise child care?"

"We'd better toss some ideas around in the steering committee although I'm finding them hard going. The committee is becoming a talking shop rather than an action group. There are so many differing views," Rab was gloomy as he contemplated another long rambling debate. Murdo was equally concerned.

"Sometimes "alliance" seems furthest from their minds. Perhaps we should remind them of the original concept of all working together."

We should get you on to that, with your golden tongue," Rab brightened as he planned the shape of the next meeting.

Although he had demurred he had been voted Chair of the Steering Committee of the S.P.A. with the proviso that it should be on an interim basis until after the elections. He himself was not standing, preferring to remain in the background. Catriona, however, was revelling in her new interest in politics, spurred on by Murdo who was content to concentrate on his music. Natasha, a foreign national, swashbuckled her way round the country cajoling women into standing for councils and the Assembly.

"I like your home," Rab observed as he gazed at the picture postcard scene before him, "You've made almost as good a job of it as I have at Drumannan."

Murdo was pleased.

"We do our best, don't we, Catriona?"

Catriona was gently mocking.

"Money helps, gentlemen, doesn't it? She enquired sweetly.

CHAPTER TWENTY ONE

RUTH, BELLE, AND THE ARCHAEOLOGISTS: NAUGHTONWOOD

Ruth and Belle met two archaeologists by appointment in the cottage in Naughtonwood. The stout woman shook Ruth's hand vigorously,

"I've heard a lot about you, Lady McFranklin. The story of your detective work which led to the discovery of the Fish Cross lives on in St. Regulus."

The Professor of Archaeology at The University of St. Regulus eyed Ruth curiously.

She saw before her an elderly woman, tall, stick thin, erect. Her blade-like nose dominated the sun-wrinkled face, the tight mouth giving her a grim appearance, only lightened when her eyes twinkled at the recognition of her earlier contribution to knowledge of the Picts.

"That was a long time ago but I count it as one of the successes of my career. I would like to introduce you to my friend, Belle Ramsay, the daughter of my benefactor. Belle has a vested interest in this place as well as a keen interest in the Picts. I have the property for my lifetime: Belle and her brothers inherit it on my death. So you see we must ensure that any archaeological work done is with her agreement." Ruth turned enquiringly to the other archaeologist.

Let me introduce my colleague Dr. John York. He is the technical expert who keeps me up-to-date with the latest gadgetry in the field."

Ruth sized them up. They were the people she and Belle have to trust with the excavation. Angela Bull had quite a reputation as a field archaeologist, having organised successful digs in Angus and Easter Ross. She had published several research papers which had received respectful attention in scholarly circles. She was reputed not to suffer fools gladly, causing tears among students and volunteers on digs. Her favoured dress was khaki tops and shorts and an Australian bush hat pushed back from her broad reddish bespectacled face.

Dr. York was more of an unknown quantity. Recently arrived from Wessex University, he was tall, stooped, with a thin sharp face and lank black hair falling to one side. Predictably he was dressed in a frayed sports jacket and brown corduroy trousers and scuffed desert boots. His response to the introduction was reserved. He seemed more interested in his surroundings than in the people around him, his eyes flicking anywhere but never contacting those of the people he was meeting.

Had Professor Bull been offhand in her introduction, Ruth mused? Was there a flash of resentment in his quick glance at her? A situation to be watched, Ruth thought, as Belle responded to Angela Bull's query about the extent of the property.

"Let's walk round, Belle invited, "We'll establish the perimeter of the excavation possibilities, and then we'll show you the find. By the way our sponsors might drop in to see you later."

"Oh, God! I hope they are not going to interfere," cried Professor Bull, "It's bad enough having you two poking around."

"Dr. York smiled sourly.

"That's all we need, "Rich dilettantes playing themselves with a new hobby."

Belle bristled but Ruth laughed.

"You don't need to worry. Both of them are far too busy with their big hobby of the Scottish Peoples Alliance to be bothered with a little sideshow like this. Anyway I shall act as a buffer to make doubly certain you are left in peace to get on with your dig. As for Belle and me all we ask is that we are allowed to be occasional volunteers, enthusiastic amateurs. And remember, without the rich mens' money you would be stuck with lecturing pimply students instead of enjoying yourselves in the field," she added sharply.

With a harrumph Angela Bull thrust her bulk through the narrow door of the cottage, John York following with pursed lips. Belle shot Ruth an alarmed look.

"Don't worry Belle. Rab will be business-like and Murdo will charm them," Ruth mollified her.

They emerged into the sunlight of a May morning in the centre of Naughtonwood, a nondescript ex-mining village. The view, however, was spectacular. Ruth enthused.

"Look at those hills. I live just round the corner at Allanford but there is nothing to beat this view."

Perched on top of a low ridge to the south of the strath of the River Devon, Naughtonwood commanded a sweeping view across the mile-wide valley to the dramatic, almost vertical, 1000 foot plunge of the Ochil Hills fault to sea level. The fault line lay on an east-west axis for 10 miles, the rocky faces broken by cleft-like glens scoured by rushing hidden streams below the sparse canopy of trees clinging to impossible slopes. Prevailing westerly winds swept an endless variety of clouds along the ramparts of the hills, providing a kaleidoscope of soft green, blue, brown, grey and black colours in different weather conditions. Behind the fault the Ochils rose to over 2000 feet, a jumbled wilderness of rolling grassy tops, bracken, heather, peat hags and mosses, cut by the secret penetrating gorges.

"This view must lift the spirits of Naughtonwood folk every morning." Ruth murmured.

"Very nice," snorted John York.

"We're in the centre of the original settlement where we stand," Ruth said, ignoring York's snide remark.

It forms an ideal defensive position. To the north is the steep 200 foot drop to the Devon valley: to east and west are two small streams that debouch into deep eroded gullies running down to the river although the western one is now culverted under the Main Street : to the south is the mostly uninhabited land that used to be the great forest of Drumannan, for centuries the hunting ground of kings. This little upward-sloping lane we are on was named

The Castle. There is no folk memory of why it should be so called. Modern housing now crowns the top of the knowe, or knoll as you would call it. Of course the village has now expanded beyond the original settlement area, but old Naughton, whoever he was, picked a good spot for his "Castle".

This house, halfway up the slope where another small lane called The Stinking Wynd joins The Castle Lane, was once a small dairy. The property has a small field attached to it. Fortunately Belle's father did not allow it to be built upon. This, I think, should be the focus of your operations. Let's walk round.

"You've built an interesting theory on flimsy evidence. Don't you agree, Professor Bull," Dr. York commented.

"I'm inclined to agree," Angela replied.

"Just wait until you see the corroborative evidence below the house," Ruth shouted cheerfully over her shoulder as she led the way back.

The old Victorian dairy cottage stood, blocky, foursquare, grey stone gable end to the wind. Of typical two up, two down construction, it still had old fashioned sash windows in each small room. A kitchenette and bathroom had been added later, replacing an outside toilet. Belle's father had converted the adjoining byre or cowshed into a garage. It was to the garage that Ruth led the group.

"As you see the trapdoor is in the north-east corner of the byre, roughly made to conceal the opening to the space below when the new floor was being put in for the garage."

"My Dad was a keen do-it-yourself man," interrupted Belle, "He did all this himself. I was always telling him to remember his heart condition."

"Be careful of the steps and don't forget the very low roof." So saying Ruth again led the way.

***

Ruth and Belle exchanged amused glances. The two archaeologists were staring disbelievingly at the recumbent stone. For a long moment nothing was said. Angela Bull edged towards it almost reverently.

"This is…" she searched inadequately for a word to express her wonder.

John York was equally thunderstruck.

"The find of the decade," he exclaimed, "It's in pristine condition."

Ever the professional, he quizzed Ruth sharply.

"Are you sure nothing's been moved? I would hate to think the site's been contaminated."

"Don't worry. Belle's father knew too much about archaeology to make that kind of mistake, and I certainly haven't touched anything." Ruth responded waspishly.

"So you don't know what's on the under side," Angela asked.

No, it will require lifting apparatus to find that out," Ruth replied.

"This stone could have been carved yesterday except that of the colour on the relief work only traces remain."

"The very fact that there are colour traces is exciting," spluttered John excitedly, "Look! It's unfinished as if the sculptor had just finished work for the night."

"But there are no tools or chippings around. I don't think it could have been worked on……" She checked herself. We mustn't anticipate a proper assessment. Let's just survey the rest of the earth house. You were right, Ruth. There's no doubt about it. It is a souterrain. Look at those capping stones!"

"There's nothing else visible. We'll have to excavate to discover if there is anything underneath." John York seemed animated, circling crouched round the stone.

"If you've seen enough for a preliminary viewing I suggest we adjourn upstairs for a cup of tea. We can discuss your plan of action in a little more comfort," announced Ruth.

"The funds are in place. I'll arrange for equipment and volunteer helpers. It'll need heavy lifting gear to get that stone out of the weem. The floor of the garage will have to be disturbed, and possibly the roof. The whole area of the earth house and its surroundings will have to be examined and partly excavated. I'll arrange for Dr. York to do a geophysical survey of the adjoining field. We don't wish to waste the summer weather so I'll try to have everything in place to start in a fortnight. Do you think we can manage that, Dr York?" Angela, her eyes gleaming, was in her element planning ahead.

John York looked dubious.

"It's doubtful. But I'll try," he added hastily as she swivelled round and gave him a baleful stare.

"Belle and I will of course do everything possible to help. We'll enjoy another experience of a dig won't we, Belle?" Ruth was equally excited.

"I'll be available most weekends," Belle responded.

"Good, see you in a fortnight" Angela said cheerfully as she gathered up her notes.

As she drove off in her car she leaned out of the window and called,

"By the way, we'll have to consider knocking the house down."

Belle and Ruth were left speechless.

CHAPTER TWENTY TWO

BELLE AND RANGI: Naughtonwood

Janet McNaughton eyed her visitors suspiciously.

Rangi's not home yet. He should be in from work in about half an hour" she added with ill grace.

Belle explained how she had rescued Rangi from the riot in Aberbrothy. Janet softened.

"So that's how he came to be in such a mess, blood all over. I thought some neds had jumped him because of his race, you know. It wouldn't be the first time. Have some tea while you wait."

The widow Janet lived in an ex-council house in Naughtonwood neatly extended with a porch-cum-conservatory. The comfortable interior was cluttered children's toys and the walls were covered with smiling school photographs and family snaps.

"My grandchildren," Janet explained, "I have seven of them. No, Rangy isn't married now. He used to be but it didn't work out. That's why he's back with me for a while.

"Oh! There he is."

Rangy paused outside, studying the Mercedes that had dropped him off after the riot before entering the house.

"I was in the neighbourhood and I thought I would look in and see how you were. You seem to have recovered quickly," Belle gushed, uncertain of her reception.

"It was good of you to come. I'm fine now. What brought you to this area? I thought you lived near Edinburgh."

Rangy smiled uneasily. These were not the kind of people usually seen in Naughtonwood.

"I was visiting my father's holiday cottage in Castle Street," explained Belle.

Rangy was dumbfounded.

"Your father is Weelum Ramsay? He asked.

"Why, yes! He lived here as a boy," Belle replied.

There was a long silence.

"Is anything the matter?" Belle demanded. Rangy and Janet exchanged a long look. Eventually Rangy shrugged.

"My grandfather was John McNaughton. He was married to a Margaret Ramsay who seems to have died in childbirth. They had a son called Weelum. My Grandfather left him and joined the army, eventually going to Burma. Weelum was brought up by an aunt after taking his mother's maiden name. That son was your father. John McNaughton had another child in Burma. That child was my father. I am your half cousin," he blurted out in a torrent of words.

It was Ruth's turn to be thunderstruck.

"Are you sure?" she spluttered, "Is this a joke?"

"Here are copies of the birth and marriage certificates and the family tree," Rangi said eagerly.

Belle and Ruth examined the evidence Rangi had produced.

"So that's the answer to an old mystery," Ruth whispered," Weelum told me often that he wished he knew what had happened to his father. How romantic! Long lost cousins!"

"I'm having difficulty taking this in," Belle muttered, "I'm in a complete daze. Wait till I tell my brothers. It's so exciting. I have a thousand questions."

So saying she embraced and kissed an embarrassed Rangy and his beaming mother.

"When Rangi told me the result of his researches I was equally stunned. This calls for a celebration. I'm afraid I've only got sherry though."

The others laughed, their heads filled with a jumble of thoughts and conjectures. Rangi was relieved. He had been in trepidation about the reception Belle would give to his news that she had a half Burmese cousin. His spirits rose. She had accepted him."

Belle considered her cousin, Duncan McNaughton, known as Rangi (short for Rangoon she remembered). He bore little resemblance to her father. Small and wiry with regular features, slightly slanting eyes and a skin tinged with gold, his face showed the bruises he had sustained in the riot. His dark eyes darted from her to Ruth and back, still seeking reassurance that all was well. It must be a constant anxiety to be of mixed race at a time of increasing racial tension, Belle thought. He looks as though he has suffered his fair share of it. She wondered if her other cousins were similarly affected.

"What about my other cousins," she enquired of Janet, "I see they have children," she added with a smile.

"John lives here in the village with his wife and three children, and Jean lives in Aberbrothy with her partner and two children. Here they are," Janet McNaughton continued proudly, passing round the photos from the wall.

Ruth and Belle dutifully cooed over the smiling young faces, Belle fascinated by the array of new relatives. Neither she nor her brothers had any children she reflected and now there was a positive swarm of children of her blood.

"We must all meet soon," she declared, "and I'll introduce you to my brothers."

She wondered about Jamie's reaction but Johnny would be delighted.

Rangy looked dubious.

"I'll see what the others think," he muttered.

What would be the attitude of Brother John, a rabid left winger who scorned middle class values, including the ownership of holiday cottages? A local councillor, John McNaughton might not take kindly to Belle and her family.

"What work do you do?" asked Ruth to cover the uncomfortable silence that followed.

"Rangi's an I.T. specialist. He has a good job at Sir Rab Bruce's engineering works in Aberbrothy. He has a B.Sc. from St. Regulus University," she added to establish Rangi's credentials as an educated man, a credit to his mother. "He's only recently joined the firm, and he's enjoying it, aren't you, son."

Rangi flushed with embarrassment at his mother's evident pride.

"Are you here to sell the cottage up The Castle?" Janet enquired, "I saw some people going round earlier."

Ruth grinned. The rumour mill was working already in the village. She and Belle quickly explained the purpose of their visit and the involvement of the archaeologists.

"Well, I never!" exclaimed Janet in wonder.

Rangi was thrilled.

"An archaeological dig, here in Naughtonwood! I've been interested in the local history for years but I never imagined something like this," he marvelled, "Do you think I could help out at weekends?"

"I'll see what I can do," said Ruth cheerfully, inwardly groaning. It seemed that everyone told about the project wanted to help. She could imagine the reaction of the archaeologists trying to cope with a surfeit of over enthusiastic amateurs, all expecting to find buried treasure.

As Ruth and Belle waved goodbye to the McNaughtons Ruth reflected on the reaction Weelum Ramsay would have had to the later history of his errant father. Belle wondered what other mysteries lay in her father's past, Weelum Ramsay, Order of Merit, ex- Prime Minister of Great Britain.

CHAPTER TWENTY THREE

RANGI AND FAMILY, NAUGHTONWOOD

"A long lost cousin!" Johnny McNaughton was incredulous "Weelum Ramsay's daughter! I don't believe it."

Silently Rangi handed over the evidence of the family tree to his younger brother.

Johnny McNaughton, ex-miner, country park ranger, local councillor for Sauchen and Naughtonwood on Drumannanshire Council, dyed-in-the-wool old Labour activist, fiercely proud of his village and its mining history. He flicked the documents back to Rangi.

"What's she like, this Belle Ramsay? I'll bet she's middle class to the core. She'll have left behind her socialist origins. After all the daughter of a Prime Minister must have been born with a silver spoon in her mouth."

"She seems a very nice person," said Rangi mildly. "She accepted me and Mum immediately and was genuinely pleased to meet relations she had never heard of."

"What about the race thing?" Johnny was excessively sensitive about his mixed ancestry.

"There was no hesitation. She quite simply accepted me."

"Is the story about the archaeological dig true, then? Your mother had some story about Weelum Ramsay's old house."

"Yes! You'll never guess. Weelum Ramsay has left his house to an old flame of his, Lady McFranklin no less, and she's discovered something in it."

Johnny was intrigued, then suspicious.

"I hope they get our official permission before they start excavating."

He was Convener of the Drumannanshire Council Planning Committee. Rangi knew his brother of old. Jealous of the powers of the Local Authority, Johnny was a stickler for the rules.

"I'm sure they will," he stated. "Sir Rab Bruce is sponsoring the dig."

Johnny's brow darkened.

"That capitalist! I've crossed swords with him before. I hope he doesn't try to ride roughshod over the regulations."

Rangi protested.

"He's done a lot for employment in the county, and I work for him, remember."

"I'll give you that, Rangi, but never trust the boss class. Underneath they are all the same. The working man always comes off worst."

Rangi grimaced. Johnny was off on one of his rants again.

"Come off it, brother. You are a dinosaur. It's time you caught up with the modern world. I've got to go now. By the way, Belle Ramsay wishes to meet you and the family sometime. She specially wants to see the children."

Reluctantly Johnny agreed.

"Aye, well, I suppose she is family in a funny kind of way. Weelum Ramsay's daughter! My cousin!" He shook his head, still trying to take it all in.

CHAPTER TWENTY-FOUR

RODDY AND THE SCOTTISH PEOPLES ALLIANCE

Roddy Neilson looked forward with some trepidation to his meeting with the instigators of The Scottish Peoples Alliance. Disillusioned with the Labour Party and increasingly concerned about the state of the country, he had gravitated to the S.P.A. and its appeal to responsible people to devote three years of their lives for the good of the country without thought of personal ambition or party advantage.

Sir Rab Bruce, Murdo and Catriona McMannan interviewed him in the Bruce Tower, seated in front of the picture windows of the opulent drawing room, the windings of the River Forth a silver snake below. Roddy stressed his theme in a powerful presentation, subordinating policies to a minor place in his exposition.

Murdo was suitably impressed with his evident sincerity: Sir Rab and Catriona were less so.

"You know the stock of politicians is so low among the public that people might not look on you as much of an acquisition to our cause. What do you say to that?" Rab observed with a piercing look at an uncomfortable Roddy.

Roddy shrugged resignedly.

"I'm only too well aware of that. All I can do is stand by my record. I'm corruption free. I have always put the public good first. I was always loyal to colleagues who, I thought, had similar standards and principles. My loyalty was misplaced one time too often,"

Catriona intervened.

"Mr. Neilson, you are a socialist. Socialist principles have been shown to be defective: socialist politicians have been shown to be venal more often than not. How can you possibly help us without changing your views," she added waspishly.

"I thought I had been indicating to you that I was indeed doing just that. Socialism must adapt to changing times. I am adapting," Roddy maintained forcefully, "I am offering considerable experience of devoted public service, and I am offering complete commitment."

Sir Rab intervened.

"We'll let you know, Mr. Neilson. We are interested but you will appreciate the anxieties we have about recruiting an ex-Deputy Leader of the Scottish Labour Party.

***

"Have you had any word from Natasha? Catriona asked Rab.

"Yes, she's been delayed, still trying to convince her parents of the merits of living in Scotland and the virtues of her wonderful son-in-law," Rab joked.

He was, however, troubled. Natasha was needed to exercise better control over her vast assets in the West.

"We'll just have to manage without her for the present. Now, what about Neilson?" Rab challenged, "Murdo, you championed him. Defend your position."

Rab settled back in his custom-built chair-foot rest, drinks holder, racks for papers, directional lights, a swivelled laptop computer and phone, and a heated seat, all electronically controlled. Playfully he activated a spotlight, focusing it on Murdo.

"Hey! Tell me where you got the chair. I must get one too," Murdo was an avid collector of gadgets.

"We should mount a publicity campaign to demonstrate that Neilson's secession from the Labour Party was an indication of the success of our Movement as a coming force in the land, particularly if important figures in the other parties follow suit. I would like to see Neilson as a mentor to those of our people who are unaccustomed to public speaking, debate, committee procedures and public administration. He could emerge as a prominent minister in a future Assembly." Murdo was waxing enthusiastic.

"I like the man. He is generally recognised as a straight arrow, as they say.

"I don't trust him," snorted Catriona. "Neilson's background and career don't impress me one little bit. And he's personally ambitious, jumping on the bandwagon when he sees a winner."

Rab smiled coldly.

"That's putting it a little strongly, Catriona. I don't entirely trust him either, but I see some merit in Murdo's plan. Let's make him a kind of workhorse- but we'll keep a close watch over his activities."

CHAPTER TWENTY FIVE
BELLE AND RODDY: QUEENSTOWN

Belle was smouldering, gin and tonic fast disappearing in hurried gulps, showing her suppressed anger.

"You've thought this action through and accepted the invitation to join that half-baked organisation, The Scottish Peoples Alliance. It's a rich man's play thing. Sir Rab Bruce and Murdo McMannan are no doubt well meaning but they'll tire of the game - the compromises, the backbiting, the failures, the increasing opprobrium of a fickle public. It'll end in tears, you'll see, Roddy."

Belle felt tense and anxious. Her thoughts had been full of excitement about the impending dig, and confused wonder about the revelations concerning her new relatives. She had hoped for a relaxed evening discussing her news with Roddy over a quiet drink. Instead he had sprung this sorry tale on her. There had been no consultation. It was presented as a fait accompli. So much for their personal relationship!

"I was afraid to discuss it with you, Belle. I was only too well aware of what your reaction would be. My decision would have been all the more difficult. My mind is made up. I think the S.P.A. is a tidal wave of change. It could herald a new era of probity and honesty in government. God! It's badly needed.

The news bulletins daily contain reports of race riots in London and Bradford, anti-Scottish demonstrations in Newcastle, the burning of "white settler" homes in the Highlands, and the bullying of children speaking with an English accent in Scottish schools. The latest Health and Safety Regulations about police and firemen exposing themselves "unnecessarily" to any risk of danger had resulted in scorn and derision in the media and among the public. Another lame ruling on Human Rights had set a murderer free on technical grounds added to a general lack of faith in an already tottering legal system. The worldwide downturn in the economy was having a disproportionate effect on the U.K.causing the government to take panic measures to try to avoid mass unemployment. In Scotland the opposition parties had successfully paralysed the minority government by defeating every proposed action.

Belle, radical measures are needed to save the country."

Belle gave Roddy a sad, considering look. The catalogue of woes facing the country was lengthy and appalling, but did he really think the S.P.A. could better matters? He had not felt it necessary to discuss his defection with her. The distance between them was widening. Did she really want to return to their previous loving intimacy? She was unsure. The migraine crept up on her, knifing into her head. She was full of foreboding.

Roddy recognised the signs and slipped away. Belle was becoming very difficult to live with. Did he want to continue like this? Roddy, too, was full of foreboding.

CHAPTER TWENTY SIX

RANGI: ABERBROTHY

Rangy was puzzled. Bruce Engineering occupied a riverside site in Aberbrothy, employing 2000 people, providing a much needed fillip to the economy of a once thriving industrial town. The Company made equipment for the oil industry and housed a substantial research facility. A recent grant from the Government together with a major input from Drumannan Holdings, the conglomerate owned by Sir Rab Bruce, was funding advanced research into wave, tidal and solar power for the generation of electricity. The search for alternative sources of power was causing oil interests to invest heavily in such research. Bruce Engineering was in the van, piloting exciting new technologies.

The intense security surrounding the research facility was what puzzled Rangy. Lesser mortals like him, working in other parts of the vast complex were barred completely from "the boffins' place" as it was known. The fact that there was even an inner ring of security within the closed area piqued his curiosity further. His interest in a striking-looking Chinese woman whom he had observed entering the research complex almost daily contributed to his keen interest in the place, particularly when she began to nod to him in passing.

Eventually he plucked up courage to ask her to join him for coffee in the canteen and she agreed with a friendly smile. Dr. Cheong Su was an engineering graduate researching tidal and wave power. She had recently been recruited from an academic post in a university in her native Singapore. She found Scotland cold and beautiful. Her little flat in Milltown-of-Devon nestled at the foot of Milltown Glen where a turbulent burn gushed from the Ochils. She was interested in exploring the hills which were a complete contrast to the ordered environment of her island home and gratefully accepted Rangy's offer to be her hill-walking guide. She thought Rangy's history romantic and somewhat sad.

The thirty-five year old, plump, yellow, slightly moon-faced, slanting eyes, ever-ready white-toothed smile, and pony-tailed jet black hair enchanted him. He fell for her like a ton of bricks. Soon, two lonely people, they became constant companions, both with bad marriages behind them, but eager to start a new relationship.

Cheong Su talked enthusiastically about her all consuming interest- the problem of making tidal power a cost efficient way of producing electrical power. She was dismissive of the solar power project, idly wondering why Drumannan Holdings were so keen on it.

"We'll have a breakthrough soon, Rangy," she declared, "if I can convince my superiors that I am on the right track."

Rangy wondered about the difference between her exciting research work and his own humdrum computer training job. Cheong Su was impatient with him.

"We are who we are. There's chemistry between us, Rangy. We click. Soon you will sleep with me."

Rangy's heart turned over.

CHAPTER TWENTY SEVEN

THE NECHTAN STONE

The winch cable tautened, taking the strain of the weight of the massive stone. The initial inertia overcome, the stone slid along the rollers laid on the floor of the souterrain before inching up greased planks on an incline leading up to ground level.

Triumphant, Professor Angela Bull turned to the onlookers.

"What do you think of my modus operandi?" she crowed, "Dr. York was convinced it wouldn't work."

The Pictish sculptured stone now lay on the floor of the cow shed converted to a large garage by Weelum Ramsay.

"I'm afraid we had to destroy part of the garage floor to form the ramp out of the souterrain," Angela explained, "The next step is to turn the stone over and examine what's on the other side. See, we have some cushioning material on which the stone can fall when we tip it over. Before we do so, however, Dr York and I will bring you up-to-date on the progress so far.

Ruth, Belle, Sir Rab Bruce, Murdo and Catriona McMannan, a collection of students and a few curious villagers, absorbed by the proceedings, crowded closer to the two archaeologists.

Adopting lecture mode, Angela Bull addressed the group.

"The previous owner of this house, Mr. Ramsay, discovered the existence of the stone when he was renovating this cow shed into a garage. The stone lay in a souterrain (or weem or earth house as such underground structures are variously known) which lies partly under the garage and partly projecting beyond its northern wall.

Mr. Ramsay bequeathed the property to Lady McFranklin, leaving instructions as to the location of the stone. She immediately recognised the importance of the find and, in collaboration with Mr. Ramsay's daughter, Belle, found two sponsors to finance an archaeological investigation of the site.

Dr. York and I have carried out a preliminary survey and have concluded that the site merits a full scale investigation.

A superficial examination of this stone shows it to be a class 11 type sculptured stone of the Pictish period. As you can see, it is a shaped rectangular slab made of reddish sandstone, roughly 8 feet in length, 2 feet wide, and 12 inches thick. Because it is carved in bas relief on a flat background as opposed to the incised carving on class 1 stones of an earlier time, we can date it to the seventh or eighth centuries A. D. What we find on the reverse side should confirm this hypothesis, particularly if there is Christian symbolism on it.

Its position in a souterrain is puzzling. Souterrains were in use at a much earlier time in history. They were, as the name suggests, underground chambers built with massive stones, low-roofed and usually somewhat banana-shaped. Their use is obscure, but it has been suggested they were used for storing grain. New ones are discovered sometimes when farmers are ploughing fields, or are disturbed by excavations as happened here. It may be that the later Picts continued to use these structures. We just don't know. The fact that the souterrain is empty apart from the stone is equally puzzling. Why is the stone there? It was not used as a workshop. It is a confined space and there is no evidence of stone chippings, etc. the kind of thing one would expect to find in a stone mason's workplace. The only tangible evidence is a scattering of seeds which will be analysed at a later stage.

Dominating the exposed side of the stone is a large carving of a fish, probably a salmon. Above the fish are two abstract symbols, common to other Pictish stones. The symbols are what are known as the Crescent and V-Rod and the Double Disc and Z-Rod. Many theories have been advanced as to the meaning of these symbols and representations of animals but the mystery of their meaning remains. I certainly don't wish to advance any ideas about the symbols on this stone at this early stage in our investigation, if ever.

On the lower part of the stone is carved a hunting scene, similar to the ones on other stones. We can distinguish hunting from battle scenes depicted by the apparel and weapons the people are shown wearing and using.

The edges of the stone are decorated by intricate interwoven designs typical of Celtic Art.

A most interesting feature of our stone is the lettering along the bottom. There is a row of indecipherable words on the top row, although one of them could be Nechtan. Such lettering has been seen before on another stone. Below is the beginning of a row of letters which is in Latin. The first word is Regnum, the second is Nechtani, and the third contains only a syllable and a half formed letter. It almost looks as though the mason has been interrupted in his work.

The relief on our stone is remarkably well preserved. I don't think there is any doubt that it has never been exposed to weathering. In conclusion, this sculptured stone is one of the most exciting Pictish finds ever made.

Dr. York took over.

"I have little to add to what Professor Bull has told you," York spoke stiffly, obviously rattled by Angela's boast about extracting the stone her way.

"I have conducted a preliminary geophysical survey of the garden and adjoining field. There are a number of anomalies below the surface. These anomalies require more detailed examination. Old mine workings, however, complicate the issue. Local sources inform me that at least one shaft was visible in the field in living memory."

He inclined his head in acknowledgement to Rangi McNaughton, standing on the fringe of the crowd. A study of mining records for the immediate area of Naughtonwood show considerable activity. It is likely that older shallow workings, which were common, will also exist. I think, however, that it would be worthwhile opening a few trenches."

"What would you be looking for exactly," interrupted Murdo.

"Possibly another souterrain, the remains of dwellings, workshops, fortifications. Who knows?" John York was dismissive, "Any evidence of occupation."

Angela Bull resumed her commentary.

"It is probable that people have lived on this site for many centuries. Demolishing the house, certainly the garage might yield important information."

She beamed at Belle and Ruth expectantly.

"No way," spluttered Belle.

"There is much to be done before we consider that course of action, Angela," intervened Ruth smoothly, "Perhaps we could discuss the matter later. Meantime, tell us about the name Nechtan inscribed on the stone. What's significance does it have?"

"Ah, Nechtan! A common Pictish name if the king lists are anything to go by. This Nechtan must have been an important personage to have his name on the stone. It's significant, too, that this village is called Naughtonwood - Nechtan's wood. In the eighth century the countryside to the south of Naughtonwood was the area of an extensive stretch of forest, later known as the great forest of Drumannan. We might garner more information about Nechtan as we excavate. At least we can be pretty sure the Picts were here then.

Let's find out more about our stone meantime. Are we ready to ease it over?" she enquired of her team of students."

With a chorused, "Yes," The volunteers heaved the stone on to its edge.

"Gently now!" admonished Angela, "Lower it to the cushion."

The stone landed with a muffled thud. What was revealed drew a gasp from the onlookers. A massive Christian cross covered the whole area of the slab. Its intricate carving seeming to leap out at the viewer, so startling was the relief. The cross was surrounded by Celtic designs and patterns of extraordinary complexity. The overall effect was awesome, conveying the intensity of the religious fervour that had inspired it.

"It surpasses the ones in Glamis and Aberlemno," gasped John York and it's in absolutely pristine condition."

"A prime example of a class 11 stone," exclaimed Professor Bull, "The person who sculpted this was an outstanding artist."

There was a general hubbub of delighted comment, laughter, even a small cheer. Everyone crowded round, excitedly pointing out individual sections to each other, trying to take photographs, and, in some cases touching the stone. Angela Bull became alarmed.

"Everybody back," she roared, ushering people towards the garage door, "You've all had a look. Now we need to conduct a detailed examination in private, before deciding where to store it in safety."

"I know the very place," Sir Rab interjected swiftly, "the museum in Bruce Tower has tight security."

"All in good time, Sir Rab," replied Angela testily, "That decision can wait."

Just then a camera flash startled her.

"I trust that is not a press photographer," John York bawled, puce with rage.

A T.V. camera poked through the garage door and a microphone was stuck under his nose.

"For God's sake clear these people out of here. This is no time for the media to barge in. There will be a properly organised press conference later."

She vigorously shoved the hapless T.V. reporter bodily out of the door.

"Who leaked this story to the media?" she demanded literally spitting with fury.

"I'm afraid I did." stated Catriona levelly, "I was meeting some reporters about the film I'm working on, and casually mentioned the discovery. I thought it would be good publicity for archaeology in general and this dig in particular."

"Publicity! Who needs publicity?" She shot a withering look at a cool Catriona and stormed into the house which had been transformed into an office and work place for the archaeological team.

In the confusion that followed Dr. York organised the students into a security screen to clear the garage, leaving the small group of sponsors stunned by the altercation. Sir Rab was the first to recover as they filed into the house. "What's done is done. We'll have to devise a proper security system to avoid further incidents like this. Leave it to me, Professor Bull. I'll put my security chief on to the problem immediately."

"Thank you, Sir Rab, but the damage is done. I shudder to think what my colleagues in the field of archaeology will make of this fiasco. We'll get little peace now," she replied angrily, "Now, if you'll excuse us, John and I have work to do." So saying she and Dr. York marched out.

"So it's John now," Ruth smiled. "She obviously thinks she has to close ranks against interfering sponsors when she calls Dr. York by his first name."

Belle laughed.

"A little diplomacy is required here. Murdo, you're a smoothie. What do you suggest?"

Murdo twinkled. I think a sweetener from the McMannans is necessary. Maybe I could volunteer to provide that additional digging machine Angela was muttering about."

Belle grinned.

"A man after my own heart. Catriona, I think you should lie low for a bit."

Catriona flushed.

"They're a touchy pair. Publicity never did anyone any harm."

The publicity will do the cause of the Scottish Peoples Alliance no harm either," observed Sir Rab slyly, "You're a wily bird, Catriona."

Catriona smiled demurely.

CHAPTER TWENTY EIGHT

THE ELECTION CAMPAIGN 2011

Roddy Neilson threw himself wholeheartedly into the preparations for coming local and national elections. The signs were encouraging. The enthusiasm in the country for the Scottish Peoples Alliance was undiminished. Large turnouts at rallies, wide favourable media coverage and the emergence of a block of solid candidates for office, both local and national, had blown away the traditional parties. Opinion polls gave the S.P.A .more than 50% of the vote with the other parties nowhere. Some candidates turned out to be charismatic. A Professor of History at the University of Wallacetown. a well known figure for his books and T.V. programmes on Scottish history, had thrown himself into the fray; the managing director of a medium sized plastics company had produced pragmatic ideas for industry and had projected them well in the media; a middle aged married woman whose children were grown up became an overnight star, her commonsense debunking the sillier policies of Health and Safety and sentencing of prisoners; Catriona McMannan, consummate actress as she was, entranced the younger generation of voters, ably backed up by the Triple M pop group. A number of candidates had outlined sensible ideas on education, the legal system and the environment. The problems of deprivation was the one area where there seemed to be no consensus view. This difficult area was a worry to Roddy as was the selection of a small number of candidates who had revealed themselves to be eccentrics, self servers, publicity seekers and rabble rousers.

Sir Rab Bruce was sanguine. This was to be expected he opined. Some rogues and oddballs will always slip through the net. A strong administration will curb any excesses. Roddy was forced to agree.

"Who do you reckon the members will elect as their leader if - sorry, when we get in?" mused Murdo McMannan.

"The outstanding candidate without doubt is Professor Latto of Wallacetown University," replied Roddy, "I'll certainly give him my vote."

"Agreed," added Sir Rab, "he has caught the imagination of the public with his demolition of the S.N.P.'s half baked aspirations, especially in view of their abysmal record in the present minority government. Reneging on their promises about policing and their failure on local Income Tax revealed them for what they are- just another set of politicians promising the earth and back-pedalling as soon as they attain office."

His disdain for all politicians caused a chuckle from Murdo but a thoughtful frown from Roddy.

"That might be a problem for us. We must put a curb on our wilder spirits."

"Well, it's over to you and Catriona now, Roddy. You'll be on the spot. Murdo and I have done our job. We've provided financial support and publicity to rouse the people. Let the people now act through their independent representatives." You have the respect and liking of the middle of the road voters and Catriona is the darling of the younger ones.

A political career has no interest for me. I just want a Scotland that encourages thrift, hard work and enterprise and a respect for law and order. I want a Scotland that is proud of its achievements but eschews stupid posturing like "the best wee country in the world" nonsense. I want to help develop Scotland as a technologically advanced country with successful industries. I want my own enterprises to be in the van of these developments."

Roddy was somewhat taken aback by Sir Rab's vehemence. There was a messianic look in his eye and his voice had risen to almost a shout. Murdo applauded.

I'm not really a political animal either, unlike Catriona. In fact if it hadn't been for her I don't think I would have become involved to this extent. My true interests lie in Scotland's cultural heritage.. I'm content to work in that context."

A month later the Scottish Peoples Alliance swept the polls, first at local, and then at national level, gaining control in the major cities and surrounding areas and a huge majority in the Scottish Assembly.

Roddy Neilson retained his seat in Queenstown.

Catriona McMannan defeated the new labour leader in the Paisley Constituency.

CHAPTER TWENTY NINE

BELLE: EDINBURGH

"St. Bernard's College will be closed," The Under-secretary steepled his long bony fingers and regarded Belle Ramsay with speculative eyes.

"I'm doing you a favour by giving you this information in advance of the official announcement. The representations of you and others in favour of retaining the College were carefully considered but the view was taken that amalgamation was the best option among those considered. All our efforts must now be directed towards making the transition to a new super college on two campuses a success."

Belle remained silent. She had expected this outcome but it was a shock nevertheless. She reflected soberly on the ruins of the career she had started on with such starry-eyed optimism, the collapse of Bartock Publications and the precarious state of her relationship with Roddy. A year ago her life had seemed settled, successful and with the future marked out for both her and Roddy, her partner. Even her recurrent nightmares and migraines were becoming less frequent. Her status as the daughter of a Prime Minister had eased her path although it irked her at times. The publicity over the Nechtan Stone, as the Naughtonwood discovery had come to be known, had dredged up the tragic stories of her mother and father. The media scrum had descended on her and her brothers for their memories of the events of the past and the romantic story of Weelum Ramsay's boyhood home. The replay of old newsreels and the rehash of newspaper coverage had sparked off nightmares and the subsequent migraines. She felt the beginnings of a migraine gathering now, spiking her sight with silver.

"I'm not sure I want to be a part of the new set up," she declared, "redundancy is an option as I understand the terms of such closures."

"I'm sure we would all greatly miss your contribution," said the Under-Secretary with manifest insincerity, "but the decision is yours."

"If you'll excuse me," muttered Belle, "I have another appointment."

"Surely," he responded heartily, relieved that the interview had passed off without rancour.

"We're well shot of that firebrand," he whispered to himself as he escorted her gallantly to the door.

Unfortunately the next crisis for Belle was not so clear cut. Bartock Publications was threatened with receivership, workers' control having finally succumbed to the consequences of putting workers benefits before investment, marketing and updating processes and practices. Evidently too customers' needs were a low priority. Previous warnings from the Trustees had been ignored. The total lack of realistic business practice had the inevitable consequences. Now the work force was "demanding" that the government should bail them out "as a worthwhile experiment in workers' control".

Belle and the other Trustees now had to decide whether to seek a take over from another firm or allow Bartock Publications go to the wall. After a bitter discussion, with the trade union representatives arguing for an approach to the government Belle managed to persuade them to allow her to approach an entrepreneur with a view to a salvage operation. Her only condition was that the work force should agree to redundancies, a pay cut and restructured working practices.

Belle came away from the meeting with a sense of foreboding. She wanted to save the company in memory of her mother but she doubted if it would be possible. Her dark mood was compounded by the lack of progress in the archaeological dig. Ruth, usually optimistic, told of dissension between Angela and John York. The investigation was going nowhere.

CHAPTER THIRTY

SIR RAB BRUCE: DRUMANNAN

Sir Rab Bruce was inordinately proud of the changes he had brought about in Drumannan, Aberbrothy and the surrounding area. The regeneration of Bruce Tower and the construction of his dream mansion on the site of the old one were the icings on the cake. The massive engineering works, which was transforming an area of heavy unemployment and associated deprivation in a derelict industrial town into a vibrant and prosperous community, operated on a worldwide basis, serving the needs of the oil industry. Although Bruce Engineering was only a small part of his Drumannan Conglomerate of multi-national companies, it was his first love. Drumannanshire was where he had started on the long hard journey to his present billionaire status. The addition of the research facility was the result of his personal intervention when senior executives were pressing for a Californian location. Aberbrothy was also being developed as the global headquarters of Drumannan Holdings, providing a further range of employment opportunities.

The modern buildings and state-of-the-art infrastructure that were being created, with its shopping malls, restaurants, hotels and leisure facilities, was a far cry from the grimy industrial town of the first half of the twentieth century, or the hopelessness of the "charity shop" streets of the latter half of the century.

Not content with his pre-eminent position in the business world Rab was deeply committed to improving the lot of the Scottish people and to the preservation and development of their culture. He gave anonymously to charity, created bursaries for deserving scholars and supported a range of Arts programmes.

He was not, however, the perfect philanthropist. Like most powerful men he was accustomed to getting his own way. His business interests came first. He could be ruthless. The present minor issue facing him was to illustrate the point.

"Ms. Ramsay, I have had my accountants run the rule over Bartock Publications. What they found was a company in deep, deep trouble - in effect a basket case. There is no way I would become involved in trying to rescue such an enterprise." Sir Rab closed the thin file in front of him with finality.

"Will you not at least listen to my case?" Belle asked incredulously.

"You haven't got a case, Ms. Ramsay," Rab replied with a grim smile.

Belle bit her lip.

"Sir Rab, the livelihood of a hundred employees is at stake here. I have extracted a promise of staff redundancies, pay cuts and revised working practices to effect a sea change in attitudes among the workers. A new management team will be put in place. I thought you were a champion of working people."

"Belle, if I may call you that in view of our mutual interests in our heritage, I champion "working" people. So far as I can make out, this lot is a bunch of layabouts who think that society owes them a comfortable feather-bedded life."

Belle exploded.

"You're typical of the hard-faced capitalists my father used to rage about. All you care about is profit. Workers are discarded when they are perceived to have served their purpose. People's lives are ruined and communities wrecked. As for your Scottish Peoples Alliance, its ideas are half-baked populism, disguising the fascist tendencies underlying them. It will all end in chaos, just you wait and see," Belle's rant ended with her quivering, near to tears.

"Your partner, Roddy Neilson doesn't seem to think so," observed Sir Rab icily.

"More fool him!" Belle threw back at him as she stormed out of the capitalist's plush haven.

Sir Rab lifted the phone.

"Buy Bartock Publications when the receiver makes a "fire" sale."

CHAPTER THIRTY ONE

NATASHA BRUCE: DRUMANNAN

The Lear Jet swept in to land at Edinburgh Airport. Its sole passenger - Mrs. Natasha Bruce - composed herself to face her husband. She examined herself in her handbag mirror. The reflected face was strained and gaunt through the carefully applied make-up. Be upbeat and try to conceal the worry she cajoled herself.

Rab regarded her quizzically, holding her at arms length, her eyes level with his own.

"It's so good to see you back, Natasha. Do you realise how concerned I've been about you? You're looking well," he said, lying in his teeth. In truth she looked dreadful but he was determined not to reveal his worry.

"Are your parents well? The words tumbled out uncharacteristically. Rab was usually undemonstrative, especially in public. It was a sign of the anxiety he felt.

"I'm fine, my bonny Scotsman," Natasha trilled, "I was sad to leave my parents but I'm so glad to be home. I can't wait to see Bruce Tower and the view to the Ochils."

Natasha threw back her head swinging her mane of auburn curls and linked her arm to Rab's, whispering,

"Has your bed been cold?"

Rab ushered her into the Rolls, grinning at her mischievous eyes.

After an exchange of domestic and business news and mutual rejoicing at the success of the S.P.A. in the elections. Natasha relapsed into silence, staring unseeing out of the car window.

"Something's wrong, Natasha," murmured Rab softly, "Is old Boris acting up again?"

"Well, yes but it's more than that. I eventually persuaded the pair of them to come to Scotland after a lot of argument but there is now some difficulty over exit visas. I pulled all the strings I could to no avail. The authorities have never forgiven my late husband for taking assets out of the country. This prevarication seems to be pay back time."

"I thought Russia was becoming more civilised," said Rab disgustedly, "It seems I was wrong. Have you explored every possibility?"

"Do you mean bribery? Of course I have. Why do you think I delayed my departure for so long? I tell you. I tried every possible thing short of smuggling them over the border. I was told the case would be reviewed in the future. Fat lot of good that is to people already in their seventies." Natasha's shoulders slumped defeatedly.

Rab had nothing to offer her. If she with her contacts had been unable to resolve the matter there was little he could do.

Tearfully Natasha told Rab of her fears that if she ever returned to Russia the authorities might refuse her an exit visa. She might never see her parents again… She might even face a prison sentence.

Rab whistled as full implications of what she was saying dawned on him. He tentatively put his arm round her in a clumsy attempt at comfort. Shaking him off angrily she cried,

"Rab, I'll just have to make the best of it - a peculiarly Russian problem, living in fear of the state. Generations of my countrymen have had to experience something similar or worse. Do you wonder why we are melancholy at times? I refuse to let it get me down.

I'm going to withdraw gradually from my overseas commitments and concentrate on working for the good of my adopted country. We can be together most of the time. I'll be the lady of the manor and do good deeds. I can help Catriona with her constituency work. I'll even learn how to play Bridge."

Rab chortled.

"Please, no! There's nothing worse than husband and wife playing together."

"Then we'll just have to play other games she whispered, biting his ear.

Natasha had put on a brave face but she was sorely troubled as they drove up the crag and tail ridge to Bruce Tower.

CHAPTER THIRTY TWO

CATRIONA: QUEENSTOWN

Catriona McMannan, Member of the Scottish Parliament for Paisley East, gazed over Queenstown Loch to the re-roofed Palace. She felt euphoric. Her film acting career had reached the stage when she could pick and choose the parts to play and the timing of them. Recently, however, she had been eclipsed by Murdo and his Pop group Triple M. which had topped the charts yet again. Her election had boosted her self esteem. The adulation of the public had reached new heights and it was dawning on her that what she needed was something more than celebrity status but power. Her election had paved the way. She thought of Eva Peron, a heroine to her since childhood. But she would not depend on a powerful man. She would achieve power by her own efforts. Murdo had been a boost to her career up until now but she had to develop an independent base. His unfailing good humour, his all consuming interest in music and the Arts generally, would be a complement to a new career, but no more than that.

A beautiful woman, Catriona at the age of thirty was in her prime. Her body was svelte and toned, benefiting from regular workouts with her personal trainer. She aspired to be a leader of fashion, frequenting expensive fashion houses, although she was sometimes criticised for being too daring in her choices. Paying scant heed to her belittlers, she continued along her idiosyncratic way, amused by the occasional furore her clothes, or lack of them, caused. Confident, poised, Catriona was ready to strut a larger stage.

Her latest move had caused puzzlement among the media gossip columnists. It did not conform to the stereotype of celebrity women. Previous disastrous instances were quoted. She kept her own counsel.

Catriona was awaiting the arrival of fellow M.S.P., Roddy Neilson, to discuss with him the forthcoming election of the leader and executive committee who would form the nucleus of the new Scottish Government Ministerial team.

Catriona had prepared her ground carefully. She had to ensure that Roddy secured a senior position and she herself at least a junior one. As a mentor to a substantial number of aspiring M.S.P.s he should receive enough support she thought. He might, however be diffident about putting himself forward, given his "tainted" status as an ex-Labour Party adherent. Her own ambitions were pretty certain to be achieved due to her popularity with the public. She had, however, to guard against petty jealousies, particularly from other women and possibly from residual opposition from male chauvinists. It would do no harm to have Roddy firmly on her side and convinced he himself should aspire to a senior position.

The Polish maid showed Roddy into the luxurious drawing room with its plush furnishings and modern art on the walls. Catriona was wearing her favourite black dress, a la Hepburn, low cut and barely brushing her knees. Her bobbed dark hair framed high cheek bones and a startlingly red lipsticked mouth. Her wide cornflower blue eyes smiled at him as she swung an impressively high heeled shoe on crossed legs.

"How nice to see you again Roddy. I'm suffering from election fatigue. I expect you are the same. Murdo's on the golf course this afternoon. I've ordered tea. Does that suit you?"

Roddy was staring out of the expansive window.

"Do you know I think I can see my house from here? There it is on the hill at the back of the town. Sorry! I do apologise. Yes, I confess to being more than a little weary of all that campaigning. The work on the Palace is well ahead of schedule. You and Murdo are to be congratulated on initiating such a magnificent project."

"Murdo and I were born here you know. This house and the Palace restoration are the culmination of a dream," Catriona rose to join him, ringing for tea.

"We need to have a clear strategy for this meeting, Roddy," she continued, "Otherwise you know how these occasions can degenerate into chaos."

"I am only too aware of that possibility," he laughed," I've been involved in too many similar jamborees."

"I admire your style, Roddy. You are so steady, dependable, and articulate. Just the qualities we need for a First Minister."

Somewhat taken aback by Catriona's directness and confusedly pleased by her flattery, Roddy contrived a suitably self- deprecating smile.

"It's very generous of you to say so, Catriona, but I understood that our little group was to take a back seat when the organisation was up and running. I envisage a role for me as an adviser to our colleagues who after all are novices."

"You underestimate yourself, Roddy." Catriona re-seated herself carefully smoothing down her dress. "I am willing to campaign on your behalf, if you put yourself forward."

Roddy was silent, considering the proposition. He had come prepared to discuss with her the advantages of Professor Latto as Leader and First Minister.

"I had rather thought you would agree with me that Bill Latto was eminently suitable for the post"

"He is an outstanding personality but he hasn't got your experience, Roddy. You would provide the stability we need."

Roddy shook his head stubbornly.

"I carry too much old baggage to be suitable," he stated, "Latto is "clean" untouched by party allegiances. I will give him my vote."

"I suppose you're right," Catriona sighed reluctantly, "but you must at least stand as his deputy."

Roddy could see himself in that position. He was pleased that the suggestion had come from her. With a display of reluctance he accepted her proposal and they put their heads together to map out a strategy for acquiring the two appointments.

The time passed quickly. They identified likely support, tactics for the meeting and the best way to present their case.

Roddy felt drawn to this vibrant young woman, his pulse quickening as she placed a hand on his arm to emphasise a point. As he rose to go he raised the matter Catriona had been angling for.

"How about your position, Catriona?" Your brains, your flair, your beauty and your popularity make you an ideal candidate for ministerial office. I hope you will be on our ticket as well. As a team we should be irresistible."

Catriona breathed a sigh of relief. She had begun to think he was like so many others - sexist. He had put her brains before her beauty even if he had shown himself susceptible to feminine charms. Her plan had succeeded.

Roddy thought Catriona McMannan the most intelligent, beautiful, sexy woman he had ever met.

CHAPTER THIRTY THREE

RANGI AND JADE: THE OCHIL HILLS

The bog cotton trembled, the lazy breeze barely tickling the white tufts. Bleached summer grass rolled in waves over the folds of the hills. The Ochils back country drowsed in the unaccustomed heat, distorting the stark outlines of the mighty pylons of the wind farm in the middle distance. The motionless sails proclaimed their lack of power. The hills seemed barren, the only bird life a buzzard speck, gliding, detached and remote. Even the ubiquitous sheep were absent, victims of the demise of the hill farmer.

"An unnecessary waste of money!" snorted Dr. Cheong Yu, lying on her belly in a nest of heather as she squinted at the bulldozed tracks scarring the approach ridge to the pylons.

"Don't get on that hobby horse again," grunted Rangi McNaughton, his back resting against a full rucksack as he gazed dreamily at the pellucid blue sky.

"On your feet, you lazy man! Have I to drag you to the top?"

Ben Cleuch summit, an ugly scatter of rocks, was still half a mile away and 300 feet higher.

"There's plenty of time," moaned Rangi, "You just want to get your teeth into my delicious filled rolls. My new recipe-----"

"Enough!" cried Dr Yu, otherwise known as Jade, whose voracious appetite was a standing joke between them.

"Hello! Here's someone in a hurry."

A lone woman was eating up the height in lithe steps, her walking poles stabbing the steep slope leading up to their resting place on Maddy Moss. As she drew near Rangy made out the slim figure of Belle Ramsay.

"Belle!" he called out, laughing, "fancy meeting you up here!"

Belle broke stride, recognition dawning. She plumped herself down beside the pair.

"You're scarcely out of breath. You must be very fit," Rangy commented admiringly, "This is my friend, Jade"

"How nice to meet you," said Belle with a wide smile, "I've heard a lot about you."

"Nothing derogatory, I hope," responded Jade with a sidelong pleased look at the reddening Rangy.

"Why don't you join us here for a picnic," he offered, "Presumably you are heading for the summit."

They settled down, producing flasks of tea and wolfing Rangy's elaborate sandwiches.

"Actually I'm working off the frustration and anger caused by a meeting I had with your employer, Sir Rab Bruce. The pair exchanged glances as Belle recounted her rebuff from the tycoon.

"I thought he had a social conscience," she said bitingly, "How wrong could I have been!"

Jade and Rangy listened sympathetically. Both were becoming disillusioned working at Bruce Engineering. Jade related how she was being increasingly starved of funds to develop her research work in spite of a Government grant. More and more of the money was being diverted into the solar power research. The fact that she thought she was on the verge of a breakthrough into making tidal power a commercially viable proposition seemed to cut no ice with senior management and she was becoming, not only disgruntled, but increasingly suspicious about what was going on. Rangy had looked up the C.V.s of one or two of the scientists in the solar power laboratories and had discovered that they had done little previous work in that field. Their expertise seemed to be in transportation. Jade confessed that she had been puzzled by the reluctance of her colleagues to chat about their work but had put it down to security consciousness.

"What a fool I was," she exclaimed, "I didn't suspect anything was amiss."

Belle listened to the pair with dismay. What had her partner, Roddy, got himself into? Something fishy was going on at Bruce Engineering. She had to find out more before broaching the subject with him. But how?

"Do you think you two could find out more about what's going on," she asked.

Jade looked dubious.

"Security is so tight that it is very doubtful if we could ferret out anything more. What do you think, Rangy?"

"There is one possibility. I've been asked to advise new staff at Sir Rab's own office at Bruce Tower. I'll be working late there for a week in addition to my own duties."

"And I could come to pick you up because your car's broken down," Jade said thoughtfully. It's unlikely that we will turn up anything useful but it's worth a try."

Belle urged them to be careful.

"You don't want to risk your jobs. Let's keep in touch anyway."

Gathering up her gear she prepared for a quick dash to the top of the Ben.

"I won't wait for you two. I have a meeting later."

The morning silence was abruptly shattered by the cacophony of a passing helicopter.

"Bloody helicopters! Servicing the bloody, bloody wind farm!" bellowed Jade.

CHAPTER THIRTY FOUR

THE DIG: NAUGHTONWOOD

"The Nechtan Stone has become so popular that people are falling over themselves to obtain it." Professor Angela Bull said sarcastically, "We have done all we can here to examine and classify it.

The Nechtan Stone is by far the finest example of Pictish sculptured stones ever found. Because it was fortuitously protected from the elements the relief work on the stone is still as sharply delineated as though it had only recently been sculpted. The evidence of colouring on such stones is confirmed by the substantial residue of red colour on the finished side, the one with the cross. The quality of workmanship is high. It can be dated to about the first half of the eighth century. Strangely the sculpture is still incomplete, very frustrating for us archaeologists because it had the beginnings of an inscription in Latin and another one in an indecipherable language which we assume to be Pictish. The only word we can read in both inscriptions is significant - Nechtan. The symbols are still a mystery. The fish symbol, also found at nearby Pitfairn, seems to be important. It is carved larger than is usual on such stones. This stone, however, takes us no further forward in our understanding of them. The cross on the reverse side of the stone is a truly spectacular example of Celtic Art, equal, or surpassing other similar stones.

The problem now is where to locate the Nechtan Stone. Naturally we will carry out a further series of tests on it at the University. A number of people and organisations have laid claim to house it. So far, the Royal Scottish Museum, Drumannan Council Museum, Sir Rab's Museum in Bruce Tower, the Terence McCool collection in Queenstown Palace and last, but not least, the Naughtonwood Residents' Association, led by Councillor John McNaughton, Rangi's brother, have demanded that the stone be erected on a suitable site in the village."

The response to this announcement was mixed. Sir Rab scowled; Murdo looked nonplussed; Ruth gave a weary shrug; and Belle was horrified.

"Of course it should be left in Naughtonwood. Where else?" she shouted.

The Professor was non-committal.

"There are costs involved. This stone cannot be left open to the weather like some of the other stones. It may have to be kept in a controlled environment. The upkeep would be considerable."

"Exactly!" muttered Sir Rab, "Sentiment can't override practical considerations."

"The new Queenstown Palace would be the ideal place. It is a national focal point with the state-of-the-art facilities, not some tin pot provincial museum like yours, Rab," said Murdo mischievously.

Sir Rab glowered.

"You see what I mean, everybody," observed Angela Bull wryly.

"I hate this kind of wrangling," moaned Ruth. "I agree with Belle. The Stone should be here, and we should all support the raising of funds to make it possible."

"Well that's one problem for everybody to think about," Angela stated, but there is a more pressing reason why I called this meeting. Dr. York, please explain."

"The investigation is going nowhere." declared John York. "We have no evidence from our surveys to support further work on this dig. All the anomalies the geophysical surveys have turned up related to old mine workings residual spoil, slag and so on. The whole area is a fascinating prospect for an industrial archaeological study but it is barren so far as earlier periods are concerned. The Nechtan Stone is all we have. The dig should now be closed down." He turned to Professor Bull for support.

"Reluctantly I have to agree with my colleague. In spite of my better judgment, to the extent of falling out with John, I have kept things going. I'm afraid I was wrong. The dig will have to cease work: anything further will be carried out in the lab at St. Regulus University."

There were murmurings of disappointment from the group of sponsors.

"Is there no possibility of extending the search to a wider area?" asked Ruth.

" You can see for yourself that modern housing developments have almost entirely replaced the old mining village ,far less any earlier remains," explained the Professor." "We considered the possibility but dismissed it as unproductive."

Belle had positioned herself as far as possible from Sir Ralph. Now she spoke diffidently.

"My cousin, Rangi McNaughton, as you know, lives in the village and has been in conversation with the occupant of the cottage at the top of The Castle lane. The cottage is one of the few remaining old buildings in the village apart from this one. Dauvit Hunter, the old man who lives there with his wife, Kirsty, have been watching the work on the dig over their garden wall. He told Rangy that his garden was difficult to cultivate because when he tried to "double dig" it to two spade depths he always hit stone but not a natural rock formation. Large flattish stones seemed to extend over much of his garden ground. He wondered if that might interest you."

Dr. York sniffed.

"Probably local stones! Of no particular interest!"

But Professor Bull perked up.

"They could just be the capstones of another souterrain. It might be worth a look. Do you think the guy would allow us to investigate?" she asked.

"Hold on!" Sir Rab intervened. "After what I've heard I see no good reason why we should spend more money on this project."

"Oh, Rab! Be generous. We can't afford to leave any stone unturned." Murdo laughed at his own unintentionally humorous remark but Ruth and Belle were quick to support him.

Sir Rab shrugged.

"Well, I suppose a day or two won't make much difference."

Angela was pleased to receive the respite.

"It won't take long to do a geophysical survey, will it John?"

"Only a few hours," he replied stiffly.

"Right. Belle, get Rangy to introduce us to his friends, Dauvit and Kirsty." She ordered, full of fresh enthusiasm.

***

"Aye," coughed Dauvit rheumily. Ye kin dig up ma gairden, provided ye pit it back the wey ye fund it."

"We surely will," beamed Angela," and there will be something in it for you."

"It'll gie us some excitement in oor lives," cackled Kirsty, "but whit's in it for me?"

"We won't miss you out, Kirsty," Belle reassured her.

Eyes gleaming, the old couple sanctioned the digging of trenches in their unkempt garden if the survey warranted it.

Dr. York sniffed disapprovingly.

CHAPTER THIRTY FIVE

RANGI AND FAMILY: NAUGHTONWOOD

"What's this I hear about the Nechtan Stone being displayed in some Edinburgh museum?" Johnny McNaughton was apoplectic with rage. The Stone belongs to the people of Naughtonwood, and it stays right here, Rangi. Tell your fancy archaeologist friends that I'll fight any attempt to move it."

"Calm down, Johnny. No decision has been taken. In fact there is strong support for your point of view. Belle Ramsay and Lady McFranklin both want it to stay here. Why don't you meet them and organise a rational campaign to make sure that happens instead of going of at half cock. Rangi reflected that he had invested a considerable effort over the years trying to stop his brother doing just that. He was finding it increasingly difficult to cope with his outbursts. On this occasion, however, the fact that there were allies in the so called enemy camp mollified the fiery Johnny.

"Is that so? I must meet this Belle Ramsay after all, the old lady with the title, too, if she'll deign to see me!"

Rangi smiled to himself. Johnny's views on titles, particularly those of geriatric Labour peers, were virulent.

"Sure, I can arrange that, Johnny. You'll like them."

***

"I've been dying to meet more of my new found relatives. Your mother is always talking about you, Lisbeth and the children."

Belle embraced the demure Lisbeth and the bashful Peter and Duncan, careful only to shake hands with Johnny. She knew Scottish men and their aversion to overly familiar physical contact with strangers. Ruth was equally correct, shaking hands with her host and fussing over the others. Lisbeth relaxed, ushering Rangi and the two women into her living room, untidy in spite of her attempts to eradicate the depredations of the boys..

Amid the laughter and chaos of the attempts of the boys to assist in handing round tea and home baking, and Johnny's hopeless efforts to play the heavy father, rapport was quickly established. Rangi was absurdly pleased. He had feared an adverse reaction from his brother, or at least a cold formality. Belle and Ruth had, without effort, scored a victory. There was still wariness about Johnny but the genuine pleasure of the women at meeting him and his family had pushed his class hatred well into the background.

The only disappointment for Belle was that Johnny had rarely met her father whose reclusive habits had distanced him from the villagers during his holiday visits. Johnny, however, respected him if only because he had refused the honours ex-Prime Ministers were usually accorded. Weelum had died titleless.

Eventually Johnny buttonholed Ruth, sensing that she had more power and influence than Belle, who was more interested in the boys than in more extraneous matters. Forthrightly he asked Ruth,

"What are chances of the Nechtan Stone remaining in Naughtonwood?"

Ruth looked at him consideringly.

"As you know there is a growing feeling in the country that discoveries of this nature need not necessarily be housed in the capital city. There is, however, a strong argument that Edinburgh is the best place to keep national treasures. This Stone is unique in its quality and is an obvious candidate for display in a museum there. So you see the problem.

Johnny was having none of it.

"The Stone is staying here. I'll get the Drumannanshire Council on my side. If necessary I'll organise protests and even direct action to keep it in this village."

Ruth laughed.

"Mr. McNaughton, with all your experience as a Councillor surely you know that there are lots of negotiating ploys that can be put into effect before you resort to such measures. Can we not put our heads together and work something out?"

Reluctantly Johnny subsided, mollified by her charm and astuteness.

Ruth thought Johnny should certainly persuade Drumannanshire Council to propose that the Nechtan Stone should remain in Naughtonwood. Meantime she would try to get other influential people onside.

"It won't be easy. For instance, the First Minister is all for concentrating finds like this in Edinburgh. Be warned. It will be a long hard slog to change the mind set of the archaeological establishment and the civil servants."

Johnny snorted, still unconvinced, but he acquiesced in her strategy.

CHAPTER THIRTY SIX

RUTH: NAUGHTONWOOD

Ruth dreamed, mouth slack, drooling slightly, stick thin figure angular on the cushioned garden lounger. Only the tiny puff of exhalation and the occasional twitch of muscle indicated that the old arthritic body lived. Ruth dreamed of another heat drenched summer day long ago by a burn in the Ochils when a sinewy trout was scooped from a basin sized pool and deposited in her lap by a laughing young man.

Jerking into consciousness, she groaned, easing her aching joints, and focused on the tanned faces of Belle and the two archaeologists regarding her with sympathetic amusement.

"I thought you were supposed to be helping us," accused Professor Angela Bull, A fat lot of good you are doing, sleeping in the sun."

The faintest twinkle in her eyes belied her hectoring tone. She laughed as she helped the old lady to her feet.

"I do believe you are a spent force, Ruth, dreaming of past glories," grinned Belle.

Ruth smiled ruefully. Ten years ago she would have snorted, releasing a flow of sarcastic riposte. Now, aged seventy-nine, she was indeed slowing down. Her dream had suffused her with melancholy, so sharp-edged and real was the image of that young man, Weelum Ramsay, a future prime minister, and herself the laughing girl by the pool, and the world at her feet.

She had enjoyed a long, varied and distinguished career after a wistful childhood, deserted by her mother, and living with a gentle, middle-aged father at a loss how to cope with his earnest sharp faced daughter in the town of Allanford.

Ruth became an intellectually hard student of History at the University of St. Regulus, head over heels in love before ditching her student lover as the result of a jealous conspiracy.

Her memories of school and university days remained bright in her mind, the snatch of a tune or a long forgotten smell bringing overwhelming nostalgia. She puzzled, however, over great blocks in her recall of her later career.

She had been a teacher in various schools in Scotland, England and Army schools in Malaysia but details were absent.

An unfortunate affair when she was a lecturer in History at Wallacetown University stuck in her mind as did a failed marriage to a Liberal M.P. when she was a Chief Education Officer in England.

As a senior official in U.N.E.S.C.O. Ruth had traveled the world, often involved in high politics, particularly in Africa.

She puzzled as to why so many of these experiences were like jigsaws with pieces missing. Even the conspiracy that dogged her career was hazy in her memory save for its climax when a coup directed against the legitimate government of the United Kingdom was attempted.

Ruth was largely responsible for the failure of the plot, risking her life in the process. Weelum Ramsay, Prime Minister of the country at the time, her student lover, turned out to be a victim of the chief conspirator, then a fellow student at St. Regulus University, when he jealously branded Weelum a homosexual, causing the split with Ruth.

Ruth became a national heroine. A grateful nation rewarded her by making her a baroness.

Now she was Lady McFranklin, a venerable old woman, full of years and honours, and recently diagnosed as being in the early stages of Dementia.

Still erect at five foot ten inches in height, Ruth eyed the two archaeologists warily.

"What do you want me to do? Nothing too tedious I hope."

She took malicious pleasure in accusing them of allocating her to the most unproductive areas of the dig or to the most tiresome of the students to supervise.

"Au contraire, Ruth. We have a breakthrough. We want to make sure you are on the spot when we uncover the evidence. Come on, dear. Mr. Hunter's garden seems to have come up trumps."

Ignoring Ruth's now wide awake barrage of questions, she stalked off, followed by an excited John York, trotting at her heels. Belle waited for Ruth.

"It must be something extraordinary. York's positively bubbling over."

CHAPTER THIRTY SEVEN

THE DIG: NAUGHTONWOOD

A crowd of students and curious villagers lined the wall fronting the garden of the Hunters' home. The side and rear of the house was crisscrossed with trenches. At one Dr. York was inserting a fibre optic cable into a crack between two large stones exposed at the foot of the shallow excavation.

"We're pretty sure these are the cap stones of another souterrain. It is hollow underneath. John's going to have a look before we excavate further. It might even contain another sculptured stone." Angela knelt down beside her colleague.

"Well, can you see anything?" she demanded imperiously.

There was a sharp intake of breath from York. He said nothing as he manipulated the cable, peering through the eye piece. His hands shook as he tried to focus.

"John!" the Professor expostulated, "Tell us!"

At last he drew back from his scrutiny.

"This is the finest moment of my career," he croaked, "There, have a look."

Angela took his place, slowly exploring with the device. It was the turn of Ruth and Belle to implore.

"Angela, what's down there?" Belle was positively dancing with excitement.

Angela spoke in a hushed whisper.

It's a treasure hoard, a massive one. I can see a heap of silver ornaments and other artifacts, some gold, lots of coins; even cloth and wood."

Dropping the eye piece to her lap she stared at the little group around her with shining eyes.

This is an extraordinary event. We must exercise the utmost care in what we do next. Dr. York and I will make a detailed plan of action before we open the souterrain. Meantime clear the site - and find a large bottle of Champagne.

***

Fascinated, the small crowd of onlookers watched as the hole was enlarged. The entrance to the souterrain, low and dark, was gradually being exposed. It had been carefully concealed under a layer of rubble. Now the heavy stones of the roof, already cleared, were revealed to be supported by massive walls.

At last enough was dug away to make it possible to edge through, albeit on all fours. Anxious to be first, John York pressed forward trailing a cable with a light attached. Smiling ruefully, Professor Bull did not exercise her prerogative as leader of the project. She followed after him, clutching her own torch.

Neatly stacked wood and hide open containers were filled with what seemed to be silver and gold jewellery. Decorative shields, ornamental swords, a collection of unstrung bows and heavy iron-tipped spears lay heaped against a wall. Wicker baskets contained what seemed to be clothing. Two cauldrons occupied pride of place among an assortment of containers for liquid. The souterrain was crammed full of artifacts.

The two archaeologists flicked their torches to and fro over the low-ceilinged cavern. Again banana-shaped, it was larger than the one found lower down The Castle lane. Everything was covered by a thick layer of dust. Careful to avoid disturbing anything, Angela and John exchanged delighted glances. This exceeded all their expectations. It was indeed the most important find in the history of the exploration of Pictish remains.

Crawling out, they generously offered their assembled sponsors the opportunity to peek in briefly. Ruth, Belle, Sir Rab and Murdo all took advantage of the offer, gingerly crawling to just inside the entrance, fearful of incurring the wrath of the archaeologists by accidentally touching something.

It was an exuberant group who hugged each other, marvelling excitedly, explaining to students what they had seen, speculating on how the treasure had come to be there. The euphoria was interrupted by the Professor who beckoned to two of the students with some proficiency in photography.

"Take as many photos as you can from different angles. Later, when we get proper lighting in, we'll have the place photographed professionally to obtain a definitive record."

John York was hopping about, scowling.

"Are you sure you want anyone else in there? The site might be contaminated."

Angela eyed him levelly.

"I'll make the decisions, John. Let's talk to the media this time in a proper way."

The garden had been surrounded by a plastic screen, shielding the excavation from view and stopping the curious from obtaining access. Now Angela and John emerged into the Lane to confront the small crowd of waiting media.

"We have made a major discovery of a substantial amount of artifacts in what seems to be an undisturbed souterrain. An initial look has revealed that it will require a meticulous, detailed inspection to establish the full extent of the find. I would therefore ask you all to bear with us while we carry out the study. Meantime I can make available some photographs of the inside of the souterrain. That's all I want to say at this juncture."

So saying she slipped through the screen to the outrage of the reporters. Fortunately a police presence had been arranged, preventing any incursions on to the site. Dr. York threw a sop to the media as he followed Angela.

"I'll give a press conference later to tell you how I found the treasure," he shouted.

Angela withered him with a look.

"You'll do nothing of the kind. Just remember that this is a team effort and I am in charge."

CHAPTER THIRTY EIGHT

DR. JOHN YORK

John York seethed inwardly. Angela Bull was being most unfair to him and his part in the dig. He was surely entitled to a modicum of respect as the Deputy Director of the Investigation.

This episode was just one of a succession of insults, put downs, and indifference to his talents. He was a bitter man, in his late forties, still not having achieved the kind of academic success he craved. This was to be his big chance. He was determined to achieve his share of the academic recognition the Nechtan Stone and the Calabar hoard would bring. Sullenly he brooded on ways to make sure his name came to the fore.

As Angela Bull strode away she pondered on the conversation she had had with an archaeological colleague at a recent conference. He had expressed surprise that Dr. York had surfaced at St. Regulus University. It appeared that some years before he had left a dig in the Middle East under a cloud of suspicion. Artifacts had been going missing during times when he had been supervising excavations. For lack of evidence the losses had been blamed on the activities of casual workers but some of the circumstances of the disappearances suggested that it would have been difficult for workers without access to protected areas to have been the culprits. Nothing was ever proved but Dr. York moved on.

At the time Angela had dismissed the slur as academic tittle tattle. Now she was beginning to wonder about the character of her recently appointed colleague.

CHAPTER THIRTY NINE

THE TREASURE: NAUGHTONWOOD

"Weelum Ramsay's house makes a useful headquarters for the dig," Professor Bull stated, "but it is not secure enough to house everything we remove from the souterrain. I would like to transfer all the artifacts to our lab at St. Regulus."

"May I make a suggestion?" Sir Rab interrupted. "The University is a long way off. I can offer you the facilities I have nearby at Bruce Tower Museum. If there is anything else you need I will see that it is made available. Security is no problem."

The group was planning its next move. Angela had explained that when the position of each of the artifacts had been mapped out and photographed it would be removed for closer examination until finally the souterrain was completely emptied. The cavern would then be sealed until it was decided what was to be done with the two souterrain sites.

The Professor looked interested in Sir Rab's proposal.

"Are you quite sure you could provide what we need? It would save a lot of time in travel."

"Out of the question," Dr. York intervened. "We must have the facilities of the University."

"You have obstructed every sensible suggestion that's been made ever since the beginning of this project. And you had the gall to try to claim the credit with the media just then. I've had enough of you. Keep quiet for a change." Angela boomed. "Let me have a look at your facilities, Sir Rab, before I make a decision."

Ruth and Belle thought the idea of working from Bruce Tower a good one. It would allow them to keep closely in touch with the ongoing developments. Ruth, particularly, was keen to be involved in making an inventory of the discoveries. The meeting broke up, everybody avoiding York's eye in some discomfort. It had been a long time in coming Ruth thought with a secret smile but he had asked for it. Murdo was more sympathetic to the ashen-faced man, putting his arm round his shoulder to console him. He was angrily brushed off with a snarl.

Ten days later the bulk of the Calabar Hoard, as it had been nicknamed by the villagers and adopted by the diggers, had been transported to the museum premises in Bruce Tower. Proudly Sir Rab had shown Angela round, impressing her with the extent of the security arrangements. Already the Hoard was being examined and classified. Ruth, eager to be of assistance, travelled from Allanford every day in spite of Natasha's wish to have her stay at the Tower House. The two archaeologists, however, gratefully accepted the offer.

CHAPTER FORTY

BRUCE TOWER HOUSE

Natasha beamed at her dinner guests. The dining room in the Bruce Tower House was furnished with blonde Finnish furniture, the table seating twelve comfortably. Abstract paintings on the stark white walls were subtly lit by concealed lighting. Uncomfortable-looking chairs, ergonomically fashioned, surprised the guests with their form-fitting ease. Belle whispered to Roddy that it was obviously Natasha who had been responsible for the décor. It did not look at all like Sir Rab's style. She had thought long and hard before accepting the invitation to dinner but Ruth had persuaded her to swallow her pride for the sake of the Nechtan project. Roddy surveyed the room with curiosity. So this was how millionaires lived. The guests had just completed a tour of the house, charmingly guided by an exuberant Natasha. No sign of the strain Sir Rab had detected when she arrived back from Russia, Murdo mused. She was concealing it well.

It was Sir Rab who was ill at ease, Catriona thought. Her antennae, sensitive to atmosphere, told her that something was amiss. Ruth, seated next to John York, was having difficulty in sustaining a conversation with him, so dark was his mood. I wonder why he accepted the invitation she wondered.

Professor Angela Bull was enjoying the ambience of this most luxurious of houses, absently responding to Natasha's questions about the treasure. Natasha laughed at the story of the Calabar nickname, questioning if Calabar really meant haven on the hill in Gaelic. All agreed it was a good story whatever the truth of it. Catriona, ever publicity-conscious, welcomed the easily recognisable names- Nechtan's Stone and the Calabar Hoard. Dr. York sniffed.

Angela and her team had settled in well at the Bruce Tower Museum. All the artifacts had now been transferred from the souterrain and an inventory had been made. She passed the list round the table.

"Hot off the press! Have a quick look just now. I'll give a preliminary assessment of the findings soon."

Ruth added excitedly.

"When I was helping with the inventory I was amazed by the number of things that have never been reported in previous finds. Wood, leather, and fabrics are just as interesting as the more exotic stuff."

Murdo was fascinated by the musical instruments.

"The carnyx and the harps are astounding finds too. I wonder if it will be possible to discover the sounds they make."

PRELIMINARY INVENTORY

3 Gold torcs (1 damaged)

2 gold chalices

4silver brooches

8 silver cloak pins

4 gold rings

6 silver hand pins

3silver spoon bowls

6 silver bracelets

1 heavy silver chain

7 other silver chains

4 silver bowls

1 silver hanging bowl

1 casket

3 silver combs

4 silver sword pommels

2 sword chapes

1 damaged piece of chain mail

1 ornamental silver shield

1 ornamental silver helmet

2 leaf shaped plaques

1 small cauldron

2 damaged round shields

3 leather tunics

5 helmets

6 spears

6 swords

3 wicker baskets full of woollen robes and cloaks

2 pairs of embroidered shoes

1 fur cloak

6 earthenware pots

2 harps

1 carnyx

265 assorted coins

14 painted pebbles

The general discussion that ensued was interrupted by Angela raising another vexed question.

"If the row over the Nechtan Stone was bad, just think of the fight there's going to be over the ownership of the treasure and its ultimate resting place. The second souterrain was largely in the Hunters' garden but partly in Ruth's or Belle's property. It will be considered Treasure Trove and will have to go to Edinburgh to be assessed. Half the value will go to the landowners and half to the finders. But who are the finders? The archaeological team? The sponsors of the project? The University? Where will the Hoard be displayed? A national museum in Edinburgh? Drumannan Council Museum? Bruce Tower Museum? The University? Queenstown Palace? Should it remain where it was found?"

Ruth groaned.

I suspected this would happen. All this in-fighting and back-biting appalls me. I wish I had never instigated this search. The whole thing is becoming a nightmare."

"That's the reality of it," declared Roddy. "You should know that matters of this kind are never simple."

"I suppose so," sighed Ruth "I've been away from things too long."

"What do you think?" Angela turned to the other guest, a senior civil servant responsible for overseeing Treasure Trove matters.

"You have laid out the problems very succinctly," came the suave reply from the portly figure of Mr. Farquhar Rose, but my concern is merely to assess the value of the find and to decide on the recipients of its value in monetary terms." He smiled thinly.

I agree delicate negotiations will be required to determine where it should be housed. The odds are of course that a national museum will be favourite. After all it is the capital city where most of the relics of our national heritage are displayed."

Catriona intervened.

"As Minister of Culture I must agree with Farquhar. " With a faint smile she sipped her wine as if that settled the matter.

"Murdo was furious.

"I disagree most strongly, Catriona. Surely the trend is to spread these national treasures around the whole country, not concentrate them in Edinburgh."

"Hear, hear!" cried Belle." They should be housed in the area where they were found."

"You see what I mean?" enquired Angela quietly' with a dismissive shrug.

Sir Rab had made no contribution to the discussion. Now he leaned forward to gain the attention of his guests.

"You may have been wondering why I've been so pre-occupied. He paused, uncharacteristically gulping his whisky.

"I have just been tipped off that the Daily Bulletin Newspaper has me all over its front page in tomorrow's edition. I have been accused of giving a substantial donation to the Labour Party in return for my knighthood. Also the recent Labour Administration has been accused of awarding my organisation a massive subsidy as a further reward for my help. The fact that these accusations are completely unfounded will not prevent a media feeding frenzy. I only hope it does not harm the Scottish Peoples Alliance."

There was a stunned silence.

CHAPTER FORTY ONE

SIR RAB BRUCE: DRUMANNAN

The muddy path squelched as the two joggers vainly tried to avoid the results of a recent heavy downpour of rain. The track led from Drumannan across moor land to Gartmorn Loch. Against the backdrop of the Ochils the tranquil Loch with its wooded island lay in a shallow valley fringed with stands of trees and shrubs. The autumn colours gave the scene picture postcards feel, ignored by the joggers.

Heads down, Sir Rab and Natasha Bruce were gloomily assessing the impact of the week long media blitz on Sir Rab's reputation. The word "sleaze" dripped from the headlines. "Ill-gotten gains", "lavish lifestyle", "trophy wife", and other trite phrases bespattered the stories, together with photographs of Bruce Tower and House, the Bermuda villa, and the London flat.

"Fight back, Rab," adjured Natasha anxiously. "You can't just take these attacks lying down."

Rab had maintained silence, going about his normal routine, ignoring the media scrum that tried to pester him. He was ruminating on the peculiarly Scottish, and to some extent English, attitude to success in others. The Scots saying "Wha dis he think he is? I kent his faither." Just about summed up the attitude, contrasting with the American respect for the go-getter, the guy who has made a million, a role model to look up to, and emulate. He was trying to control the element of self-pity that was engulfing him as he pounded along, splashing straight through puddles, ignoring Natasha's anguished yelps as he kicked mud over her elegant jogging attire.

He had done so much for the community. Although not on the scale of the benevolence of Andra Carnegie, the Scottish-American who had lavished his accumulated wealth on gifts to the Nation, Sir Rab had nevertheless, spent millions on his bursary scheme "The Lad O Pairts" to help impoverished students to receive an appropriate education, and more millions on "Be Your Own Man" a scheme to assist people back into work, or to start their own business. His community projects, "Responsible Citizens and Caring Communities", were active in many Scottish towns. His industrial enterprises had provided regular employment with a fair wage for many.

This was his reward, a kicking from the media, politicians, even people who had benefited from his vision.

"My initial inclination is to turn my back on the lot of them, shift the emphasis of my business to the U.S.A., Europe and the Far East, and move my personal assets out of the U.K. Apart from anything else I would save a lot in tax."

"Try not to be sullen and resentful, Rab," Natasha cautioned. "Organise support. Refute the allegations."

Rab grunted. He was an angry man, ready to lash out. Grimly he concentrated on his running, matching it to the younger loping stride of the fit Natasha. Crossing the inflow at the eastern end they rounded the head of the Loch and headed west along the northern shore on the old wagon way.

"Isn't this where the colliery was?" asked Natasha, hoping to take his mind off their problems.

It was a neat ploy of hers to stop him over-exerting himself on these expeditions. After all he was now in his fifties. He drives himself too hard she mused. Ask about the names of Rangers football players of certain years was always good for a five minute break while he recalled obscure names of obscure players. Questions about local history was good for a long break while he reminisced about his childhood wanderings around Drumannan, or expounded on the exact nature of an archaeological site.

She was only partially successful on this occasion. He paused briefly, pointing out the overgrown remains of the pithead buildings of the old colliery. He did not elaborate, resuming his steady jog. Scowling, Natasha followed. Little was said as they completed the circumnavigation of the Loch before heading for home. At last Sir Rab stopped short, causing her to cannon into him, cursing.

"Sorry darling. You're right. I must fight back, but on my terms."

Two days later a laconic statement was released to the media. It revealed that Sir Rab Bruce had been awarded his knighthood by a Conservative Government, and that he had never given money to that Party. He had spent a total of £100 million pounds on his charitable enterprises. The Government money for research amounted to one tenth of the amount his organisation was investing into research into developing alternative sources of energy for the country. He would continue with his work for the good of the country he loved and would remain in Scotland as a taxpayer. He hoped that more Scots would be encouraged to emulate and better his achievements.

CHAPTER FORTY TWO

PROFESSOR BULL: PUBLIC ACCLAIM FOR THE CALABAR HOARD

The discovery of such a comprehensive collection of Pictish remains created enormous public interest. The media splashed the story, interviewing the Archaeologists, student helpers, volunteer workers, the sponsors and the villagers of Naughtonwood. Photographs, background pieces on Naughtonwood, historical information about the Picts, comments from historians, filled the T.V. and Radio channels and the newspapers. Sightseers flocked to the village and to other Pictish sites. The general public took a renewed interest in the past of the nation.

Sir Rab, Murdo, Ruth, Belle and Rangi tried unsuccessfully to keep in the background but were hounded for interviews. The story of Belle's father and mother was rehashed to a fascinated audience.

The main interest, however, focused on Professor Bull and Dr. York who spent hours trying to be patient as they explained the significance of the finds.

The Nechtan Stone was exhibited around the country while Angela talked about what was known about the complexities of the symbols on the sculptured faces. She developed a standard potted history of the period, its people and customs.

***

"With virtually no written sources the language and culture of the Picts could only be glimpsed through the evidence of archaeology. The carved stones that dot the countryside of north east Scotland assumed a significance that they might not otherwise have had given more historical evidence.

The craftsmanship and artistry as shown on the sculptures revealed an affinity with the natural world, particularly the animals. A range of familiar and exotic animals, birds and fish are depicted on the stones. Whether these represented the names of tribes, noble families or some other category of people is not clear. It is generally agreed, however, that they have some symbolic significance. The Nechtan Stone, for instance, shows a large fish, most probably a salmon, as does a similar stone found nearby by Lady McFranklin.

Much more puzzling is the large number of abstract symbols depicted on the stones. Below is a chart showing the symbols that have been recovered around the country.

Many theories have been advanced as to the meaning of these symbols but no scholar has yet come up with a convincing explanation of their meaning. Two of the most common appear on the Nechtan Stone- the crescent and V-Rod and the double disc and Z-Rod. The mystery is yet to be resolved.

Two other features of the stones deserve mention.

The first is the depiction of scenes from everyday life, hunting parties, battle scenes, and in one instance a humorous picture of a Pict on horseback drinking from a horn.

The second is clear evidence of the spread of Christianity among the Picts during the early medieval period. The stones dated from the early Pictish period show no Christian symbolism or scenes. About the 8th Century A.D, however, the stones display a great deal of Christian influence. A variety of Christian crosses are carved on many stones, some of which are ornate, showing a high standard of artistry. The Nechtan Stone is a superb example of Christian symbolism. Indeed, the cross carved on one side of the Stone is probably the finest of its kind.

A feature of the stones is the Celtic art carvings that decorate them. The intricate knot work and intertwining representations of flowers and vegetation are common throughout the Celtic world, not only on stones but in the work of monks transcribing biblical texts.

Finally, The Nechtan Stone teases us with the hope of discovering some clue to the language of the Picts. On a square panel on one side of the Stone is the Latin inscription "Regnum Nechtani" below a line of indecipherable script the only word of which is recognisable is Nechtan. Sadly the inscription is unfinished as if the sculptor had been interrupted in his work. "Regnum Nechtani" means Nechtan's Kingdom or land. From this we can deduce that our Nechtan was a very important personage. It is possible, even probable, that Nechtan was the King of the Southern Picts or even the whole of Pictland. Two intriguing puzzles!

The Calabar Hoard is hugely important for the insights it gives us into the lives and culture of the Pictish people. The art, the craft, the weapons, the clothing and the containers and utensils of the time are now available for us to study. Never before have so many artifacts been found.

For instance we can say with certainty how shields, swords, armour, musical instruments were fashioned; the types of clothing that were worn and how they were made; and the kinds of containers and utensils that were in use.

Of particular interest is the treasure trove of jewels and ornamental articles that were found. Two golden torcs, or neck pieces, presumably worn by important, rich, people, perhaps as a badge of rank are the most important of the finds, adding to the presumption that someone of royal blood lived in Naughtonwood Three magnificent chalices, richly decorated, again confirm the owner's wealth and status. The exquisite designs of the brooches, cloak pins, bracelets and plaques reveal the remarkable skills of the craftsmen.

The presence of a cauldron which seems to be of purely ornamental use points to the lingering of pagan practices. That is, however, conjecture.

To sum up, these discoveries will take years to analyse in detail. There is no doubt, however, that we will know a great deal more about our Pictish heritage when the studies are complete."

These populist lectures did much to foster more public interest in archaeology in general and the Picts in particular. Angela Bull revelled in the media spotlight, becoming the latest in a line of archaeological pundits much in demand on the T.V. circuit. John York fared less well, his dark brooding presence overshadowed by his ebullient colleague. Relations between them were strained, and it showed. Gradually he was dropped from the interviews, sullenly nursing his bitterness.

CHAPTER FORTY THREE

DISASTER: DRUMANNAN AND ABERBROTHY

Ruth muttered to herself as she set the security alarm at Bruce Tower Museum. Pausing at the gatehouse she asked the guard to double check that she had done it correctly, uneasy about her failing memory. The stout security man, indulgent as always, heaved himself to his feet and went to the Museum to reassure her that she had indeed secured the premises. On his return Ruth asked him where his colleague was.

"Oh, he's checking Sir Rab's personal office. Mr. McNaughton is just finishing up there. His partner has arrived to drive him home." He added, smirking. "You know, the Chink-er Chinese lady." hastily correcting himself under Ruth's hostile stare.

Ruth, lonely in her medical misery, had chosen to work late, writing descriptions of some of the artifacts from the Calabar Hoard. She always found release in such tasks, imagining the people who had made and used them, and still revelling in the thrill of discovery. She would pick up a takeaway meal in Allanford on the way home.

***

The Bruce Tower stood blocky, four square and silent, flood-lit and proud against the night sky. A black clad figure emerged from the Museum entrance carrying a box which was loaded into a waiting vehicle. Three times the figure went inside, returning with more boxes. The vehicle drove off down into the dimly lit road that led to Drumannan.

An hour later an explosion sounded from the direction of Aberbrothy, a sudden bloom of radiance eclipsing the lights of the town. Almost immediately another smaller explosion blew out the windows of Sir Rab's personal office, setting it on fire. In the confusion that followed no one noticed the body of Natasha Bruce lying partially covered with debris outside the office. Rangi McNaughton and Dr. Yu were however found, gagged and tied up, stuffed in the back seat of her car.

Sir Rab, startled awake by the appalling crack of the explosion, shouted for Natasha, only to discover that she had not followed him to bed. Sprinting downstairs to the source of the noise he was pulled up sharply by the searing heat on his face. Checking that the sprinklers were working, he quickly organised dishevelled staff who had appeared to man fire extinguishers and call the fire brigade. Only then did he spot his wife, motionless and bloody, in the hallway outside the offices. With a cry he plunged forward, braving the nearby inferno. He threw off the shielding debris and dragged her clear. He knew she should be moved as little as possible so screamed for someone to get an ambulance. Natasha was semi-conscious, moaning his name over and over and repeating the word sorry, sorry, sorry.

"Try to be still, dear," he whispered, comforting her. "The ambulance is coming."

He was confused. What could have happened? A gas explosion? What was Natasha doing here at this time of night?

The emergency services were quick to respond. Natasha was whisked to hospital in Wallacetown, accompanied by Rab, still in his pyjamas. Some one had produced a dressing gown and slippers. Before the ambulance drove off a member of his staff informed him that there had been an explosion at Bruce Engineering.

The fire was soon extinguished. The two security men were found in their cubby hole, breathing stertorously in a drugged sleep.

***

The doctor spoke tiredly. It had been a long night.

"Your wife has been concussed. She has a number of broken ribs, a broken arm, a wound on her shoulder and another near her left kidney which I am concerned about. She has superficial burns. Her condition is serious but not life-threatening."

Rab gulped in relief. It had looked much worse.

"Can I have her moved to a private clinic?" he questioned.

The doctor regarded him in a hostile fashion.

"Lady Bruce is in no condition to be moved. She is getting the best possible attention here."

Rab accepted the reproof.

"Can I see her?" he asked more humbly.

"You can look in for a minute but she's in no fit state for visitors."

Natasha was unaware of his presence. She was in a drugged sleep. All he could do was to lean over and kiss her.

***

The tidal and wave power research laboratories at Bruce Engineering had been partially destroyed by a massive explosion which had also totally destroyed the adjoining solar power research building. One dead body had been found. The remainder of the engineering works was largely unscathed since the two research facilities were at some distance from the main factory buildings. It was soon established that a gas leak was not responsible for the explosions. Initial findings suggested that they had been caused intentionally. It was sabotage.

***

The guests at Bruce Tower House, evacuated from the building after the explosion, were allowed back into the main house by morning. Bewildered and upset by the fire and the injury to their hostess they exchanged rumours anxiously. It must have been a gas leak. Natasha was dead. Two intruders had been caught and tied up. The security guards had been shot. Gradually the true facts emerged.

Angela and John York agreed that they would continue working in the Museum. When they made the security locks inoperative and entered they recoiled in shock. The silver and gold objects were missing. Unable to take in what they were seeing they rushed about, hoping to find that they had been misplaced. The realisation dawned that the Treasure had been taken except for the bulky items.

The police were informed and the Museum was sealed off. Ruth arrived from Allanford, trying in spite of her shock, to console Angela who was weeping inconsolably. Dr. York, tight-lipped and angry, railed,

"The Treasure should never have been brought here in the first place."

The police inspector was brusque.

"I want no one to leave until I have questioned them. People have been injured, one killed. The explosion was caused deliberately and a burglary has taken place. Until I get to the bottom of what went on last night everybody is suspect."

Sir Rab had returned from the hospital to collect some clothes. Reluctantly he was excused for a short while to visit Natasha. He was informed that he would go under escort. Indignantly he bristled at the imposition. The inspector was adamant.

"You do realise that your own life might be threatened."

Sir Rab looked appalled. The others stared at him wonderingly.

CHAPTER FORTY FOUR

REACTION TO THE DISASTER

Belle's car screeched to a halt outside Ruth's house in Allanford. Rushing straight in without waiting for a reply to the doorbell ring, she gabbled,

"Ruth, what's happened? I heard the news on the car radio and tried to phone you. Are you alright? What about the others? It said one person was in hospital."

"Hold on, Belle. I'm fine. Sit down and I'll tell you what I know. Have a cup of tea."

Ruth seemed relatively composed but her hands shook as she filled the kettle.

Quietly she described to Belle the events of the previous night as she knew them. Belle was appalled.

Natasha badly hurt? The Treasure gone? Sabotage? I can't believe what I'm hearing."

She ran her hand through her hair distractedly. A sudden thought caused her to stop in mid flow.

"My God! What about Rangi and Jade? You said they were tied up. I must contact Rangi at once."

"Don't worry. I've been on the phone to Rangi. He and Jade will be here shortly to discuss matters," Ruth soothed her.

The two of them relapsed into silence until Belle started off again, flinging a flurry of questions and speculation at Ruth, interspersed with imprecations directed at the unknowns who had stolen The Calabar Hoard. Irritated, Ruth deflected the barrage by saying she had run out of milk and asking her to fetch some from the nearby convenience store. Reluctantly Belle agreed, almost flouncing as she departed in a huff.

When she returned Rangi and Jade had arrived, looking subdued. Calmed down, Belle questioned them soberly.

"I know I encouraged you to pry into Sir Rab's secret operation but I hope you didn't do anything illegal."

"Certainly not!" snorted Jade angrily. "We had a look at the stuff in his office but he is too canny an executive to leave anything important lying about. He is obviously a "clear desk" man. Neither he nor his team of assistants and secretaries were guilty of any oversight."

"Their computers were all protected by security codes," added Rangy.

Did you see who overpowered and bound you?" asked Ruth.

Wu shook her head.

"It was so totally unexpected. They came from behind. We had no chance. They were strong and quick. I did hear a woman's voice shout but it wasn't English."

"If they wanted the Treasure and knew where it was why blow up Sir Rab's office?" wondered Rangy. "Do you think the burglary was a cover for the real objective, destroying the office and the research complex?"

"The two incidents could be unrelated," suggested Belle.

"Too much of a coincidence," replied Jade. "It doesn't seem at all likely."

"Who could have stolen the Treasure, then? Professional thieves? "

There was a thoughtful silence. Eventually Ruth sighed.

"I suppose we are all suspects."

Jade and Rangy exchanged glances.

"We think you should know that both of us are suspects. We have been warned by the police to make ourselves available for further questioning."

CHAPTER FORTY FIVE

NATASHA AND SIR RAB: WALLACETOWN

Natasha is still sedated. I'm hoping to be able to see her later. Sir Rab, haggard and dishevelled, paced the floor of the hospital waiting room. Catriona and Murdo had sped to Wallacetown when he phoned to tell them what had happened. Sympathetically they mouthed the inadequate phrases people use when at a loss as to how to comfort the distraught. At last Rab sat down.

"Why Natasha was up in the middle of the night and in the office suite I just can't fathom. The explosions were clearly sabotage. Some one, or some organisation, did not want my people to develop their research work. The burglary at the Museum must have been an attempted cover up although I can't see how that could have explained the explosion at Aberbrothy."

"Could it have been some crackpot or group of weirdoes who were incensed by the media stories about you and decided to exact retribution for your alleged wrongdoings?" Catriona speculated.

"No, it was specifically aimed at the research facility," Rab replied, "That's the line the police are pursuing."

"But who could have stolen the Treasure?" Murdo asked, "I'll bet it was John York. He was so jealous of Angela."

"Murdo," protested Catriona, "You've absolutely no evidence to support that suggestion. It could be crooks or cranks; it could be anyone, a villager for example. Perhaps that councillor, Rangi's brother for example, always going on about the rights of the villagers."

"I 'm not sure of Rangi McNaughton's own position. I know he was doing some work in my office but he shouldn't have been there so late. He's under suspicion along with his lady friend, Wu."

Catriona and Murdo were disbelieving.

"Surely not!" exclaimed Murdo, "He's Belle's cousin."

"It could be Belle herself," said Catriona maliciously.

"Or that partner of hers who's besotted with you," Murdo insinuated softly.

Rab got up and resumed his pacing, annoyed by their bickering.

"Idle speculation will achieve little," he threw at them. "At the moment I'm more concerned about my wife."

Contrite, Murdo apologised. Catriona had the grace to look guilty but said nothing. The uncomfortable silence was broken by the entrance of a nurse who beckoned to Rab to accompany her. Murdo and Catriona made to follow but she shook her head.

"Only her husband. No other visitors."

White and peaked Natasha attempted to smile. Various monitoring devices attached to her by tubes and wires were warily skirted by Rab so that he could lean over and kiss her.

"How are you feeling? Are you hurting?" he enquired gently.

Natasha tried to shake her head, grimacing as the movement sent a wave of pain through her body. Weakly she attempted to speak..

"I'll be O.K., Rab." She managed before her eyes closed.

Rab sat tensely by her bed, frightened to disturb her further. After a while she spoke again.

"I'm sorry, Rab. I'll tell you about it later."

The nurse intervened.

"I think you should leave now. She is still very poorly."

Murdo and Catriona saw immediately from Rab's face a he entered that he was upset.

She doesn't look good. They tell me she'll pull through but I'm worried. I want to call on top specialists to ensure she gets the best treatment." Rab abstractedly pulled a mobile phone from his pocket and replaced it. I can't remember if I can reach my daughter on this thing. She is at our place in Bermuda.

"She kept saying she's sorry, sorry. I don't know why. Could you stay here, please? The police want me back at Bruce Tower. They think I might be in danger so they've provided me with an escort."

The other two looked at him in astonishment

CHAPTER FORTY SIX

THE ARCHAEOLOGISTS: DRUMANNAN

The west wind scudded across the Central Belt gap until it hit the Drumannan ridge, buffeting off the Tower crowning the crag and tail outcrop. The Museum rooms echoed as it redounded against the new double-glazed windows. Modern technology had insulated the Tower from the elements. Air conditioning sustained an even temperature, allowing the archaeologists to work in comfort. The police had asked them to make an inventory of the missing items of the Treasure under police supervision.

Their hearts were not in it. The remaining artifacts, excellent material for intensive study of clothing, domestic containers and weapons did not have the romance of the missing silver and gold pieces. Angela Bull knew the remaining items were of equal importance but the thought of all that historical material perhaps being melted down by ignorant thieves filled her with despair. She recalled what had happened to the Norries's Law Hoard in the 19th Century.

John York was in sullen mood, his anger spent, as he contemplated the disappearance of the chance to publish a series of academic papers that would make his reputation as an archaeologist. Petulantly he scored off yet another item from the original inventory, a silver torc.

"Let's go over to the house and have a cup of tea, Dr. York. I can't settle to this."

The two had reverted to formal terms since their disagreements.

"I think not. I prefer to carry on here," he announced frigidly, "I suppose we must make the best of a bad job and finish off here. I am going to make a written request that everything that is left is immediately transferred to the University as I originally asked."

"That's your privilege."

Professor Angela Bull stalked out of the Museum leaving a bemused policeman and a seething York.

CHAPTER FORTY SEVEN

THE INVESTIGATION

The Chief Constable of Central Scotland Police glowered at Inspector Charles Orr.

"What on earth's going on at Aberbrothy, Orr? This report makes strange reading. Is there any terrorist connection?"

"There may be. It's too early to say." Inspector Orr was on the defensive. The investigation was always one step behind what the Chief expected.

"And what about the involvement of Sir Rab Bruce and his wife? This story will run for weeks in the media if you don't produce a quick result." Orr noticed the use of the word "you". If things were going well no doubt it would have been "we".

"Anyway, elaborate on your report."

Charles Orr gathered his thoughts before replying.

"As you can see from the report, the explosions were probably sabotage. They were specifically targeted at the research facilities and Sir Rab's personal files. He has no idea who might have carried out the attack. When we are allowed to interview Lady Bruce we might get information about the intruders. Meantime the forensic team are ferreting about to obtain evidence.

The burglary at the Museum is puzzling. It has been bruited that it was a cover for the explosion at Bruce Tower House but it hardly explains the one at Aberbrothy. It may be coincidental that the two incidents occurred on the same night.

My team has questioned everyone who was around that night. There are possible suspects. The Head of Security at Bruce Engineering has disappeared. The security guards could have conspired with the raiders by allowing themselves to be drugged after revealing the security codes. The staff at the House might have been involved. The Bruce Engineering employees, McNaughton and Yu, have given a pretty thin excuse for being in Sir Rab's office at that time. The woman, McFranklin, who was working in the Museum earlier, is a possibility, but she is nearly eighty years old. The presence of Lady Bruce at the scene of the explosion is a mystery. She may well have disturbed the intruders. We just don't know." Orr paused.

The chief Constable interrupted.

"You'll have to find out what kind of research was being done. Was it secret defence work we don't know about? Or was it what it purported to be, research on solar power?"

"I'll have to question Sir Rab and his executives about that, sir. I didn't want to lean too heavily on him in view of his wife's condition." Orr replied uneasily.

"Yes, yes, of course. Mustn't forget the casualty. What about the unidentified body at Aberbrothy?"

"No clues about his identity. He was dressed all in black, very athletic, but there is nothing to tell us who he is. I am almost certain he was one of the attackers. There are no missing employees. We have circulated a description of course."

"Well, keep me informed. If you need more help let me know. I want this cleared up quickly."

In Naughtonwood Dauvit and Kirsty Hunter were discussing the news with a cluster of neighbours in hushed tones. Lady Bruce had died. Rangi McNaughton had been arrested. The Calabar Hoard had been stolen by "thae English." Bruce Engineering would shut down. Bruce Tower was about to collapse. Rumours abounded. Dauvit spat.

"Ah kent nae guid wid come o' this."

CHAPTER FORTY EIGHT

RODDY AND CATRIONA: EDINBURGH

"The Trident Nuclear Submarine Base is to be transferred to a site in south-west England." Professor Latto, First Minister of the Scottish Government, surveyed his Cabinet Members bleakly. "The Conservative Government at Westminster is using operating costs as a reason for shifting the base from Faslane. The real reason is that they are preparing for a possible move towards independence by the Scottish people. What they don't seem to realise is that the cumulative effect of the measures they are taking, such as abandoning the Barnet Formula for Scottish expenditure, culling the number of Scottish M.P.s, refusing to allow them to vote on so-called English matters, all of that is actively pushing Scottish opinion towards the break-up of the United Kingdom. This Trident proposal is the latest. And it might be the straw that broke the camel's back. I thought our overwhelming defeat of the Scottish National Party had proved that we wanted the Union to continue. It seems I was wrong."

Amid the shuffling of papers and muttered expressions of concern as Cabinet Members digested this disturbing turn of events, Roddy Neilson, Minister of Justice, voiced an opinion held by some.

"Taking nuclear weapons out of Scotland might be no bad thing. The benefits in employment opportunities are far outweighed not only by the inherent dangers of having these weapons here but the morality of having nuclear weapons at all."

There were murmurings of support from a few of the others but Catriona McMannan, Minister of Culture, was shrilly indignant, saying that the move would be the precursor to taking all defence spending out of the country, and that in turn could spark an exodus of manufacturing and investment from Scotland. The Scottish people would be reduced to the status of second class citizens in the Union. Most Members supported this view. The First Minister agreed.

"We respect your views on nuclear arms, Roddy, but Scotland cannot opt out of this uncertain troubled world. The refusal of the previous S.N.P, Government to have nuclear power stations built in the country was an example of a blinkered attitude to the realities of the world as it is. Nuclear power is needed. Scotland must play its part.

I am going to seek a summit meeting with the U.K. Prime Minister as a matter of the greatest urgency to assure him of our Unionist credentials. We can swallow the financial limitations imposed on us and the tinkering with M.P.numbers and duties but we must resist the weakening of our economy. As an earnest of our commitment we will volunteer to have nuclear power stations in Scotland."

Roddy was crestfallen He had exposed his Campaign For Nuclear Disarmament past, wrongly assuming that he would receive substantial support from non-politicians. It would appear that he had badly misjudged the solid citizens who were his new colleagues. These people were a far cry from the idealistic campaigners of his youth. His attempt to intervene again to extol the virtues of alternative power sources was equally badly received. Again Catriona McMannan was to the fore in decrying their capability to supply the nation with enough affordable power.

"Roddy knows as well as I do that research into wave and tidal power is making slow progress. Wind power is now acknowledged as not being cost efficient and mars the countryside."

Roddy shot Catriona a surprised glance. She was fairly putting the boot into him. Levelly she returned the look, cool, detached.. Dimly he began to be aware that she was moving rapidly away from the close alliance they had forged when the new Administration was formed. He had ruefully accepted her scornful rejection of his advances. Completely undone by her beauty, her flirtatious charm and her deliberate cultivation of his support in achieving a ministerial post he had made a fool of himself by confessing his adoration. Not only that, he had attempted to kiss and caress her. Her sudden change from charm to icy withdrawal had jolted him into a realisation of his teen-age-like behaviour and he had apologised. She had accepted his contriteness graciously and afterwards their relationship as close colleagues had continued as if nothing had happened. Now, however, clear differences were emerging. He was being cast aside. Grande dame sans merci!

Catriona had seized the opportunity to discomfit Roddy. Envious of his powerful position as Justice Minister, suspicious of his socialist past, she chose her moment carefully, judging that opinion was on her side. With some guilt she reflected on how she had manipulated him to acquire her position. Poor Roddy! Totally infatuated! She calculated her next move. People must start briefing against him in the media. A few dropped hints among her supporters would start the process.

With a dazzling smile she leaned forward, listening raptly to the First Minister.

CHAPTER FORTY NINE

RODDY AND BELLE: QUEENSTOWN

Driving home to Queenstown Roddy steeled himself for an encounter with Belle. Their relationship was reaching its nadir. Since her voluntary redundancy from her post at the college and the demise of Bartok Publications, Belle had become largely sullen and withdrawn, occasionally punctuated by outbursts of ungovernable rage. The temporary euphoria following the discovery of the Calabar Hoard had been eclipsed by the shock of its theft. Sometimes she ranted at him, at Sir Rab, at the Scottish Peoples Alliance, at the robbers, at the Westminster Government. Mostly, however, she was uncommunicative, offering only the briefest of responses to attempts at conversation. The frequency of her migraine attacks had increased. And she dreamed. The nightmares crowded in, always the explosion, the blood, the shattered body. Belle was psychologically a mess, and Roddy was at the point of walking away.

He had determined to tell her of his intention on several occasions but his nerve had failed him. Today he would finally break the link and end their partnership. Already he had rented a flat in Edinburgh.

Belle hardly reacted to Roddy's muttered explanation as to why he wanted to leave her. She felt relieved that matters had come to a head. Roddy's defection to the S.P.A. had seemed to her more than a political move. It was a betrayal of all the history of her family and its proud tradition of social conscience and principled public service. The tragic memory of her parents overshadowed and overwhelmed her perception of events. Roddy was a traitor. She was glad he was going.

Something told her she was being irrational, confused in her thinking, that the past should not colour her being like this. But the memories of glad days, clear purpose, achievement, hope and certainty could not be put aside. She could not come to terms with a world of human folly, deceit, greed, and, above all, violence. The I.R.A. bomb was having an effect a generation after it had exploded. The particular irrationality of her attitude to Roddy's defection puzzled her. It was not as if she had followed her parent's idealistic socialist beliefs. To her mind all politicians and politics in general epitomised all that was venal in human beings, recent events just proving her point. Roddy had shown himself to be part of that corruption. Better that he go.

Dully she listened as he detailed how they should go about the separation, acquiescing without demur to his proposals.. He eyed her cautiously. It was so unlike her usual combative self.

"Do you agree with the arrangements?" he enquired.

"Fine with me!"

CHAPTER FIFTY

CATRIONA AND MURDO: QUEENSTOWN

"You were right about Roddy Neilson." Murdo McLean McMannan gazed pensively at the wispy tendrils of mist trailing across the loch below the Knock House. His C. N. D. performance in Cabinet was a huge misjudgment. I remember the misgivings Sir Rab and you had about him and I'm now inclined to agree. I didn't mind his New Labour background but I thought C.N.D. was youthful idealism he'd grown out of. Mind you, from what you tell me the treatment you meted out to him was pretty brutal."

Catriona said sharply, "What was said is strictly between us, man and wife. I don't want any leaks from these meetings to be traced back to me."

"Don't worry, love. You know me, the soul of discretion," Murdo chuckled.

Catriona knew him as an enthusiastic purveyor of gossip.

"That's the trouble. I know you too well. Murdo, you are too open for the quagmire of politics," she scolded.

"But I thought the Scottish Peoples Alliance was going to change all that. We were going to be open, totally transparent, above politicking," protested Murdo.

"Get real, Murdo. The world doesn't work like that." Catriona searched her husband's guileless face, realising that she had to manipulate him from his innocence and ignorance of the real politic she was beginning to practise in her bid for power if he was to be of use to her. His worldwide fame was too valuable an asset to ignore.

"There's a matter I want to discuss with you, Murdo. These boneheaded Conservatives at Westminster are in danger of driving us out of the Union with their short-sighted policies. Resentment towards each other is building up more and more in Scotland and England. We need to mount a huge campaign to counteract the separatist tendencies. Here's my plan."

Murdo listened carefully. When she had finished a slow smile lit his face. "Something I can get my teeth into. I like it."

Catriona laughed teasingly. "You could even write a song about it."

"That's a good idea.. I'll have to let it gestate for a while. As you know my songs don't just appear."

Amazed that he had taken her joke seriously, Catriona indulged him.

"I'm sure it'll be a hit."

Murdo paced up and down excitedly. "Do you think Rab would join us in the scheme? I know he has troubles of his own at the moment. I hesitate to approach him."

Catriona's lissome figure moved gracefully as she glided across to the window where she slid an arm round his waist.

"Best keep it in the family," she murmured.

Murdo grinned. "Yes, a McMannan project. I've felt a bit out of things recently. By the way, I presume poor Roddy has been cured of his infatuation for you." Catriona and Murdo were plagued by admirers. Men of all ages and types were bowled over by Catriona's beauty and female pop group fans made plays for Murdo constantly. It was an element of stardom they both accepted as inevitable. Catriona maintained that when the adulation stopped their fame would be over. Fortunately theirs was, atypically, a close affectionate marriage, able to withstand the pressures of the celebrity world.

"I 'm afraid I used the man," she mused.

"Naughty girl! You'll burn your fingers one of these days." Murdo regarded his wife fondly. "Sometimes I wonder what your long term plan is. What goes on behind those impossibly wide blue eyes?"

"Are you becoming amorous, Murdo?" Catriona asked sweetly, "because if you are, you can forget it. I have ministerial papers to attend to."

Murdo cursed in disappointment.

"At least it's a more original excuse than a sore head," he muttered with a wry smile.

CHAPTER FIFTY ONE

NATASHA AND RAB: WALLACETOWN INFIRMARY

Quiet sobs broke the hush of the hospital room. Sir Rab Bruce frowned in consternation. Natasha was much recovered the doctors had assured him. She was in for a long haul as her broken bones knitted but the other injuries were responding well

What she had whispered brokenly was a revelation so appalling that he was having difficulty in all the implications.

When Natasha was in Russia unspecified officials had approached her about Drumannan Holdings and, they said, the threat it presented to Russia's prosperity as a nation. At first disbelieving, she had scoffed at the notion. Stony-faced, the Senior Man produced a dossier entitled Drumannan Holdings Research Programme.

According to the document, the so-called Solar Power Research Programme was a cover for research into the viability of a hydrogen powered engine which, if successful, would replace the petrol engine. Such a development would be a tremendous blow to the oil industry in general and to Russian oil production in particular.

Natasha was interested to know how her countrymen had procured the information and, importantly, how it had remained a secret within Drumannan Holdings. Rab and she kept their business interests apart but she thought she might have picked some hint of what was going on. A flash of resentment crossed her mind. On reflection, however, she recognised the need for total security. No wonder the Russians were so worried. Every oil producing nation in the world would be falling over itself to buy up the rights to the discovery.

But how far had the research progressed? There had been a proliferation of such research in recent years. None of it with much success

"What makes you think this any more credible than other premature claims?" she demanded.

"We have reason to believe that a breakthrough has been achieved and in a very short time a working model will be ready for trial," replied the Senior Man.

"Even so, why are you talking to me? I have nothing to do with Drumannan Holdings. In fact my oil interests will be affected also." Natasha was nonplussed.

"Ah, but we think you can help us," intoned one of the wooden faces.

Natasha shouted angrily.

"I have no influence in my husband's business interests. They are quite separate from our domestic life. If you wish to do a deal with Sir Rab Bruce you should approach him."

"That's as may be," said Mr. Senior Man." "By the way, have you been in contact with your parents recently?" He regarded Natasha detachedly, waiting for a reaction.

Realisation dawned on Natasha. It was not necessary to articulate the threat. Throat dry, she stammered, "I'll do my best to persuade my husband to negotiate with you if you grant exit visas to my mother and father."

"That's not quite what we had in mind, Natasha Molotov. We want that research programme terminated." Mr. Senior Man gave her a considered look. "We want your help in destroying the facility."

"I couldn't possibly do that," screamed Natasha.

"You would merely facilitate the destruction by helping the operatives to gain entry. It shouldn't be difficult for the Chairman's wife to obtain codes for the entry system for example and act as a guide to the office part of Bruce Tower House."

Appalled, Natasha rose to storm out.

"Nyet, nyet, nyet!" she exploded.

"Think of the unfortunate events here in recent years- the strange accidents, the assassinations, the poisonings, the fire bombings. The days of the Siberian gulags are gone. In the New Russia, however, accidents do happen. There are rogue elements that do not look kindly on millionaire exiles and their relatives. He smiled thinly. "Old people are particularly vulnerable."

Natasha was shaking with anger. "You are reverting to the old Soviet Union days. I thought we had distanced ourselves from all that. I'm not without influence in the West you know, nor is my husband. We can bring pressure to bear on the Government. If you are acting unofficially you might suffer grave consequences."

"The well being of Mother Russia is at stake, Natasha Molotov," one of the wooden faces said flatly, "Perhaps you should ask your parents if they have yet heard that their dacha has been destroyed by fire."

Natasha was subdued now. Her stomach was churning and she felt sick.

"I will have to think about this," she muttered.

"Well, let us know your decision tomorrow. I'll set up a planning meeting for 2 p.m."

As Natasha informed Sir Rab of this encounter his anger grew, mottling his face with suppressed rage.

"Surely you didn't succumb to that kind of blackmail, Natasha," he thundered.

"There's a lot more, Rab," she sobbed.

That night her father was set upon outside his flat. Ostensibly it was a mugging. He was not badly beaten up, but it was a clear warning. Her old father had been targeted. Natasha heeded the warning. She attended a number of meetings with people who seemed to be Spetznaz, or ex-Spetznaz, she was not sure which.

After her return to Scotland she was contacted by an assault group. She obtained entry codes to the Aberbrothy complex and guided the group who blew up the office in the Bruce Tower House. There must have been a fault in the fuses the operatives used. Both explosive charges went off prematurely, causing her injuries and the death of one of the so-called Spetznaz.

"I'm so sorry, Rab. I've committed a terrible crime but I couldn't help it," she appealed to him, eyes brimming, face distorted. The thought of my mother and father being subjected to the brutalities of the Russian regime was too much for me. I couldn't refuse to carry out the orders of the swine. God help Russia!" She turned her face away against his intense fury. It was not, however, directed at her. He sprayed a stream of obscenities, jumping from his seat, striding up and down the room. An alarmed nurse poked her head in the door. With an effort he brought himself under control.

"Try not to worry, darling. You've got it off your chest. Now just relax. I'll be here for you, no matter what happens." He squeezed her hand, kissed her and held her close, careful of her injuries.

Turning to the nurse he implored her to calm Natasha down.

"Please give her a sedative. She's under intolerable stress."

Inspector Orr was at first disbelieving. When he realised the implications of what Sir Rab had told him, his mind reeled. Sabotage by Russians! In Aberbrothy! On his Watch! The security services would have to be involved. The repercussions would go straight to the top. If the allegations were proved they were way above his pay grade. He would have to verify this man's statement by getting into that hospital room as soon as possible.

"You realise how serious this confession is for your wife, sir. We'll have to interview her thoroughly and get a written statement."

"Please don't put too much pressure on her, Inspector. She's very fragile," he pleaded.

We'll do our best, sir but we have a job to do," Orr responded bleakly.

Sir Rab phoned his legal department.

"I want to engage the best legal team in the land to represent my wife," he ordered peremptorily.

CHAPTER FIFTY TWO

THE INVESIGATION: ABERBROTHY

The Chief Constable rubbed his chin thoughtfully.

Much as it goes against the grain I'll have to shoot this one upstairs, Orr. Interview this Russian woman immediately she's fit for it. I want a report straightaway. Orr departed on the run.

The Anti-Terrorist Squad and M.I.5. reacted quickly to the encrypted message circulated to a select few senior officials. Ministers were informed and the COBRA Committee activated. Aberbrothy quickly became a scene of new urgency. The explosives were identified as of Russian origin. The dead operative's body was given a more detailed examination without yielding further clues as to his identity.

In her hospital bed Natasha Bruce wanly responded to the questions, trying to recall everything that might be relevant to aid her interrogators. Unfortunately she had no information to add about the theft of the Calabar Hoard or the whereabouts of the Russian operatives. She had not been told where their base was and how their extraction tactics were carried out. A call went out to airports and seaports to look out for possible suspects but the authorities knew it was a vain hope. They would be long gone.

Natasha was formally charged and refused bail. Police Officers guarded her room.

A brief statement issued by the Police to the media caused a buzz of excitement.

"A woman has been charged with complicity in the criminal events leading to the explosions at Aberbrothy and Drumannan.

CHAPTER FIFTY THREE

RANGI AND JADE: DRUMANNAN

They were not asked to sit down. Rangy McNaughton and Cheong Yu (Jade) shuffled uncomfortably in the unfamiliar surroundings of the Bruce Tower Museum, acting as a makeshift office for Sir Rab Bruce and his personal staff after the destruction of the office in his house.

Sir Rab stared at them, stony-faced.

"I refer to the events leading up to the explosion. What were you doing in my office so late at night?"

Rangy cleared his throat nervously.

"I was preparing a presentation of a new computer system for your office staff. It was to be installed next week and a training session was considered necessary."

"And I merely came along to run Mr. McNaughton home because his car was being repaired," added Jade.

"Till midnight? I find that hard to believe," snorted Sir Rab. "There was more to your presence there than that."

Jade exchanged looks with Rangy. She had made up her mind to make a clean breast of her actions. With hindsight it seemed extraordinarily naïve for her to even attempt such a hazardous stunt. Genuine curiosity was one thing. Snooping in the way they had done was reprehensible. She sighed. Rangy looked at his feet in misery.

"Both Rangy and I had become suspicious about what was going on in the Solar Power research facility. As you know I am a senior researcher in the Tidal and Wave Power section and I could never understand why my colleagues in the Solar Power research section were so reticent, secretive even, about what they were up to. When Rangy traced their qualifications and records of previous employment he discovered that they came from quite different fields of study from that which would be expected of scientists researching Solar Power. We decided to do a little poking around to satisfy our curiosity, no more."

Sir Rab remained impassive.

"What about you, Mr. McNaughton? Is this your story too?"

Rangy stuttered, "Exactly, Sir Rab. I encouraged Miss Cheong Yu to try to find out more. It was my curiosity that got us into this mess."

Sir Rab said nothing, continuing to stare at them coldly. At last he made a decision.

"I believe your stories. My investigations show that you seem to have had no connection with the sabotage. What you did was foolish in the extreme. I can scarcely believe that two experienced professional people would embark on such a daft enterprise. Did you really think that a hurried rummage through my office would reveal the secrets of one of the most exciting developments in reducing dependence on oil? You are a pair of bumbling fools. For that reason I am not going to ask the police to question you further. I will say this is an internal company matter. What I am going to do is to dismiss you both."

He resumed reading the papers in front of him. It seemed the interview was over.

Jade took a deep breath.

"Sir Rab, as you no doubt are aware, my individual research work on Tidal and Wave Power was yielding interesting results. I am near to producing a prototype unit that would generate power at an economic price. I was almost ready to have it field tested when the explosion damaged the facility. I believe the destruction has caused only a relatively short delay to the project. In six months I could be ready to test the equipment."

"Miss Cheong Yu, I am well aware of your work but I place great store by loyalty and trust in my business dealings, particularly in the case of employees. You have both betrayed that bond. I can easily replace you with equally qualified people. You will not return to your posts. Your personal effects are waiting for you outside."

Sir Rab had carefully balanced the advantage of retaining Jade because of her successful breakthrough in Tidal and Wave Power. He calculated, however, that it was only a matter of time before other scientists would emulate what she had achieved. He was willing to take the risk that a new team at Bruce Engineering would still be ahead of the field. Jade did not know that her prototype was undamaged although he had let it be known that everything had been damaged beyond repair. The evidence had been bulldozed to make way for reconstruction before Jade was allowed into the remains of the building.

Rangy was deeply depressed. Yet another promising start in his career was in ruins. At his age he would find it difficult to find a position commensurate with his qualifications and ability. He would have to settle for a lowlier job, if indeed he could find anything. He confided his despair to Jade on the way home to Milltown-on-Devon.

Jade was equally concerned about her own career. From being an eagerly head-hunted near genius she was now going to have to contend with the rumours that would spread about her in the small world of research into alternative sources of energy.

Miserably they picked at the Chinese takeaway meal they had bought. Rangy was too despondent to cook. Even Belle's arrival to commiserate with them failed to lift the gloom. There was no progress in the search for the Calabar Hoard. Various claims had been made. The Sons of St. George mockingly announced that it was buried at Glastonbury; a dissident I.R.A. group claimed it was in their possession, a further punishment for Weelum Ramsay's opposition to them all these years ago; a Muslim extremist group boasted that it had been spirited away in Afghanistan. It was rumoured that the Russians had taken it. A Scottish Independence group claimed they had hidden it at Arbroath Abbey to ensure it remained in Scotland. It was even said that the villagers of Naughtonwood had been responsible for its disappearance. But the police had no leads to follow up.

Belle's own problems were sympathetically discussed, Belle failing to convince the other two that she was unaffected by her break up with Roddy and her redundancy.

The three of them made arrangements to climb Kingseat Hill the next day. Then they got drunk.

CHAPTER FIFTY FOUR

RANGI: MILLTOWN-ON DEVON

Rangi read the note with disbelief.

Rangi,

I have returned to Singapore.

               Jade

There had been no indication that Jade contemplated leaving. The cold abrupt note completely undid him. Sick, dizzy, stumbling, he fell into a chair, his mind incapable of accepting what he had just read. Frantically he rehearsed the events of the past few days. Jade had talked of jobs she had applied for, about a possible expedition to the West Highland Way, about the haughty Catriona McMannan. There was not the slightest hint that she was even thinking of returning to her native land.

Rousing himself, Rangy checked the bedroom, hoping against hope that her clothes would still be there. The suitcases were gone: her side of the wardrobe empty. He smashed the door closed, humiliation overwhelming him. Had she no feelings for him? Had she been using him as a convenience while she was in Scotland? He grimaced bitterly. Once again he had been rejected.

As a young boy he had been puzzled that he looked different from the other children. His father brusquely told him not to worry: it had never bothered him. Rangy's peers soon cruelly made him realise that he was not one of them. School children were merciless in their baiting of the different and vulnerable. He was small and sensitive unlike his "hard man" father. His school days became torture, his mother the only haven of refuge from persecution. Things improved at secondary school where he effaced himself. An anonymous member of most classes he made few friends and did little to impress his teachers. Nevertheless his marks were good and his staunch mother supported him against the inverted snobbery of Chinky McNaughton, his father, who professed to scorn education as a waste of time but who secretly resented the fact that he himself had been denied the chance. Eventually Rangy made it to university, acquiring a degree in Computer Science. At last he could face the world armed with his professional qualification.

Silicon Glen beckoned and he quickly established himself in a multi-national company which promptly folded. A succession of similar jobs followed, puzzlingly not resulting in promotion to more senior positions. A brief relationship with a girl, who confessed to be intrigued by his slanty eyes, came to an end when she became even more intrigued by a fellow with a Jesus beard and a hippy history. His mining village socialism was severely dented by his experience as a would be shop steward. The cynicism of his erstwhile left wing colleagues appalled him.

The recent fiasco at Bruce Engineering and now the desertion of Jade was more than he could bear. Resentment was boiling in him-resentment of his colour, his background, his ex-colleagues, social activists, capitalists, Jade, Scotland in general. Sullenly he opened a bottle of whisky.

CHAPTER FIFTY FIVE

RANGI AND FAMILY: NAUGHTONWOOD

Johnny McNaughton was curiously subdued when Rangi and he discussed the robbery of the Calabar Hoard. Instead of his usual fiery outburst of indignation he accepted the story in a matter-of-fact way.

"We might have expected something of the sort. There are too many vested interests at play here. Any one of them could have carried out the robbery. The Treasure should never have been moved."

Rangi was in no mood to put up with His brother's nonsense. He scoffed.

"What about security, Johnny? Where in the village could it have been safely stored?"

"Well, all the security at the Bruce Tower Museum didn't prevent the theft," Johnny grunted. I just hope criminals didn't steal it to melt down for the worth of the silver."

"Don't even think that, Johnny."

Rangi had never contemplated that possibility. He was appalled.

"It has probably happened countless times in the past. Grave robbers and all that! The theft has made me all the more determined that the Treasure will stay in Naughtonwood if it is ever recovered." Johnny muttered gloomily. I've got to go now. By the way, I was sorry to hear about you and Jade."

With an embarrassed wave he slid out of the door.

CHAPTER FIFTY SIX

THE ARCHAEOLOGISTS: St. REGULUS UNIVERSITY

The Vice Principal of St. Regulus University rubbed his eyes wearily before replacing his spectacles.

"Angela, why is so much of my time taken up with dissatisfied, resentful, academics who think they have been slighted, insulted, overlooked or bullied?"

Professor Angela Bull smiled politely. The old boy had been around long enough to know that it was par for the course. Such problems were endemic in academic circles and it was part of his job to deal with them. He must be feeling bilious this morning.

"So, I've examined the complaints of Dr. York and I've seen your comprehensive rebuttal. There is a clash of personalities here but he seems unduly sensitive and resentful. He also has misrepresented some of the facts. I interviewed him about his accusations regarding your conduct. He did not take kindly to my suggestion that perhaps he had skewed the "actualite" in his favour. He tendered his resignation, accompanied by some intemperate remarks about our way of doing things here at the University. I accepted it. Clearly he was never going to fit in, particularly with you as his Departmental Head. He has applied for a post in Italy. He has a villa there, you know. So the matter is settled.

I must, however, caution you to try to be more diplomatic in your dealings with staff and students. You do have the reputation of not suffering fools gladly."

His eyes twinkled as Angela smiled ruefully.

"I'll try to do better, Vice Chancellor.

"What about the Pictish remains? I presume there is still a great deal to be learned from the remaining artifacts. The Calabar Hoard! An amusing and catchy title!"

The Vice Chancellor had followed the unfolding events closely. An historian, he realised the importance of the contribution archaeology could make to the study of the so-called Dark Ages.

Angela snorted. "A cheap gimmick! Archaeology is too serious a subject for such journalistic nonsense. Yes, I hope the finds will reveal much that we did not know about the domestic life, dress and weapons of the period. I and my team will produce a preliminary report soon. Of course if the stolen artifacts turn up it will take a lot longer." Angela swore, apologised, and burst into tears.

The Vice Principal was appalled. Where was the tough professional woman he had worked with for years, crossing swords with anyone who opposed her and usually winning? He was at a loss.

"Angela, I know it was a terrible blow to……" Words failed him. He sat miserably until the storm of tears gradually diminished, petering out into sniffles.

"Do you feel better now?" he enquired hopefully.

"No, I bloody don't," she shouted as she stumbled out of the room.

The Principal swung to and fro in his comfortable swivel chair. He recalled Angela Bull as a thrusting young lecturer, embroiled in a dispute with her head of Department.

A product of a famous girls' school in Sussex she had graduated with first Class honours in Archaeology from Durham University and had acquired extensive experience of field work before coming to Scotland.

The cause of the furor was the remains found at the site of a projected housing development on the eastern outskirts of Queenstown. Angela had advanced the theory that Queenstown Loch in earlier times had extended much further to the east than at present, exactly where the new houses were to be built, and that the remains were those of a crannog (or lake dwelling). There was some fragmentary evidence to back up her theory, not enough to convince Dr. Robin Christie, the Head of the Archaeology Department. After a battle of wills, Christie reluctantly gave her permission to excavate the low mound at the centre of the site.

Angela's prediction was brilliantly proved to be correct as the excavation produced abundant evidence of the existence of a crannog dwelling. Artifacts from everyday life in the Iron Age and the remains of timber posts on a base of boulders were recovered.

When the University published an account of the findings the main credit was attributed to Dr. Robin Christie. Angela Bull was mentioned as an assistant on the project.

Righteously indignant, she raised the matter with the University Court and obtained their support. Dr. Christie was reprimanded for professional misconduct and resigned his post soon afterwards.

Now, ten years later she had been thwarted on the brink of another triumphant archaeological success by the theft of The Calabar Hoard. The Principal sighed again. He hoped she would be able to survive the blow.

CHAPTER FIFTY SEVEN

MURDO, BELLE AND RANGI: QUEENSTOWN

What if I told you the Calabar Hoard is at John York's house in Italy?" Murdo McMannan looked consideringly at Belle and Rangi.

"You've absolutely no grounds for making that assertion, Murdo." Belle protested. "Just because you don't like the man, and think he's shifty, doesn't give you the right to accuse him of robbery."

Rangi frowned in concentration. "You know I worked with York as a volunteer. Well he treated me off-handedly, never trying to explain anything and giving me the most mundane jobs all the time. But, yes, on occasion he did act furtively when we were removing the artifacts from the souterrain."

"Still no reason for an accusation!" Belle grunted.

Murdo resumed their stroll round Queenstown Loch, its waters slate-grey, a stiff breeze whipping up little waves and lines of foam. The autumn colours of the bushes and trees surrounding the Loch caught a glint of sun. The swans clustered in the expectation of food, curtseyed as they passed, ignoring the mute pleas of the birds.

Murdo outlined a far-fetched plan.

"I would like the pair of you to go to Italy and set up a sting operation against York. I suspect that, if he has the Treasure, he will want to sell."

Belle and Rangi stared in disbelief." Don't you think I'm in enough trouble without becoming involved in another daft adventure?" Rangi spluttered.

But Belle was intrigued.

"There's nothing illegal about someone asking an archaeologist if he has any artifacts for sale. If he bites we'll know he's guilty. If, on the other hand, he is indignant, or promises to look out for suitable pieces we can be pretty sure he is clean, unless of course he has taken them for his own pleasure of ownership." Murdo was persuasive, turning on his full charm.

Rangi was still suspicious.

"How would you set up the sting?" he enquired, "It still sounds less than feasible to me."

Murdo intervened.

"Listen, you two need a break. Belle, your break up with Roddy and Rangi, the collapse of your professional career, all that stress has made it very desirable for you to have a holiday away from your difficulties. As a concerned friend, I'm willing to cover all your costs. The fact that you carry out a small deception operation while you are there should add spice to your holiday. It would be a bit of fun if nothing comes of it. If York has the Treasure it would be a triumph.

Here's the plan. I had occasion to use a private detective agency in Florence a year ago when a picture of mine was stolen from my villa near Cortona. They retrieved it for me quickly and expeditiously by means of a sting operation. I'm sure they would do so again, given their previous success. All you would have to do would be to confront York with the evidence on tape and video, or melt away into the darkness if you drew a blank. Does that scenario overcome your objections, Rangi?

Rangi was still dubious.

"It seems an awful lot of money for a slim chance that you are correct in your supposition."

Murdo laughed uproariously.

"I have an awful lot of money, Rangi."

CHAPTER FIFTY EIGHT

THE STING: TUSCANY

The Tuscan town of Montecatini shimmered in the autumn haze hundreds of feet below its tiny twin Montecatini Alto perched high above on a spur of the Apennines. Seated in a restaurant in the sloping piazza of the village, Belle and Rangy toyed with their glasses of the so-called house red wine. Their lunch had been typical tourist fare-Crostini, Ravioli, Veal and Tiramisu. Rangy belched softly, apologising to Belle who smiled wanly.

"Not used to Italian food, Rangy. I suppose we should be enjoying the break but I am too emotionally drained to appreciate the scenery, the weather, the atmosphere, the whole Tuscan thing."

Rangy had never been to Italy before. In his depression he was prepared to dislike the experience but to his surprise he was intrigued by the country and its inhabitants from day one. Montecatini was a town with a magnificent Spa where elegant Italian men and women drifted around with string bags containing mugs from which they swigged a selection of mineralised water from the various taps while listening to live music. To the south and east stretched mile after mile of the tree nurseries which supplied Europe's garden centres. The old German Gothic battle line loomed over the town in the foothills of the forested Apennines. Further into the hills old villages topped eminences and spurs, each with its church tower. Summer-bleached stream beds awaited the winter spates. Further north the hills became mountains with winter ski slopes. The towns on the River Arno plain all seemed to have an austere historical town centre and modern developments of housing and industry sprawled around. The people, commercially friendly in the tourist industry, somewhat dour in the everyday life, took the weight of the centuries for granted. Rangy, a north European tourist, gawped in wonder. In a happier period of his life he would have thrown himself into a frenzy of sightseeing. As it was his excitement was damped down by his latest failure to establish himself as an ordinary Scot with a career and a family. Could a person of mixed race ever overcome the sense of not belonging? He gazed bleakly at the carefully tended memorial to the war dead across the square. His mind roved over recent events and in particular with his failed relationship with Jade.

The late autumn day was chilly and they had chosen to wait for Murdo's private detective inside the restaurant, keeping a look out for his approach. He was late. Belle's melancholy mood matched Rangi's. She remained withdrawn, a tension headache developing into a migraine. Why had she agreed to this wild goose chase?

Her introspection was interrupted by a scusi from a bald, portly man with a black bar for eyebrows and a bushy moustache over a mouth full of crooked tobacco-stained teeth. In his fifties, he was dressed soberly in a cheap dark suit, dazzling white shirt, a conservative maroon tie, and slip on patent leather shoes.

"Ms. Ramsay, Mr. McNaughton," He spoke in accented English, stumbling over Rangi's name. "Mr. McMannan asked me to meet you here."

Belle appraised him dully. So this was the wonder private detective Murdo had hired. He was certainly no Sherlock Holmes but then what did she know about that seedy side of life. She decided to bide her time and observe how he operated. Rangy was even more jaundiced in his view. Brought up on a diet of tough guy American private eyes, he was disbelieving.

Scrambling to his feet he greeted the newcomer coldly.

"Are you Signor Francesco Caproni?

"At your service," beamed the Italian, "Mr.McMannan has told me about your quest and has indicated how you want to proceed. Perhaps I should sit down and explain my part in the operation."

Belle was contrite. The man was clearly amused by his reception.

"Please excuse my bad manners. May I order you a drink?

"Not when I am on duty," twinkled Francesco, "I watch your English police soaps so I know what is expected of me."

They all laughed. At least he has a sense of humour Belle thought.

"I trust you are both enjoying your stay here. Tuscany is pleasant at this time of year. Now to business. I have made a start to my enquiries. Would you like me to fill you in?"

"Please do," said Rangi expectantly. Perhaps some purposeful activity would shake them out of their depression.

Francesco and his two colleagues had established the whereabouts of the small cottage John York had inherited from an aunt. It was situated in a foothills hamlet a few miles from the nearby town of Pistoia. York spent his days pottering about in his garden, tending the sprawling tomatoes, vines and olive trees, or visiting places of archaeological interest in the neighbourhood. He dined regularly in the only trattoria in the village which did a thriving carry out trade in pizzas and the like and boasted a one choice menu for lunch and evening meals. The offering was really quite good Francesco reported. He had already dined there once or twice.

He had made a point of discussing Etruscan remains with his colleagues and had produced a genuine artifact for the other two to examine, hoping that York, sitting at one of the five tables, would have enough Italian to pick up what the conversation was about. The next step would be to pretend to buy a piece of pottery from one of his companions. He would ignore York save to wish him a casual good evening in English for it was common knowledge that he was British. The hope was that York would be intrigued enough to enquire about Francesco's interest in antiques.

"What do you think of my plan," he paused to enquire. "I'll have a glass of wine after all." He spoke in rapid Italian to the waiter who smilingly brought a bottle of red wine to the table.

"A local red, not for the tourists," he explained, as he urged them to try a glass.

"What if he ignores the bait? asked Rangi churlishly. He was still uneasy about the operation. "And how will you develop the situation if he does?"

Francesco laughed. "No problem. I have plans B and C. I have a hunch, however, that he will approach me. He pretends not to be interested but I know he is listening to the talk."

"And what do we do?" enquired Belle, amused by the deception and eager to participate.

Francesco was alarmed.

"Please keep out of sight. Do your tourist thing. Go to Florence, Sienna, and San Gimigniano. He's done all that. You won't run into him there. Avoid Pistoia though. He shops there."

"Oh!" Belle was disappointed, Rangi less so. "Is there nothing we can do?"

"Absolutely not! Your big scene will be when you confront him but that might be some time yet."

The rest of the afternoon was spent listening to stories about some of Francesco's past cases. Later, Rangi conceded that perhaps he was not such a bad chap after all.

Three days later Francesco returned to meet Belle and Rangi in their plush hotel in Montecatini Terme. Murdo McMannan spared no expense in booking their holiday. Each had a suite with sitting room and balcony. It was to Belle's suite that they repaired with Bellinis in hand. Francesco's prediction had proved to be correct. Dr.York had engaged him in conversation the previous evening in the village restaurant, expressing interest in Francesco as a dealer in antiques. Francesco explained that he was in the area to meet some of his network of local contacts. York was particularly interested in Etruscan artifacts and suggested he might be interested in acquiring some in exchange for two pieces of antique silver ware he owned.

Francesco paused in his account of the events, waiting for the reaction of Belle and Rangi.

"So Murdo McMannan was correct after all," Belle exclaimed, "York has the Calabar Hoard."

Even Rangi was convinced, but with his usual reservation.

"What do you have to offer in exchange?" he demanded, "You can't expect him to buy a pig in a poke."

Francesco gave him a pitying look.

"Murdo had already thought of that. I have a delicate Etruscan figurine from his villa in Cortona to show York with the promise of more if his silver ware merits it. I told him I had a client who would be interested in ancient Celtic artifacts. He told me an amateur with a metal detector had uncovered the silver ware in a field in Fife, and had contacted him, not wishing to turn his find over to the authorities as treasure trove since he was operating illegally in a farmer's property. York had bought the artifacts at much less than their true value. He wanted to dispose of them outside Britain. I had the impression, however, that he only had the two pieces, nothing like the quantity that was stolen."

"He might be selling in small lots to avoid the suspicion if a large quantity appeared on the market at one time," Belle suggested.

"True. We'll have to wait and see. I have set up a meeting with him at my hotel near Pistoia so that we can view each others goods and agree an exchange or part exchange. I've set up the room with a hidden camera and sound recorder and I would like you two to be in the adjoining room with my colleagues. You can make an entrance and confront him at the appropriate moment." Francesco was sweating and tense as he outlined the plan. It seemed watertight but much could go wrong. They discussed details for some time before phoning Murdo to inform him of progress and gain his consent to the denouement. Murdo was gleeful.

"I knew it was York. I just felt it in my bones. Go ahead. And let me know immediately when you've trapped the bugger."

***

"I have here a silver torc and a chalice from the Pictish period, probably eighth century. They are in mint condition. It seems they were found in a metal container."

John York was nervous, his voice cracking as he explained the detail of the two pieces. "I would expect a price in the region of 20000 Euros as well as the Etruscan figurine."

Francesco pursed his lips.

"I have led my client to believe that there were many more pieces available. He'll be disappointed to discover that there are only two."

"I'm afraid that's all I have. My metal detector friend only unearthed what you see in front of you," York muttered, dismayed that Francesco would back out of the transaction.

"Ah well! I'm sure my client will still appreciate the two pieces. They look like fine examples of Celtic Art. Your price, however, is too high. They haggled for some time before agreeing a part exchange and 15000 Euros to York.

"Good! A done deal," Francesco beamed.

York, secretly delighted to have covered his tracks so easily, stated pompously, "I accept your terms."

Belle and Rangy stepped into the room.

Dr. John York reared back in shock. His face drained of colour.

"What-what are you two doing here?" he spluttered. "Get out! Out!" His features turned mottled red, mouth working, and spittle flying. He plunged forward, arms outstretched to push and punch. Rangi directly opposite, ducked away.

"I'll kill you, McNaughton. I always knew you were a little yellow weasel. Belle felt almost sorry for the man, as Francesco restrained him with some difficulty, his colleagues coming to his assistance.

"Get them out of here, Signor Caproni." He paused. The awful truth slowly dawning on him.. He had been entrapped.

"You can't prove anything," he screeched.

"Oh, but we can," Belle intervened icily. "We have a recording and a video of your conversation with Signor Cabrelli."

York swore, and swore again. "I'll get a lawyer. I'll plead entrapment."

"The evidence of the torc and the chalice will still be there," said Rangi quietly. "You'd better calm down and listen."

John York snarled at him, the hatred gleaming in his wild eyes.

"You can hand over the artifacts to be returned to their rightful owners or we can arrange for you to be handed over to the British police who are actively pursuing the thieves of the Calabar Hoard," Belle stated.

"But I only took—"Too late he realised his mistake. "Anyway the ownership is in doubt."

"It matters little who owns the Treasure," Rangi hissed, "You are a thief." His antipathy to the man was apparent.

"I'll say I packed them by mistake during the transfer to Bruce Tower Museum," York attempted to bluster. The others looked at him contemptuously.

"It won't wear, York," Belle said quickly, "The voice and audio recordings reveal that you were trying to sell the stuff."

At last York seemed deflated, staring dully at the floor. Belle continued.

"I'm going to phone Murdo McMannan. Sir Rab and Professor Bull. I'll propose that you give me the silver so that I can return it to the University. The two items will be discovered among the remaining artifacts, concealed in some clothing. You will not be prosecuted but these recordings will be retained as evidence of your theft if you cause any more trouble for the University. In that way your reputation will be preserved as will the good name of St. Regulus. Do you agree to these terms? The alternative is prosecution and wide publicity."

York was silent, mouth working. At last he ground out,

"Agreed."

"Thank you, Dr. York. I'd appreciate it if you would leave us now."

York sullenly shambled out of the room, a broken man.

The next morning Francesco bade Belle and Rangi farewell at Pisa Airport.

"A job well done," he called as they disappeared through the security barrier. "Benissimo!"

CHAPTER FIFTY NINE

RODDY, CATRIONA AND THE FIRST MINISTER: EDINBURGH, 2012

The Deputy First Minister of the Scottish Assembly, Roddy Neilson, listened with alarm as Professor Latto sombrely reported that the construction of the new aircraft carriers would be carried out at English shipyards. The Westminster Government deemed Clydeside and Rosyth to be unsuitable.

The Scottish Peoples Alliance had been in Government for over a year and had performed much better than critics had forecast. The law and order crackdown was largely successful. Many more police deployed more effectively had transformed the public perception of their ability to make the streets safe for law abiding citizens. The justice system was beginning to be seen to respect the rights of the victim rather than the criminal. A new education policy emphasising the three Rs was enthusiastically received by the teaching profession and the public. Discipline in schools was strict: disruptive pupils were excluded and parents held to account for the misdemeanours of their children. The work-shy were faced with stern policies which brooked no "bleeding heart" misplaced sympathy although genuine cases were dealt with fairly. Reduced business taxation was already producing an upsurge in business confidence. All this good news was tempered with the need to find the necessary finance by cutting back on other aspects of Government. Local government suffered severely: services were curtailed: staffing levels were reduced drastically. Expenditure on capital projects ground almost to a halt: new road programmes were .abandoned: school building was significantly reduced. The public grumbled but recognised the need to accept the consequences of the new priorities.

Relations with the Westminster Government, however, were deteriorating, and anti-English feeling was growing. This decision to ignore Scottish shipyards would exacerbate the situation. Professor Latto, able and sure-footed though he was in holding his Ministers together and pushing through sensible policies, was finding it increasingly difficult to maintain the Unionist stance of the Scottish Peoples Alliance. Already there was back room talk of forging an alliance with the rump of the Scottish National Party and pressing for independence.

Roddy, impressed by Latto, and convinced of the wisdom of staying in the United Kingdom, desperately cast about for tenable arguments to support the S.P.A. policy in the face of this rumbling discontent.

"This news is most disappointing but it is not the end of the world. We should concentrate on updating our technological base. For instance, I have learned from a reliable source that our researchers have made a major breakthrough in a cost efficient method of utilising tidal and wave power. I also understand that development work on hydrogen powered engines is at an advanced stage. Elsewhere new methods of extracting and utilising coal should make it possible to profit from the large coal reserves still untapped beneath our feet in

Scotland. Our scientists and engineers are at the forefront in the field of medical research. The potential is there if we have the courage and drive to overcome setbacks such as the loss of the ship contracts. We don't need handouts. Scotland can stand on its own two feet as a vibrant and successful part of the United Kingdom." Roddy's eloquence swayed the waverers in the Cabinet, earning a smile of gratitude from the increasingly careworn First Minister.

Catriona, however, demurred.

"I applaud what Roddy has so convincingly argued. Notwithstanding what he said, however, I am furious at this affront to our national integrity. It is clear that the Conservative Government at Westminster do not trust us with key defence contracts. I have heard rumours that R.A.F. airfields in Moray and at Leuchars are to close and the nuclear submarine base at Faslane will be moved to the south coast of England. We cannot tolerate this undermining of our position as an integral part of the United Kingdom. It almost seems as though the Conservatives are hell bent on driving us out."

There were murmurs of agreement around the table. Professor Latto intervened.

"I intend to seek a meeting with the Prime Minister at the earliest opportunity to reaffirm our position our commitment to the Union and to protest in the strongest possible terms about the cumulative thrust of the Government's recent policies. He was grey and sweating. He was well aware that the tensions in the country were mounting. Bullying of English children in Scottish schools was becoming endemic, as was the reverse in schools in England. Attacks on "white settler" homes, demonstrations outside the House of Commons, ugly incidents at football matches between Scottish and English clubs marred sporting rivalry, in rugby the Calcutta Cup match at Murrayfield was boycotted by a substantial number of both Scottish and English supporters. Jock bashing in England was common. Organisations such as the Sons of St. George and Hearts of Oak in England and Flower of Scotland, the Reivers and the Bannockburn Boys attracted bigots and ignoramuses in their respective countries. Platitudes by politicians calling for restraint and moderation were having little effect. The very fabric of the Union was at risk.

After the Meeting the Private Secretary of the First Minister approached Roddy.

"Minister, I am concerned about Mr. Latto's state of health. As you know he is a workaholic and the strain is beginning to tell. We are off to London tonight. When we return would you have a word with him, suggesting he should ease off a bit?"

Roddy readily agreed. He too had noticed the effects of the heavy work load of the First Minister. He was becoming uncharacteristically irritable, often late for appointments, and eating on the run. Some of his decisions recently had not been up to his usual standard. A fluent speaker, he had under-performed in the Chamber. Roddy resolved to confront him with a demand that he have a medical examination and consider taking some time off.

The next afternoon he received a phone call from Bill Latto.

"Roddy, things are pretty bleak. My meeting with the Prime Minister did not go well. He listened politely to my protestations of loyalty to the Union, was non-committal about our successes in Government, and stonewalled my questions about the future policy of the

United Kingdom Government towards devolution, finance, and Scottish problems generally."

Roddy had hoped that Latto's obvious sincerity and integrity would have impressed the Prime Minister.

"Were there any chinks of light at all?" he asked. "He couldn't have been completely negative surely."

I'm afraid so, Roddy. We'll have to rethink our position. I'll start to work something out on the plane home. Meantime you try to find time to do the same, please."

Bill Latto sounded a beaten man, so unlike his usual incisive self. Roddy rang off, deep in though. Matters were much worse than he had envisaged.

Late that evening Roddy was telephoned by the Permanent Secretary to the Scottish Office. The First Minister had suffered a stroke on the plane from London to Edinburgh. The plane had been diverted to Newcastle Airport and Bill Latto had been rushed to hospital. He died two hours later.

Roddy was aghast, reviling himself for not acting sooner to try to avert such an occurrence. As Deputy he automatically became Acting First Minister pending an election for a new First Minister. All S.P.A. Members of the Scottish Assembly would be entitled to vote. In view of the deteriorating economic and political situation an election would have to be held as soon as possible.

The election was arranged for three weeks later.

Roddy felt he was in a strong position to become the new leader. His supporters launched a campaign on his behalf among his fellow M.S.P.s, based on his excellent record as Justice Minister. It came as no surprise that Catriona McMannan had also thrown her hat into the ring. She announced her candidature amid a throng of supporters. Her women colleagues- the sisterhood - as they were called - predominated but a substantial number of men made it clear that they preferred her to Roddy. You are worthy but staid, said one of them, and I haven't forgotten your old Labour and C.N.D. background.

Roddy was crestfallen. It was acknowledged that he had done a first class job as Justice Minister and had supported Latto loyally. Now it seemed that people were briefing against him. The charismatic Catriona was active in the corridors, tearooms and watering holes, charming her colleagues with her wit and elegance.

The result of the vote was Catriona McMannan 72, Roderick Neilson 48, with the others either absent or abstaining.

Bitterly disappointed, Roddy let it be known that he would not continue in office, suspecting that Catriona would not re-appoint him anyway. She made no attempt to persuade him to reconsider.

CHAPTER SIXTY

THE WEST LOTHIAN ANSWER

In simultaneous raids the statue of Winston Churchill and the Wallace Sword were spirited away. After much media speculation and Government and Opposition posturing the Sword was deposited outside the Houses of Parliament and the Statue outside the Scottish Assembly building. Attached notes attributed the stunt - for that was what it was - to:

The West Lothian Answer- a Kingdom United.

A week later the Scottish manager of a famous English football club was kidnapped just after a game. A world famous English pop star with a farmhouse retreat in Scotland disappeared after appearing at T in the Park. Both were released unharmed three days later having received extensive media coverage. Beaming, they displayed placards displaying the words:

The west Lothian Answer- a Kingdom United

The police vowed to deal sternly with anyone wasting police time.

The multi-millionaire pop star, leader of the Triple M group, made an appeal to anyone living in England or Wales who had been born in West Lothian or had parents or grandparents who had lived there to send him proof of their origins and he would give them free tickets to his next gig in their area and an invitation to the opening ceremony of the re-roofed Queenstown Palace. Similarly anyone living in West Lothian who was born in England or Wales or who had parents or grandparents who had lived there would receive the same reward.

The appeal caught the public imagination. He was inundated with calls. The B.B.C. ran a series of programmes in which participants recounted their family history, demonstrating how intertwined peoples lives were. The extent of the intermingling of Scottish, English and Welsh people was revealed in a startling fashion.

I.T.V. networked a sit-com series lampooning nationalist bigots in industrial towns in Scotland and England. Major television stars guested in the series. The Kingdom united in laughter.

The Bruce Bus Company, whose principal shareholder was Sir Rab Bruce, offered free holidays to families in selected unemployment black spots in Scotland and England whose breadwinners had found work after a period of unemployment and had held down their position for a minimum of one year.

With all this publicity as a backcloth Scotland's First Minister, Catriona McMannan, joined the Prime Minister in a meeting at which she acknowledged the need for a more equitable distribution of funds among the different parts of the United Kingdom, for the reduction in the number of Scottish M.P.s at Westminster, previously bitterly opposed by other Scottish Parties. She did, however, oppose strongly another plank of Conservative Government policy, the exclusion of Scottish M.P.s from aspects of Parliamentary business. She questioned the seeming policy of excluding Scottish-based firms and locations from more and more Government contracts. She reversed the previous position of the Assembly on the building of nuclear power stations in Scotland.

Impressed by the record of the new Scottish Administration in the fields of law and order, education and the encouragement of a work ethic the Prime Minister and his colleagues pulled back from their concerns about Scotland's commitment to the Union and pledged to work closely with the First Minister and her colleagues to bolster the United Kingdom.

Catriona returned to Scotland, triumphant.

In celebration, Triple M pop group, husband Murdo to the fore, announced a series of gigs across the U.K., with an admission charge only sufficient to cover costs.

The West Lothian Answer

A United Kingdom

The cumulative effect of these initiatives went a long way to stem the narrow nationalist sentiment in the country. Extremist groups like the Sons of St. George and the Bannockburn Boys continued to try to stir up trouble and the S.N.P. prattled on about Scottish Oil. It seemed, however, that the Union was safe.

CHAPTER SIXTY ONE

BELLE AND FAMILY

Surprised, Belle re-read the letter from her brother, Jamie, They had not spoken since he had accused her and her friends of failing to obtain a position "commensurate with his talents and qualifications" in Bruce Engineering, A junior position in the Public Relations Department was apparently beneath his dignity and seniority. When Belle had tartly reminded him that he had been "between jobs" for some considerable time and had failed to retain a string of previous appointments and that he should be glad of any job, he had stormed off in a huff. Nevertheless, with an ill grace he had accepted the offer of Second Assistant Public Relations Officer.

Belle had tried in vain to restore normal family relationships to no avail. Jamie coldly spurned her invitations to visit. Later Belle had learned indirectly that he had married. Hurt and angry that she had not even been informed she reluctantly added the estrangement to her list of life's disappointments. Now this friendly note asked her to visit him and his wife.

Belle drove slowly towards the end of the cul-de-sac of spanking new houses, each with four bedrooms, a double garage, and a conservatory. The one at the very end Jamie had said when giving her directions. How could he afford a place like this Belle wondered to herself? As a junior employee of Bruce Engineering he had been living in a one-bed roomed flat in Wallacetown.

Jamie seemed happy and relaxed, grinning as he introduced Belle to his wife, Mary, and a ready made family of two early teenage boys. Mary, it turned out, worked as a Personal Secretary in the offices of Bruce Engineering. Shy to begin with, she soon relaxed as Belle complimented her on her taste in home decoration. It was clear that no expense had been spared. A superbly equipped kitchen, shining and blonde, drew a gasp from Belle. Jamie extolled the virtues of his top-of-the-range media equipment. The boys proudly showed her their rooms, each with lap tops and play stations. A Mercedes and a Range Rover stood in the drive.

"Jamie, this is wonderful. However did you acquire the wherewithal to own all this-she gestured all around-stuff?

Jamie and Mary exchanged a quick look.

"We'd rather not discuss the matter, Belle. It's our business and we'll keep it to ourselves if you don't mind."

That reply discomfited Belle and soured the remainder of what had been a pleasant visit. As she drove off, bemused and angry, she wondered yet again how on earth Jamie had acquired such affluence.

"You should have told her, Jamie."

Not likely! Our lottery win is our secret.

CHAPTER SIXTY TWO

NATASHA IN JAIL

Natasha Bruce was tried for aiding and abetting sabotage attacks on Bruce Engineering facilities and Sir Rab Bruce's personal office, indirectly causing the death of one of the saboteurs. She pleaded guilty. In view of the mitigating circumstances she was sentenced to two years in prison with one year's remission for good behaviour. The sheriff considered that he had no option but to recommend a prison sentence in view of the loss of life and the possibility of many more casualties.

Tears streaming down her cheeks the usually ebullient Natasha looked sadly at Sir Rab across the court. He was staggered by the sentence. He had convinced himself that the story of the threats to her parents in Russia would have created enough sympathy for her to be given a suspended sentence.

The inquest into the death of the dead saboteur had been unsuccessful in establishing his identity. Russian style dental work provided the only clue. The Russian authorities, however, disclaimed all knowledge of him. No one had been reported missing. His identity remained a mystery until a month later a distraught Russian citizen appeared in Edinburgh claiming that the body was that of his brother, Yuri Yeftushenko, a serving member of the Spetznaz, Russian Special Forces. The Russian Ambassador asserted that the man was mentally ill and that his story was a fabrication. D.N.A. tests, however, proved that there was a close relationship. The man's extended family of fifteen adults rallied to support the dead man's brother, challenging the Russian Government to admit they were mistaken and to acknowledge the saboteur was indeed who his brother said he was. The subsequent furore deeply embarrassed the Russian Government which was forced to announce that the man had been a member of the armed forces but had deserted and become a renegade. The story was widely disbelieved.

In an uncomfortable position, the Government made a show of granting exit visas to the parents of Natasha Bruce, hoping that the gesture would divert attention from the case of Yuri Yeftushenko.

Natasha recovered her naturally sunny disposition and served the balance of her prison sentence cheerfully, happy to be reunited with her visibly relieved parents..

Sir Rab Bruce arranged for the final payment to be paid to the family of the dead saboteur to compensate them for revealing the duplicity of their Government. He paid off the agents he had employed to track them down and organise their protest.

CHAPTER SIXTY THREE

THE POLICE INVESTIGATION

Police Inspector Orr reviewed the lack of progress in the investigation into the theft of The Calabar Hoard. Unlike the clear-cut resolution of the sabotage incidents at Bruce Engineering and Bruce Tower House with the conviction of Natasha Bruce and the involvement of the Russians (in spite of official denials), the investigation of the robbery at Bruce Tower Museum had ground to a halt.

Several lines of enquiry still remained open and one or two people still remained under suspicion but no positive leads had emerged. The Russians would always be suspect. Inspector Orr was coming to the conclusion that professional thieves might be the culprits and it would be a matter of waiting until some of the stolen goods appeared on the market, always assuming that the thieves had not ignorantly melted down the gold and silver for a comparatively small gain.

Jack Drummond, former Head of Security at Bruce Engineering, remained a suspect. His whereabouts were still unknown. Johnny McNaughton, too, was suspect although Inspector Orr felt that his bluster about keeping The Treasure in Naughtonwood was no more than that. Extreme organisations like the Sons of St. George and the Bannockburn Boys were capable of planning and executing the theft. Such organisations must remain in the frame as possible perpetrators of the crime.

Orr sighed. Although media interest in the incident had long since evaporated the Chief Constable would still expect a report which would show the Central Police Force in a favourable light. The best approach would be to emphasise the professional thieves aspect of the case, pointing to previous examples when attempts had been made to sell stolen art had led to the apprehension of the thieves.

CHAPTER SIXTY FOUR

RUTH: AT ALLANFORD

Ruth gazed in puzzlement at her bank statement. A meticulous guardian of her personal finances, she was undertaking her monthly check on her transactions. She had just realised that she could not add up. How could she not make sense of the figures in front of her? Eight and seven makes………. The cold realisation that the disease was progressing rapidly hit her.

Slowly she lowered her pen. She had reached a critical point it seemed. How long would it be before she was no longer capable of remembering anything? Soon she would be beyond recall, her mind completely gone.

Ruth had decided when her condition was diagnosed that she would choose the manner of her death. It was time for action. First there were things to do. She leaned back in her chair, planning the sequence of events she must follow. Her affairs were in order. The house would go to Belle. Rangy would get a substantial legacy. Her Bermudan relatives would benefit from what was left. She must finish the scarf she was knitting for Belle. And she must depart with the minimum amount of trouble to others.

Her thoughts drifted. She had led a full and satisfying life with its complement of triumphs, defeats, disappointments, good fortune, despair, happiness. She felt she had made a modest contribution to the sum of human knowledge, and had tried to treat her fellows fairly, if with some severity, even acerbity, at times. She smiled wistfully. The one thing she had missed was to give birth to a child, a grief well concealed and eventually accepted as she grew older. Shaking herself out of her sadness Ruth set about her preparations.

Three days later Ruth carefully wrapped the scarf for Belle in a waterproof bag together with a note. With certain other items she placed it in her battered old rucksack, laced up her walking boots, donned her anorak, picked up her walking poles, and locked the door of her Allanford house. Forcing herself not to look back, she angled her way up the wooded slope behind the town and emerged on to the open hill. With a long hike in front of her she paced her old body carefully, making full use of her poles as she trudged eastward along the spine of the Ochils.

"She's always switching off her mobile phone," muttered Belle. "Silly old bat! I wonder where she is."

Belle had been trying to contact Ruth. There had been no response from her house phone for two days. Rangi, Murdo and Catriona, Sir Rab and Natasha, and Angela Bull had not heard from her.

"She'll be off on an expedition to some Pictish site," laughed Angela. "She's always phoning to tell me of her latest foray. I expect I'll hear from her soon."

Belle was not so sure. Ruth had always been punctilious in informing her of her movements. This silence was out of character. I'll run over to Allanford to check if she's not ill and being brave, suffering in silence. After phoning Rangi to accompany her she set off, driving along the foot of the hills from her temporary home in her father's old cottage, lent to her by Ruth.

Another spring was in full fig. The gorse bushes, calthropian guardians of the lower slopes of Craigleith, Myretoun and Dumyat, speckled the hillsides with a harsh golden yellow, the native shrubs clashing with the pink blossom of the ornamental cherries in the roadside gardens along the way.

Belle felt curiously uplifted. She was enjoying living in Naughtonwood, walking its hinterland to the south, savouring the dramatic Ochils fault line, and gossiping with Jean McNaughton, old Kirsty Hunter and other villagers as she collected her morning newspaper. Roddy was in the past, her high-flying career was history, her tortured memories were receding, her contempt for politicians shrugged off as unimportant. She must tell Ruth of her newly acquired contentment.

Rangi waited for her outside the grey, Victorian villa overlooking Allanford. He was absently shredding Forsythia blossom in his fingers as he moodily contemplated the view.

"It's funny how you can sense if a house is unoccupied, that nobody is inside. It seems to brood, sinister in its emptiness." He forced a nervous laugh, avoiding Belle's eye.

Rangi was smouldering with resentment, anger and despair, thought Belle. Racial prejudice, rejection by his socialist friends, the loss of his career, and, the final straw, the abrupt departure of Jade for Singapore, had left him a mental wreck. She was glad she had coaxed him to come along to Ruth's. He had been incarcerated in the little flat in Milltown for months, almost hermit-like. His mother was anxious about him and had asked Belle to try to "get him out of himself".

Now the pair of them circled the house uneasily.

"Does Ruth have a cleaner come in?" Rangy asked.

"Yes, only once a week. Ruth, as you well know, is an independent lady," Belle replied. "I don't know where the cleaning lady lives."

"What about neighbours?"

"I've phoned one or two but they know nothing," Belle responded gloomily. "I have a feeling something is wrong." After some deliberation they phoned the police.

"Ruth will crucify me if we've done the wrong thing," Belle declared.

The two policemen were accustomed to have forcibly to enter the homes of old people who lived alone. Quickly they effected an entry and searched the house. There was no sign of Ruth. Everything seemed to be in place. On the desk in her study was a letter addressed to Belle.

It said,

Dear Belle,

For some time I have been suffering from Dementia. It has now reached a critical stage. Therefore, while I am still in command of my senses I have decided to end my life on my own terms. My affairs are in order. My lawyer knows what to do in the event of my death.

I am sorry that I kept all this secret from you but you had many other problems.

Don't grieve. I've had a full and satisfying 80 years

All my love,

Goodbye,

Ruth

Belle sat down abruptly, passing the letter to Rangy.

"Oh, Ruth! Dear Ruth! And I never suspected." Belle blinked back her tears.

Rangy was all urgency, snapped out of his torpor.

"We may be in time to stop her. Here!" He shoved the letter towards the policemen. How old is the letter? Where can she be? Where would she go? Is her car in the garage?"

"Yes, the car is still in the garage," one of the policemen said. "Can you tell us her habits, her haunts?"

"Her walking gear," Belle gabbled. "Look for her walking gear."

Both Belle and Rangy made a dash for the cubby hole where Ruth kept her walking boots, anorak, rucksack and walking poles. Only remnants of old gear remained.

"Where did she walk?" demanded one of the policemen.

"The Ochils"" screamed Belle. "The hills were her passion. I'm sure that's where she'll be."

"Right, mountain rescue and a helicopter," chorused the policemen. We'll try and get permission for a search. Can you tell us a likely route?"

"She wandered all over the Ochils," said Rangy hopelessly. "She could be anywhere."

The police departed, promising to keep in touch.

Belle and Rangy looked blankly at one another.

"Had you no inkling of her condition," asked Rangy.

"With hindsight there were signs I might have picked upon - forgetfulness, uncharacteristic behaviour, a bit cantankerous just like many other old ladies."

"I got the same impression," commented Rangy. "She was most unsympathetic about my problems although usually she was supportive. She called me a little wimp last week." Rangy smiled ruefully.

Belle frowned in concentration.

"There is one possibility, a long shot perhaps. Ruth told me about a place in the hills she and my father trekked to when they were students. It was at the headwaters of a burn in the Ochils back country. It seemed to have a special place in her memory. As I recall the story, my father wagered that he would land a trout from an impossibly small pool, the last one before the stream disappeared into the heather. He won, landing the fish in her lap. She was all coy about what the wager entailed."

Rangy pondered, lips puckered.

"Back country suggests the streams to the north of the Ben Cleuch massif- the Devon headwaters or the Breich or the Grodwell burns. What say we start searching in that vicinity right away? We could let the police know. They'll be looking for volunteers anyway. Perhaps the Bruces and the McMannans will join us." Belle phoned them and, appalled, they agreed to help. They would hire an additional helicopter first thing the next day.

Anxious not to waste a second, Belle and Rangy drove to their homes, collected their equipment, phoned the police to let them know their intention, and set off from Milltown-on-Devon into the depths of the Ochils. An hour and a half later they were at the source of the Breich- and drew a blank. There was no sign of Ruth. By this time it was getting dark. The police helicopter that had been searching further west, departed. Glumly they settled down for the night in a peaty hollow, checking frequently for lights or sounds. The darkness revealed nothing.

Dawn filtered through an almost impenetrable curtain of mist, drizzle and cloud. With great difficulty they picked their way back down the Breich to where the Grodwell joined it, before turning back up the little stream. The new search seemed fruitless when the burn began to peter out as they scrambled desperately from pool to pool. Eventually a miniature waterfall loomed out of the mist, with a tiny pool at its base, forming a small cup in the heather.

Curled in a foetal position lay the body of Ruth, on a ground sheet with her rucksack placed neatly beside her. By her side was a half empty whisky bottle, two upended bottles of pills, and a waterproof package addressed to Belle. Blood pooled, livid purple, drawn by gravity to collect at the lowest points of her face as she lay on her side. The body felt stone cold as Rangy felt frantically for a pulse.

They contemplated the body of their friend in silence.. She had made a good job of her suicide.

"She's been dead a long time, Belle. We were never going to be in time."

Belle sank to her knees

"Poor Ruth! Imagine! All alone here on this bleak hillside! Dementia! No wonder she wanted to end it all. The thought of descending into that pit of disintegration of her being must have appalled her. But you should have told us, Ruth, let us support you. Give us the chance to say goodbye."

Their grief was interrupted by the whup of a helicopter overhead. Rangy waved and the machine settled on a reasonably level spot some yards away. Sir Rab and Natasha, Murdo and Catriona ran towards them. The drawn faces of Belle and Rangy told the others what to expect. The two women embraced Belle: the men stared down at the body. Baroness McFranklin. Grand old lady honoured and respected by the nation remembered with great affection by her friends.

The police helicopter was summoned and soon the usual incident procedures were in place. Sir Rab drew the others aside and produced a bottle of Ruth's favourite malt whisky. They solemnly toasted her.

CHAPTER SIXTY FIVE

SIR RAB AND NATASHA: DRUMANNAN

The reconstruction of Bruce Tower House was complete. The last vestige of the explosion had been eradicated. Natasha had supervised the new décor and furnishings. At last Sir Rab could relax and enjoy the panoramic view of the links of the River Forth, the mountains to the far North West and his beloved Ochils to the north

Abstracted, Rab toyed with the remote control of the massive television screen, surfing the documentary channels. Nothing suited his mood. His mind wandered. He had enormous wealth, power, and a wife he adored, yet he felt strangely dissatisfied. Even the prospect of a major breakthrough in alternative power sources failed to enthuse him. Was it an age thing? He had reached his fifties. Perhaps he had become so obsessed with work that over the years some things had passed him by. It was not that he had no other interests. He fished, played golf occasionally and badly, and was an enthusiastic Bridge player. His abiding interest in Scotland's culture and heritage completed a fulfilled life. So what was wrong?

Disturbed, he sought out Natasha and quibbled over the colour scheme in his den, although it was exactly the same as it had been before the explosion. He spoke sharply to an aide who had brought him some papers to sign, and marched out to rebuke a gardener for leaving a muddy trail on the courtyard.

Natasha forthrightly told him to see a doctor. He was acting out of character. His usual calm, considered manner was giving way to petulance and irrational outbursts, she maintained. Sir Rab scoffed but inwardly he worried. Perhaps he should advance his annual check up and broach the matter with the doctors. What he had revealed to nobody was the dizzy spells he had been experiencing, the sudden tightness in his chest, and the unaccustomed lethargy that made his jogging sessions a chore, rather than an exhilarating experience. He made an appointment for the following week before supervising the arrangements for the three-monthly Bridge tournament he sponsored usually held in the spacious lounge of Bruce Tower House. Twenty four players competed regularly, each in turn donating a prize. It was the turn of Sir Rab and he had made it known that the prize on this occasion would be a week in his Bermuda villa, much to the delight of Professor Angela Bull, an expert player who had replaced Baroness McFranklin in this close knit group of aficionados.

Six baize covered card tables were dotted about the room. With drinks trolleys, subdued lighting, curtains drawn, and plush carpet underfoot, Sir Rab's elegant, expansive lounge with its panoramic views had been transformed into the claustrophobic ambience of a high class bordello or casino, Natasha maintained. She abhorred the whole atmosphere.

"Only the eye shades and cigar smoke are missing," she snorted, making herself scarce.

In contrast, Murdo and Catriona McMannan were regular participants, Catriona coolly proficient and Murdo swashbuckling as usual in all that he did. Rab liked playing with him. His own cautious methodical approach to the game compensated to some extent by the pop singer's aggressive play. They were drawn against Catriona and Angela in the first session.

Sir Rab was feeling distinctly unwell and had thought of cancelling the event. The possible disruption to the plans of the others convinced him to carry on. Characteristically he revealed nothing of his distress to Natasha. Now he was struggling to cope with Murdo's ebullience at the table. He found himself in an overly ambitious slam game promptly doubled for penalties by Angela. Woozily he assessed his options- and felt himself keeling sideways off his chair, unable to stop himself. He was on the floor, a crushing pain in his chest, consciousness slipping. Blackness!

Catriona screamed. Murdo hurtled round the table in futile attempt to arrest the fall, but only succeeded in canting it into Angela's lap, trapping her as she struggled to rise. Rab was now on his back, breathing stertorously, deathly pale. Amid the hubbub of the startled Bridge players mobile phones were produced frantically calling for an ambulance. Some tried to move Rab, hastily desisting when screams of "don't move him" chorused from the more knowledgeable. Catriona rushed from the room to find Natasha, savagely interrupting her peaceful enjoyment of a recording of Rimsky Korsakov's music in the studio. Together the two women helter-skeltered down from the top floor of the tower to the lounge to find a shocked huddle of guests gathered round the unconscious Rab. Natasha sank down by his side, whispering incoherent endearments through her tears in a mixture of Russian and English.

"When will the ambulance be here?" she implored to no one in particular."

"It's on its way," Murdo responded, phone to his ear.

"It looks pretty bad," muttered one of the guests, a business associate of Sir Rab's.

"Shut up hissed Murdo. "That sort of remark is of no help."

The para-medical team bustled in festooned with resuscitation gear. Wasting no time they tried to stabilise their patient preparatory to transferring him to Wallacetown Hospital. Soon they were on their way, sirens wailing, an ashen Natasha by the stretcher.

The Bridge players dispersed in silence.

***

"Your husband is in the intensive care unit, Lady Bruce." The florid-faced consultant informed Natasha. "He has had a massive heart attack."

"What are his chances," whispered Natasha.

The doctor looked at her levelly.

"There is a less than 50% chance of his pulling through. We won't be able to tell for sure for a day or two. That he is in good physical condition is in his favour. I won't attempt to underestimate the seriousness of his situation though. He is gravely ill."

"I want him moved to a private clinic and top specialists to attend, Natasha shouted.

The consultant bristled. "I cannot possibly allow him to be moved. That might prove fatal. He will be well looked after here. I can arrange for another consultant to be called in if that is your wish. It will take some time, however. Meantime I suggest you try to rest. We can provide a bed.

"Just get the best. Expense is no object," Natasha replied haughtily, her Russian background showing, "Now, may I see my husband"

"You can look in for a moment. Just don't disturb him," the doctor answered stiffly.

Natasha clung to Catriona as she peered through the medical paraphernalia at the motionless figure.

***

A week later Rab was sitting up in bed shrunken and pale, his jowls hanging slack. He gazed sombrely at his friends, grouped round his bed.

"I feel angry and resentful that this has happened to me. I had such great plans for the future. Now I'm just a hulk." He relapsed into a sullen silence. Natasha stroked his hand.

The important thing is you survived, Rab. The attack would have killed most people."

"You'll soon be on your feet again," boomed Murdo. "You'll be your old self in no time."

"Don't talk rubbish, Murdo," Rab snapped. "You know perfectly well that's untrue."

Murdo reddened and Catriona intervened.

"Rab, you're full of self pity. Take some advice. Accept that life isn't necessarily fair. What's happened can't be changed. Plan your future accordingly. And you, Natasha! Your job is to help him to adjust."

With that she swept from the room, leaving Rab blinking in fury, and the others appalled by the brutality of her treatment of him.

***

Sir Rab's triple by-pass operation, deemed safe to be carried out two months after his heart attack, was completed successfully.

"One of my better days," commented the surgeon to Natasha. "He should be as right as rain after a suitable convalescence. That means absolutely no contact with work," he added sternly for Rab's benefit.

Natasha prevailed on Rab to embark upon a three month cruise in spite of his protestations that his business interests would suffer.

"Come on, Rab. If you go back too soon you might undo all the good work of the surgeon," Natasha expostulated. "I'll look after Drumannan Holdings."

"But you'll be with me," Rab cried.

"Rab, do you trust anyone else to run your affairs?"

That silenced Rab who was paranoid about subordinates who put their own careers before the long term interests of the company.

"O.K., I'll grant you power of attorney over my affairs while I'm away. There is one outstandingly important decision you will have to make. The tidal power device is ready for large scale production. It is so cost efficient that it will undercut the costs of any other power source. I do not want to patent it. I want the whole world to benefit without hindrance. New sources of cheap power are desperately needed. This will be my contribution."

The breathtaking generosity of the gift to humanity, for that is what it amounted to, startled Natasha.

"You can't be serious, Rab. Think of all the development costs to begin with. They run into millions."

"My mind is made up. A near death experience changes ones outlook on everything," Rab replied quietly.

Natasha knew that messianic mood of Rab's. He would not change his mind.

**

Natasha registered the new device with the Patent Authorities without telling him.

"I'll be dammed if I'm going to let the Leaders of Russia have free access to cheap power," she muttered, completely ignoring Sir Rab's wishes.

**

"I have two possibilities for your cruise, Rab. The first is to rent the motor cruiser of my colleague, Igor Petrov. It is one of the largest and most luxurious in the world. He would be delighted for you to have it. The alternative is to embark on the floating palace that is "The World on your Doorstep," a new concept that allows millionaires to actually live permanently or for extended periods on a 100,000 ton cruise liner, circling the world, calling at exotic locations and being present at important events such as the Olympics. You must have assets of at least £20 million to be considered. What do you think?"

Sir Rab was interested. After examining thoroughly the two possibilities he opted for the "The World on Your Doorstep", preferring to have company, albeit restricted to a select few very rich people.

"There might be some good Bridge players among them. And I can get on with my research into the Oral History Project.

CHAPTER SIXTY SIX

THE CRUISE

The huge ship slipped effortlessly through the phosphorescent Indian Ocean. Sir Rab sat contentedly on his balcony outside his plush personal suite high above the sluicing bow wave. An enormous moon bathed the scene in silvery light. The Horn of Africa, featureless and sullen, sank low on the port side.

The three day safari from Mombasa into the Kenyan game parks, the little edge of danger intruding into the pampered lives of the floating rich, had proved satisfying and exciting. Now the great liner was heading for Dubai, that artificial creation of opulence in the Gulf. Already passengers were talking of investing in real estate and wallowing in its expensive gold jewellery.

Rab was determined to avoid going ashore. He was familiar with the Middle East - its oil, its bribery, its restrictive customs. He would stay on board with almost sole use of the gym and swimming pools. He had arranged with the team of medical staff to give him a through check up although he was progressing well after six weeks of smooth unobtrusive service.

This floating community represented a cross section of the wealthy, with Americans predominating. Old money, new money, reclusive, brash, pleasant or boorish, the passengers had the style that comes with almost unlimited funds, an unconscious assurance that most people could never emulate.

Sir Rab had moved among such people for years, accepting them for what they were without being particularly attracted to their life styles. Apart from the few who played Bridge, he mixed seldom with the passengers, preferring to immerse himself in compiling an archive of the memories of the survivors of the industrial age of the Scottish Lowlands.. The desultory efforts of Ruth were being transformed into a major operation with teams of researchers combing the towns and villages seeking out from old people and families, firms and organisations with information about the lives of people working in the myriad occupations of a bygone age.

He chuckled as he recognised replicas of himself and his family among the accounts of life in the mines, the workshops and the mills. He shook his head over the memories of the Great Depression and revelled in the rambunctious histories of shipping magnates or coal owners.

Noiselessly his butler appeared with his usual nightcap of a single malt whisky, all he was allowed under his strict medical regime. He sighed. He liked an occasional cigar, and the ship even had an exclusive shop that sold the most expensive types, but he was denied that pleasure. Saying good night to the Goanese servant he settled down to enjoy his drink.

An hour later, dozing, he was seized from behind, gagged, bound and lowered over the cliff face side of the eleven-decked ship by hooded assailants. A sharp injection had rendered him unconscious just as the realisation that he had been kidnapped dawned on him.

The small wooden craft, engine switched off, had been in wait, allowing itself to drift into the path of the great ship, undetected by radar until, with a quick burst of engine power, it drew alongside. A series of grappling hooks were thrown into place and the attached ropes were climbed. Before the alarm was raised Sir Rab was being jerkily lowered into the raiders' boat.

***

Jack Drummond, on his first voyage as a security man on "The World on Your Doorstep," was first to react. He had been appalled when he recognised Sir Rab as one of the passengers and had so far had managed to keep out of his way. He had secured his position by virtue of his Military Police background, accounting for his time at Bruce Engineering by saying he was freelancing in Iraq.

On hearing the alarm he made his way from his quarters on one of the lowest decks to the nearby exit port. Already a launch had been lowered and he piled into it with another armed security guard.

"What's happened? he screamed.

"It looks like a pirate attack," laughed his colleague. "Fat chance they have against a ship this size."

Jack's walkie-talkie came to life, squawking, "Passenger kidnapped. Pursue."

The raiders craft seemed to be wallowing far astern in the wake of the slowing liner.

"I think their engine's broken down. Let's get them," shouted Jack.

The crew of two sailors gunned the engine, closing rapidly on the almost stationary boat. A burst of Kalashnikov fire shattered the glass in the windscreen of the launch, killing one sailor and showering the others with shards of glass. Jack cursed, realising the side arms of his colleague and himself were no match for that kind of fire power. As if to confirm his assessment a rocket-propelled grenade smashed into the side of the launch, hurling the other security guard to the deck, blood spouting from a gaping chest wound. Desperately Jack urged the frightened helmsman to keep on course while he blazed away uselessly with his pistol. Another spray of machine gun fire made them both cower. Jack spotted the boat's flare pistol on a shelf below the controls of the engine. Shouting to the now frantic helmsman to edge closer to the other boat he took aim at a cluster of men working on its faulty engine. At a range of thirty metres he fired. With a whoosh the flare plunged toward the group. Startled cries changed to howls of agony as the flare landed among them. A fire started and some of the men flung themselves overboard.

In the confusion the two boats crashed together, unbalancing the two remaining raiders. Coldly Jack shot them before jumping on board. A motionless figure lay, hooded, bound, gagged, helpless in the bow. After ensuring that there was no further resistance he cut the plastic bonds securing the man and removed the hood and gag, recoiling in surprise as he recognised Sir Rab.

Other launches quickly arrived on the scene, the wounded terrorists attended to, the men in the water rescued and Sir Rab's condition rapidly assessed. He soon recovered consciousness, woozy but coherent. The flotilla returned to the now motionless cruise ship.

The investigation that followed established that the raiders were Saudi Arabians. No other passengers had been molested: no bomb had been planted. The sole objective of the assailants had been the kidnapping of Sir Rab Bruce

The World on Your Doorstep was an American ship. The kidnappers were swiftly transported to Guantanamo Bay. Under interrogation they confessed that the reason for the seizure of Sir Rab was to hold him to ransom until the rights to his new hydrogen-powered car engine were handed over. It was further revealed that the men were members of the Saudi Special Forces.

This information was concealed from the World's media. In secret the American and British Governments entered into acrimonious discussions with the Saudi Government. The result was an agreement that the Saudis would invest heavily in the development of alternative sources of power, compensate Sir Rab to the tune of £100 million pounds, and begin a process of democratising their institutions

Meanwhile Sir Rab was flown home, apparently none the worse for his traumatic experience. As he joked to Natasha, as she fussed over him.

"The worst of it was, I hadn't finished my whisky."

Natasha, however, was in no mood for jokes.

"Rab, first my countrymen and now the Saudis have attempted to scupper the introduction of this engine. Unscrupulous Governments are determined to control and restrict the World's energy supplies to suit their own narrow national interest. I fear for your life.

"I'm more concerned at my foolish decision to make the tidal power device freely available to them. I should have kept some degree of control so that only cooperative democratic countries gained benefit from the discovery."

Natasha smiled.

"Don't worry, Rab. I disobeyed your instruction. Your near death experience affected your judgment badly. It warped your thinking. Making these inventions available to the world was an idealistic gesture, totally inappropriate in a climate of ruthless big business, tyrants, and governments with their own self interest paramount. They would fall on your bounty like a pack of wolves, my precious Russian Administration to the fore. Ordinary people would not benefit in the way your idealism envisaged. A relatively few individuals would cream of gigantic profits. Inefficient beaurocracies would dissipate the potential benefits. I couldn't let you do it. I was acting in your own best interests and for the benefit of Scotland as a country in the forefront of technological advance. Your patents are sewn up tightly. Only Drumannan Holdings has the right to produce these devices."

"You devious minx! You astute minx!" Rab spluttered, half laughing. Trust you to recognise the dangers of a free-for-all on rights. I still dream of a Utopia. Sadly the World is far from ready for it.

I'll tighten up security at all our plants and the homes of key personnel, and ask the Government to provide additional cover. After all, it is in the national interest. I'll go back to work tomorrow and set things in train."

Natasha exploded.

"You'll do nothing of the kind. I've ordered the Jet to be ready to fly us to Bermuda, and don't argue. It's time you saw your daughter anyway."

Rab sighed.

"O.K., Natasha, but only for a month. I must get back. First though I have to see Jack Drummond. He was a hero. He disappeared from Aberbrothy because he felt he had let me down. Well, he has made amends in no uncertain manner. I want to reinstate him immediately as Head of Security."

CHAPTER SIXTY SEVEN

CATRIONA AND MURDO: QUEENSTOWN, 2013

Murdo, Triple M, McMannan grinned as Catriona reprimanded him for driving the top-of-the-range S.U.V. too fast along the sinuous hill road. Obediently he slowed. The Ice Queen of Scotland, as she had come to be known since her succession to the post of First Minister, was distinctly nervous in cars. In contrast he revelled in the exhilaration of driving at speed in difficult terrain. He had participated in a trans-Sahara expedition recently. By comparison this little trip to Badger Country Park was tame. He parked in a clearing in the midst of regimented lines of conifers, and they set off briskly round the banks of a little gem of a loch, complete with a wooded island, fishing boats, and squadrons of raucous wild fowl.

The hoarse bellow of a stag in the adjacent deer farm startled Catriona momentarily. She was abstracted, beset by problems as First Minister. She liked to use Murdo as a sounding board for her thoughts and ideas on these walks.

"Things are not going well, Murdo," she murmured as she splashed unheeding through a muddy area of the loch side track. Catriona looked ravishing in her outdoor gear, yellow bobbled tammy offsetting her raven black hair, fashioned Goretex jacket, and multi-coloured doubled down socks over two toned walking boots. Only she could look elegant in well-used hill walking gear thought Murdo. He told her so.

"Shut up, Murdo." Catriona turned to him, leaning on her walking pole. "Serious trouble is looming."

Murdo sobered. Catriona had been pre-occupied and snappish recently.

"Tell me about it," he suggested.

She paused, marshalling her thoughts.

"There are three major issues.

"You know that people were tasked to serve a three year term as local councillors or M.S.P.s." He nodded.

"Well, the situation at councillor level is reasonable but we are hemorrhaging M.S.P.s at an alarming rate. People are saying that the job is not what they envisaged. They dislike the atmosphere of debates with cheap, taunting, political point-scoring, the feeling of being cannon fodder, the long hours of tedium, and the sniping of the media. The list goes on. Oh, there are some who have recognised that that is the reality of political life but many are disillusioned by it and are starting to drift away. Also one or two unsuitable characters got through the selection process. People are riding hobby horses; some find it almost impossible to contemplate compromise; others are just not team players. Don't get me wrong. There is a solid core of M.S.P.s who have done sterling work and many of our policies have been successfully implemented."

"But surely these are teething problems. After all your team was elected just over two years ago. Experience will improve the selection process. A fuller explanation of what is expected should deter the faint hearts. Our strategies of retaining a limited number of people for a second term will provide an element of continuity."

"That's a related problem. Few people want a second term. Those that do are finding it difficult to contemplate putting their careers on hold for that length of time. Too many retired people able to do so would reduce the appeal of our Party to younger age groups. The days of the village elders are long gone."

So it's much more than natural wastage," Murdo said thoughtfully.

"Much more! When the opposition and the media realise the extent of the problem they will be after us like a pack of wolves. In addition our big majority will disappear if the resultant bye-elections go badly."

Perhaps you were too quick to ditch people like Roddy Neilson, experienced politicians. Would it not be an idea to rehabilitate them and make use of their political skills?" Murdo challenged.

Catriona considered.

"There's something in what you say, Murdo. I'll have to give it thought. Mind you, it won't be easy to persuade them to return."

Murdo laughed.

"They are hungry for power, not necessarily for themselves, but they think they can contribute to improving society. Remember they are politicians."

Catriona linked arms with him.

"That's cheered me up a bit. Now for the next problem-the biggie.

Our West Lothian Answer campaign in favour of the Union had initial success but it is beginning to fray badly. You've seen the reports of the resurgence of extreme nationalism in both Scotland and England. The old raggle taggle groups of bigots like the Sons of St. George and the Bannockburn Boys have attracted more and more adherents; the general public is being infected by their propaganda. Every incident, however minor, is seized upon by the media and blown up out of all proportion. Things are turning ugly again. Fear of the stranger or something alien to the ways of a society seems to be an aspect of human nature politicians and social scientists are finding very difficult to eradicate by propaganda and education. Think of the Basques, the Catalans, the Bretons, and the Northern Italian Alliance, not to mention the dreadful recent history of the Balkans or Northern Ireland. And that's only Europe! One doesn't dare contemplate the rest of the world.

We thought our campaign was successful, showing that the peoples of the U.K. were inextricably mingled, sharing a common heritage. It seems we did not convince people."

Murdo was dismayed. Out of the country on a long tour with Triple M to the Antipodes, he was somewhat out of touch with the way things were going at home. Ever the optimist he had sincerely believed that his campaign for Britishness had been a winner.

"Should we mount another campaign?" he suggested. "I'm sure we could make it even bigger and better than the previous one."

"We could, and I'm sure we would do it well," Catriona smiled as she hugged her husband, "but there's another factor that is causing me the most serious concern.

That suave duplicitous Conservative Prime Minister has out-foxed me. I believed him when he said he would do his utmost to preserve the Union. The latest intelligence from Whitehall suggests that, due to the deteriorating economic situation, work on the two large aircraft carriers is to be suspended indefinitely with the inevitable consequences for our Scottish shipyards at Rosyth and on the Clyde. The naval programme is to be rejigged to increase the number of frigates. They will be built in shipyards in England "as they are deemed to be most suitable to carry out the work." Air defence is to be concentrated in England to reduce travelling expenditure. The small army presence in Scotland is to be reduced even further. All these policy decisions have been taken without reference to me and my Ministers. We have effectively been written off as a liability, as a drain on national resources, more trouble than we are worth." Catriona slumped against Murdo. "Things couldn't be worse."

Murdo was finding it difficult to take in this plethora of bad news.

"Surely there is something you can do. I had thought our campaign in support of the Union was a great success."

"That was a year ago. A lot has happened since then," Catriona lamented.

"I knew there was more trouble from the nationalists and the little Englanders but I thought they were the usual lunatic fringe without widespread support."

"You weren't forthcoming in our regular phone calls."

"I didn't want to distract you from your tour, dear. I was hoping matters would improve. In fact the opposite has happened." Catriona shrugged.

"Then what about the re-roofing of the Palace?" Murdo demanded. The Prince performing the Opening Ceremony, celebrating the rejuvenation of that ancient structure after all these years might be a unifying factor."

"That idea certainly has merit," Catriona said thoughtfully. "We could milk it for all the publicity attendant on Royal events. It's a forlorn hope, mind you. The social and economic forces stacked against moderate policies at times of deep recession are overwhelming us all. Bigotry, demagoguery, and cult figures flourish. Extremist political parties emerge. The Scottish Peoples Alliance has been more badly affected than we realised."

The usually cool and controlled Catriona was more downbeat than Murdo had ever seen his wife. To lighten her mood he suggested a quick round of Golf, a fillet steak, red wine, and an early night.

"I appreciate your sexual panacea for all my ills, dear Murdo, but I think not. I have a heavy day tomorrow. I meet the cabinet to warn them of imminent catastrophe."

CHAPTER SIXTY EIGHT

THE RE-ROOFING OF QUEENSTOWN PALACE

The ancient burgh of Queenstown throbbed to the sound of bagpipes wailing, big drums beating, people cheering, children screaming with delight, a well of noise cresting along the High Street as the procession approached from the West Port. The excitement grew to a crescendo at the Town Cross, pavements overflowing , banners waving, flags flying, every building in the curious mix of medieval, Victorian, and incongruous modern, bedecked in bunting.

The motorcade slowed and turned up the Palace Wynd, the Prince grinning as he waved in acknowledgement to the tumultuous welcome. Soldiers of the Royal Regiment of Scotland lined the narrow lane and the Palace courtyard. Unfamiliarly resplendent with its cunningly constructed new roof the Palace seemed suddenly a functioning building. It was no longer a sad reminder of past glories but a place with life and vigour. On this day it was filled with the pomp and circumstance of a royal presence, the refurbished halls and rooms thronged with dignitaries, the invited townspeople and some of the West Lothian, English and Welsh Diasporas. A glad occasion!

Beaming, Murdo and Catriona McMannan welcomed the Prince as he stepped out of his open limousine. Plain clothed security men, visibly relieved that an ancient tragedy had not been repeated, closed discreetly round their charge. (In the sixteenth century a similar cavalcade along the High Street had been brought to a chaotic halt by an assassin's musket ball gut shooting a Scottish Earl.) The danger was not yet over. Security chiefs had bitterly opposed the opening of the Palace to such a large disparate group of people but had been overruled by the Prince, a keen supporter in private of the campaign to save the British Union.

The Prince, trailing a group led by the First Minister, the sponsors of the project and the Convener of West Lothian Council toured the building, listening to the running commentary given by the Chief Architect of the project. They completed their tour in the Great Banqueting Hall, its massive fireplace dominating the space. The official party took their places on a low dais facing a selected audience arrayed below the tapestried walls. The Prince began his speech inaugurating the rejuvenated Palace.

"Accustomed as I am to viewing the roofs of buildings from a helicopter I confess the sight of this venerable old palace on its loch side promontory, with its ------"

Fidgeting in the row of seats reserved for personal guests of the McMannans' Rangi McNaughton was fuming. His resentment at the way life had treated him was boiling over.

Racially abused, career in ruins, abandoned by his lover, his pent up frustration and anger had become focused on this symbol of the racist nation he had been born into. He hated Britain and its unfair society. In front of this televised gathering he would stage a protest by flaunting the banner he had folded under his jacket under the nose of the Prince. He readied himself, poised to run to the front of the hall. At that moment someone pushed in to the seat beside him with a quick wink to Belle, his neighbour.

"Marry me," whispered Jade. "Come with me to Singapore. I have organised a house and a good position for you in my new research facility." Rangy choked, scarcely realising that Jade was actually beside him inn the flesh. He let out a strangled cry, hastily shushed by those around him. She clutched his arm fiercely.

"Everything will be fine, Rangi. Believe me." He subsided, shocked at how near he had been to committing a major blunder.

The Prince had paused, amused by the minor disturbance. His smile faded as a knife-wielding figure ran towards him, screaming, "Allah is great," Before anyone could move Murdo threw his six foot frame at the assailant smothering his approach and bearing him to the floor in a tangle of limbs. Security guards slammed into the pile pinioning the would-be assassin. Amid the ensuing commotion the Prince was bundled out of the Hall. Catriona knelt over Murdo howling, "No! No!" and trying to stanch the blood pouring from his body. Elegant white gown splashed crimson she was dragged away by a medical team which was quickly on the scene to minister to Murdo.

Pandemonium reigned in the hall, calls for calm going unheeded. Outside, rumour spread like wildfire. The Prince had been killed. The attacker had escaped. A bomb had exploded killing all those on the platform. The Prince was only wounded. The assassin was a Muslim. He was a member of the I.R.A. He was a madman. There were angry scenes as men with brown or black skins were verbally abused or assaulted. Only a loudspeaker announcement by the police quietened matters. There had been an incident in the Palace. The Prince was unhurt and had been taken to a place of safety. One person was injured. There was no cause for alarm.

The carnival atmosphere punctured, events cancelled. People gathered in little knots asking for news, dispensing rumour. Those with young children obeyed the police instruction to disperse.

Murdo McMannan was badly wounded by a knife thrust to the shoulder. His condition was serious but not life threatening.

CHAPTER SIXTY NINE

THE DISILLUSIONMENT: DRUMANNAN

Magnificently, the mansion topped the crag and tail ridge of Drumannan. The plateau on which Bruce Tower House stood had been transformed into a garden with surrounding park land, initially following the pattern of the grounds of its predecessor but with modern planting arrangements of lawns, arbours, herbaceous borders, exotic flowering shrubs and trees and formal bedding. The park was dotted with specimen trees, expensively planted at a mature size. Bruce Tower itself, medievally grim, stood sentinel alongside, grandly refurbished.

On this perfect May day, Natasha, Sir Rab and their guests sat in garden chairs on the windward side of a barbeque fire, tended by household staff. It should have been an occasion of ease, luxury and contentment for Murdo McMannan, Belle Ramsay, Roddy Neilson, Rangy McNaughton and his partner Jade, and Professor Angela Bull. Catriona McMannan was expected later in the day. The atmosphere, however, was gloomy. Anxiety prevailed, anxiety about the state of the U.K., The Union, the Scottish Peoples Alliance, the continued absence of news about the Calabar Hoard, and the slow progress of Murdo's recovery from the injury received during his heroic action at Queenstown Palace.

Natasha tried vainly to lighten the mood by inviting her guests to participate in a game of croquet on one of the immaculate lawns. Her suggestion was met with a lukewarm response. No one was interested at the prospect of mock cutthroat competition. Instead Sir Rab began what became a long, rambling discussion about the position their initiatives had reached after two years of endeavour.

"Natasha and I had hoped this would be an occasion to celebrate your full recovery, Murdo. It's clear you still have some way to go before you are fully fit again."

Murdo, gaunt and drawn, uncharacteristically sighed.

"I've been told my golfing days are over. I can no longer swing a club."

There were murmurs of sympathy from the others. Everyone knew of his obsession with the game.

"Thank goodness I can still sing." With a sad attempt at his old humour he added. "Maybe Rab will employ me as his caddie."

Enough of me, however. The doctors say progress will be slow but I will be fine apart from my dickey shoulder. Catriona should be here within the hour. I hope her latest meeting with the Prime Minister will produce results."

Sir Rab remained sombre.

"Maybe the cynics were correct when they laughed at the idea of very rich people trying to cure the ills of the country by simplistic ideas and seemingly straightforward answers to complex issues. Perhaps we were wrong to initiate the Scottish Peoples Alliance. The best efforts of Catriona and Roddy, and despite her immense popularity, have proved to be of no avail. The Scottish Peoples Alliance is crumbling; the nationalist extremists are in full cry. The English seem to have turned virulently anti-Scottish in contrast to their past tolerance of our foibles. The Conservative Government is embroiled in a fierce fight with the European Union and look like leaving or being ejected. The world economy is in freefall because of the oil shortage. I could go on but I am disheartened and disillusioned." Wearily he leaned back in his recliner, moodily sipping his Montrachet.

A gloomy silence was broken by Murdo who was equally dismayed by the turn of events.

"I was dazzled by my success as a pop star. I thought, like so many of my fellow stars before me, that I was therefore qualified to pronounce on the ills of the world and those of Scotland in particular. I was wrong."

Roddy Neilson, with so many recent setbacks in his mind, was in a depressed state of mind.

"I agree with what has been said. The S.P.A. is falling apart. We have done much good work but the concept of getting together people from all walks of life with disparate views and careers temporarily in abeyance has not worked, I'm afraid."

Sir Rab turned to Belle.

"What about you, Belle? You scoffed at the idea from the start. Are you going to say, I told you so?"

Belle slowly shook her head.

"I am deeply saddened. Although I thought the whole idea was hare-brained I secretly hoped it would succeed. It gives me no pleasure that the concept is failing. I still cling to my parents' steadfast belief in social justice. Politicians certainly couldn't deliver it. That's for sure. The idealistic S.P.A. has also failed to realise their objective. I just don't know the answer- if there ever will be one."

Rangy and Jade exchanged glances. He motioned Jade to speak.

"Sir Rab, as an outsider I offer this advice to you and the others. You can best help your country by concentrating on what you do best. Sir Rab, you now have the means to make Scotland the industrial power house it once was. Alternative sources of energy, the extraction of coal and burning it using new technology and the possibility of a new means of powering motor transport, will transform the country economically. Natasha, you are ahead of the game with your Institute of Personal Freedom, and your birth control campaigns in developing countries. (Incidentally worth more than a dozen charities in my view). Murdo, your popularity combined with your enthusiasm for the history and heritage of Scotland will provide a hugely effective leadership in cultural values. Roddy, you must stick your role as a member of the Scottish Assembly. You are needed more than ever there now. Belle you must retain a role in education. In that way you can help bring about the social justice you so desperately desire. Rangy and I wish you all well as we view the future from our new home in Singapore."

"Hear, hear!" boomed Angela. "Well said, Jade. As a completely apolitical person I applaud the dressing down you have given this sorry group. Gee up, people! The future is yours."

Murdo laughed delightedly.

"That's what we all needed a severe reprimand from the wise Doctor Yu and a magisterial rebuke from the lofty professor.

The others smiled ruefully.

"A timely antidote to our despair," Rab mused, rubbing his fingers through his thinning hair. "That's given us food for thought."

As lunch was served, barbeque style, a general discussion, sparked by champagne and red wine, sounded almost cheerful. Devouring a dripping burgher, Angela turned to Belle who, figure conscious, was heaping her plate with salad.

"Is that the sweater Ruth knitted for you? I haven't seen you wear it before."

"Well, yes!" Belle confessed. "It's superbly fashioned and I love the black and orange colours but the design of Pictish inscriptions is a bit overpowering."

"I see what you mean," Angela commented. "That thick seam on the sleeves is a bit odd."

"Yes, the horizontal lines on each side of the seams seem haphazard. They certainly don't form any sort of pattern."

Angela suddenly leaned forward, intent.

"Let me examine these marks more closely. The way they stand out from the vertical seam reminds me of something I was studying last term. They look remarkably like Ogham Script."

"What? Do you think Ruth……….? Belle couldn't continue for her excitement. "Do you think it's a message?"

"Don't jump to conclusions, Belle. It certainly is a possibility. Let's repair to the library and see if Rab can provide us with a suitable reference to Ogham."

Almost skipping Belle followed Angela to the well stocked library, filled with technical, archaeological and historical books. Angela, however, headed straight for the state of the art computer console.

"The internet is becoming the fount of all knowledge," she remarked dryly, as she keyed it up. "It shouldn't take long to track down the Ogham alphabet."

Soon the screen filled with the ancient script, examples of which had been discovered in different parts of the British Isles, particularly in Ireland.

"It is often found on the vertical edge of standing stones with the markings etched on either side. The seam of your sweater served the same purpose if I'm correct. Let's try to match the markings against the Alphabet as transliterated into Roman script and see if it makes sense."

Belle looked in disappointment as the letters

"eituolcdraohrabalac" appeared.

"These letters make no sense at all," she exclaimed.

"Maybe it's in code," Angela mused, frowning at the meaningless string.

Suddenly she gasped.

"Wait a minute. I've just remembered. The Ogham Script is meant to be read from bottom upwards."

Feverishly Belle transposed the letters.

She squealed as the word "Calabar" appeared, running on to "Hoard. The remaining letters formed the word "Cloutie."

Angela was puzzled.

"Is that a Scottish word? It sounds vaguely familiar."

"Yes, it means a piece of cloth but what possible significance could that have? Wait a minute. The Cloutie Wells! All over Scotland there was a tradition of decorating the bushes round so-called sacred pools or wells with offerings usually scraps of cloth. The practice survives to this day in one or two places."

"Of course!" Angela exclaimed. "I should have recalled that pagan rite but the word isn't very helpful here, is it? It's clear that Ruth is trying to tell us something but what?"

Belle started suddenly.

"I can remember one day Ruth and I were chatting with Old Kirsty Hunter. We had the idea of recording some oral history from the old people of the village. It's coming back to me now. Kirsty said that her grandmother told her she used to hang "clouts" on bushes round the pond, hoping that illness would be cured. Kirsty was dared to go near the place as it was reputed to be bottomless. Strange blue lights were sometimes seen around the pond. A monster lived in its depths. Perhaps Ruth is referring to the Naughtonwood Cloutie pool."

"It's possible," said Angela thoughtfully. "You're sure about your recollection?"

"Yes!" Belle was becoming more certain that the word was a clue.

"But why would Ruth…..? She couldn't have taken the Treasure," she gasped, appalled at the thought. "Why would she do that?"

Angela shook her head dismissively.

"We can't speculate at this stage, Belle. Let's go with the evidence. Ruth left you this strange gift of a sweater with what is clearly Ogham Script knitted into it as a patterned reference to the Calabar Hoard. She then adds cryptically "Cloutie." That's what we have to go on. From what you say about the Garto Pond the next step is to make a close examination of that pond."

"You mean, excavate it?" Belle exclaimed.

"Exactly that! Let's convince our worthy patrons." So saying, Angela marched back out to the barbeque party and called for everyone's attention.

The story of the sweater was listened to with rapt attention. Her conclusion was received with cautious acceptance by some, with disbelief by others. In the general confusion of comment: "Ruth would never have taken the Treasure": She was a deranged old woman": "The pattern was merely a coincidence": "The word Cloutie was meaningless": "Ruth is teasing us. Maybe she knows nothing about the whereabouts of the Treasure" Sir Rab cut through the hubbub.

"There's only one way to find out. We'll drain the pool and find out what's in it, if anything."

"I was hoping you'd say that," Angela crowed, winking at Belle. "It'll take money, permission from the owner of the land, and probably some sort of planning permission from the Council."

Sir Rab waved his hand airily.

"It's not generally known but I own most of the land in Drumannanshire, including the area round Naughtonwood."

"You old fox," Murdo laughed." I'll join you in sponsoring the investigation."

Professor Bull beamed.

The First Minister of the Scottish Assembly, Catriona McMannan, appeared through the French windows of a reception room, slowly descended the steps from the patio, and approached the group at the barbeque.

"Just in time to get the scraps, Catriona," chuckled Murdo, as he embraced her, "You look tired. Did you have a hard time?"

"I'm dying for a glass of wine and a –something sizzly, Murdo. Be a dear and get me some chicken, or even a burgher if there is any left. I'm dead on my feet."

There was a general murmur of sympathy as Catriona lowered herself wearily into a reclining chair

Belle regaled her with the tale of the sweater. Bringing the first smile to Catriona's drawn face.

"Ruth!" she exclaimed in wonder. "What a mystery woman! I hope there's some credible explanation for it all."

More general speculation followed, becoming wilder and more fanciful as the wine flowed.

Eventually Murdo posed the question everyone had been dying to ask. What happened at your meeting with the Prime Minister, if you are at liberty to talk about it?

Catriona pinched her nose delicately, frowning in concentration.

"There's no harm in telling you. I've made a statement to the media already. It will be released in time for the evening news."

Negotiations about relations between the Scottish Assembly and the Westminster Government have broken down. The Prime Minister made it quite clear that he and his Ministers felt that it would be to the mutual advantage of both nations if the Union was to be terminated and the English and Scottish nations pursued separate paths. He expressed regret that three hundred years of history should end in this way but matters had reached the stage when unrest could result in more and more violence. He therefore intimated that he would present a Bill to Parliament initiating the process of dissolution of the Union.

Faced with this fait accompli I had no alternative but to terminate the negotiations. I will now report to the Scottish Assembly"

Catriona paused as the angry exclamations from the others interrupted her.

"They can't do this. We must fight for the Union. Bloody Tories! There'll be an exodus of business from Scotland. Will the European Union accept us as a nation? The furious comments splattered around the group. At last the hubbub died down. Catriona rose to her feet. She announced,

"I'm going to recommend to the Scottish Peoples Alliance that we join forces with the Scottish National Party to take the Country into independence within the European Union. A General Election will be called immediately with that as a joint platform."

Murdo was outraged.

"You're entered secret negotiations with the S.N.P.?"

Catriona looked at him stonily.

"Yes, Murdo, I have. There was no other alternative."

Murdo spluttered,

But the Scottish Peoples Alliance was pledged to save the Union."

"Yes, indeed! And we failed."

Catriona stalked away: the others stared at her blankly.

CHAPTER SEVENTY

THE GARTO POND NAUGHTONWOOD

Garto turned out to be a nondescript piece of scrub land some way to the south of Naughtonwood village. At its heart lay a small pool of peaty water, its margins fringed by scattered rushes and other tangled vegetation. An animal track skirted the eastern edge, disappearing into the birch, elder and clinging brambles threatening to obliterate the little - used path altogether.

The regular beat of a wheezing pump disturbed the peace of the countryside, deserted save for a small group of people watching the pond being drained of the last of its water and liquid mud. The group clustered expectantly round a mechanical digger, ready to begin the process of investigating what lay buried at the bottom of the pool. Generations of gullible children had been scared away from the area by parents' tales that the pool was bottomless. In fact it was revealed to be no more than eight feet deep, strewn with old bike frames, skeins of barbed wire, assorted bottles, nameless bits of agricultural implements, and - four large bundles covered with layers of thick plastic, glistening black in the sunlight.

Amid exclamations of excitement the watchers instinctively surged forward to the edge of the empty mere. Professor Angela Bull's stentorian command stopped her half dozen student volunteers from jumping into the mud to retrieve the objects.

"You fools; there might be six feet of mud or peat in there."

Belle and Rangy, who had leapt forward as the bags appeared, retreated sheepishly to rejoin the grinning Murdo, Sir Rab, Natasha and Jade.

Angela had let them know that the pumping operation was nearly complete and had asked if they wished to be present when the excavation began, an invitation accepted with alacrity. The thrill of discovery, the hope that Belle's theory would be borne out by events, had drawn them like moths to a flame. They watched as Angela directed the use of a long pole to grab the bags and drag them the short distance to the bank.

The parcels, heavily wrapped presumably in an attempt to make them waterproof, were clearly of recent origin, unlike many of the other exposed debris. The students carried them to a makeshift shelter, an awning over a trestle table, and stood back expectantly as Angela examined them. There was nothing to indicate what was inside. A nervous laugh followed a whispered aside by one of the students that they might contain body parts.

Angela silenced the young people with a glare.

"Let's slit one open carefully and we'll soon find out," she boomed, red-faced beneath her signature bush hat.

A Stanley knife made quick work of the plastic, digging its way through the layers. A glint of silver appeared and then a jumble of cups, brooches rings and a torc.

Whoops of delight, backslapping and general jubilation followed. Belle was in tears; Professor Bull was choking with emotion; even Sir Rab was animated, excitedly pointing out a particularly fine piece of silverware to a laughing Natasha. Rangy asked if he could open the last parcel, larger than the others. Eagerly, clumsily, he slit it open. It contained more silver and gold artifacts and a small waterproof bag of transparent plastic. Inside was a letter, clearly addressed to Belle Ramsay. Everyone looked at Belle who accepted it, white and trembling.

"It's in Ruth's handwriting," she muttered thickly. The others waited expectantly

"I'm almost afraid to open it," she faltered.

"Go and sit in the Jeep," Natasha suggested, "That'll give you some privacy."

Gratefully Belle clambered into the S.U.V. and opened the envelope.

My dearest Belle,

If you ever read this letter you will have learned of my guilty secret. I realise that what I did was irrational and plain wrong. I could blame my illness for I have been aware for some time of losing control but my action in spiriting away the Treasure was more than that of a mad old woman. I was sickened by the bickering and haggling over the destination of the Hoard, the intense media attention, and the likelihood that the Stone and the Treasure would be torn away from their origins, from Naughtonwood, Nechtan's Place - I am sure it was the eighth century King Nechtan - and exhibited in some soulless museum. For better or worse I decided I couldn't allow that to happen. I had the perhaps silly idea that if the Treasure was concealed until the initial furore had died down this plea from me would ensure that all the historical remains would be allowed to remain where they should be - in Naughtonwood.

So I left a clue for you, Belle, to find the Calabar Hoard. I know you will do your best to ensure that it remains in sight of my beloved Ochils.

Your loving friend,
Ruth

Belle was in floods of tears, bowed over the steering wheel of the vehicle when Natasha appeared to comfort her. Dumbly, Belle proffered the letter. Sombrely Natasha read it out to the assembled group.

"Poor demented old woman," muttered one of the students.

Sir Rab rounded on him fiercely.

"Be quiet, sonny. Baroness McFranklin was a great lady with a passion for her country and its heritage. What she did was with the finest of intentions. I will do all in my power to ensure that her wishes are carried out. There was a general murmur of agreement. Belle whispered,

"Thank you," as she dried her tears with a sodden tissue. She lifted her eyes to the rampart of the hills and pictured an indomitable Ruth striding along the tops.

The Professor brought everyone back to earth.

"Sir Rab, may we shift all this stuff to the Bruce Tower Museum for inspection?"

"Certainly, I'll make it ready immediately," Rab responded

"Meantime there is much work to be done here," she continued.

The others stared at her.

"But we've recovered the Treasure," Jade protested.

Angela smiled.

"You are all in for a treat. These sacred pools were used by the ancients as places where they deposited all sorts of artifacts for whatever reason- to placate the Gods, to avoid the use of a dead person's belongings by others, to guarantee good health, to protect themselves from evil spirits. Who knows? We do know that many and varied articles have been retrieved from watery resting places. I think we have a good chance of finding some in this pool. Be prepared to get very wet and muddy."

Laughing she made her way to the pool, excited students in her wake. Rangy and Jade, inseparable now, nodded to each other and followed. Belle and Murdo raced after them. Sir Rab, shaking his head at such exuberance, sat in the S.U.V. to watch proceedings.

The driver of the digger had worked with the Professor before. A skilled operator, he knew exactly what was expected of him. Carefully he skimmed layers of mud from the bottom of the pool, depositing it on the bank. Soon a shout stopped the machine. One of the students held aloft what appeared to be a broken pot. This discovery was followed in quick succession by coins, broken weapons and other unidentifiable objects. Covered with mud the students toiled for hours until the discoveries dwindled and stopped.

"One last drag round the edge," pleaded the driver, enthusiastic to the last.

"O.K.!" shouted Angela. "Then we call it a day."

The blade cut through the peat at the edge of the pool and was brought to an abrupt halt by Rangi, windmilling his arms frantically.

"There's something here. It looks like a body. Yes it is."

Angela strode over and organised a careful partial excavation. An hour later the preserved body, the colour of tanned leather, lay exposed on the peaty surface. It was dressed in padded leather. By its side lay a helmet and square shield.

Professor Bull sat back on her haunches.

In an awed voice she announced,

"People, I think we have uncovered the body of a Pictish Warrior.

EPILOGUE

SUMMARY OF A REPORT TO THE PRINCIPAL, ST REGULUS UNIVERSITY BY PROFESSOR ANGELA BULL

SUBJECT

The Pictish remains discovered at the village of Naughtonwood, Drumannanshire over the period 2009-2012

1) The Nechtan Stone

A stone, sculptured in relief, found in a souterrain at 3 The Castle, Naughtonwood.

> This stone, popularly known as Nechtan's Stone, was discovered by the owner of the above property when he was converting an old barn into a garage. Excavations revealed the entrance to an intact souterrain in which lay recumbent an eight foot sandstone slab which had not been weathered by the elements. Carved on both sides, the stone proved to be of the Class 11 variety, sculptured in relief rather than incised as Class 1 stones were. The exposed side featured the Crescent and V-Rod and Double Disc and Z-Rod Pictish symbols, a hunting scene and the beginnings of an inscription in Latin and duplicated in an unknown language. Not enough of the inscription had been completed to enable the unknown, presumably Pictish, letters to be deciphered. The Latin inscription read Regnum Nechtani. Only the word Nechtan could be deciphered in the other writing. Regnum Nechtani probably means Nechtans Kingdom or Nechtans Land.

> On the reverse side of the slab was carved a magnificent Christian Cross, surrounded by intricate Celtic designs. Traces of colouring were detected on the slab.

> My department has almost completed a detailed analysis of the stone. A full report will follow shortly

Initial Conclusion.

Our initial conclusion is that the stone commemorated an important personage of the eighth century, probably Nechtan, King of the Southern Picts, or possibly of the whole of Pictland. One can only speculate as to why the stone was in an unfinished state and why it was interred. Likewise one can only speculate about the purpose of the stone. From the inscription it would seem that Nechtan was erecting it to lay claim to the "debatable land" between the Ochil Hills and the River Forth. A tantalising discovery!

2) The Hoard (popularly known as the Calabar Hoard after the nickname of the village)

Subsequent to the discovery of the Nechtan Stone, excavation at the top of the sloping lane called the Castle revealed a further souterrain which contained the finest collection of Pictish artifacts ever discovered in Scotland. Unfortunately numerous items of silver and gold were stolen soon afterwards from a transitional depository in the Bruce Tower Museum nearby and were only recovered recently. An inventory of all the items has been made (attached) but much detailed study will have to be made before a full report can be prepared.

Initial Conclusion

This discovery will throw much light on the everyday lives of the Picts, their clothing, their utensils, their weapons, and their decorations and artistry.

3) The Garto Pool

The Calabar Hoard was rediscovered in a so-called sacred pool at Garto, near Naughtonwood. Also in the pool were various artifacts, many of them broken. e.g. broken spears and swords. Importantly, the preserved body of what would appear to be a young man was revealed clad in the battle order of the early medieval period. He seems to have died as the result of a slashing blow to his throat.

Initial Conclusion

It would seem that the people of the time did venerate the pool for whatever purpose. How and why the body of a fighting man came to be in the peat at the edge of the water may never be known. Again much detailed study of both the artifacts and the body will be necessary before a full report can be made.

ACTION PLAN

An examination of all the material discovered at Naughtonwood will strain the resources of the Archaeological Department to the limit, resulting in a diminution of our teaching programme if additional staff and equipment are not made available.

a) Since the discoveries are of national importance funds should be sought from the Scottish Government
b) The cooperation of other University Archaeological Departments will be desirable.

c) The artifacts are at present housed in the Bruce Tower Museum. It is suggested that the studies be carried out there, a convenient central location. The owner, Sir Rab Bruce, has promised that any facilities we require will be made available.
d) The time scale of the operation will be three years.

Angela Bull

Head of the department of Archaeology.

BELLE

Belle Ramsay moved into the house in Allanford bequeathed to her by her friend Baroness Ruth McFranklin. After a surprise meeting with Sir Rab Bruce she was offered the post of Managing Director of a new, greatly expanded, Bartok Publications. She accepted with gratitude, and soon regained her old poise, drive and direction.

RODDY NEILSON

Roddy Neilson, the estranged partner of Belle Ramsay, found himself completely isolated after the merger of the Scottish Peoples Alliance and the Scottish National Party. A Unionist to the last, he had no alternative but to become an independent M.S.P. fighting a fierce lonely battle in the Assembly. He attempted reconciliation with Belle Ramsay. His approaches were met coolly but not entirely rejected. He took hope from this slight encouragement.

RANGI

Reunited with Jade, Rangy began a new life in the multi-racial state of Singapore as Head of Information Services in a new organisation devoted to research into alternative sources of power. Set up by Drumannan Holdings, the research facility was directed by Dr. Cheong Yu (Jade).

MURDO

A loyal husband, Murdo McLean McMannan swallowed his chagrin over his wife's defection to the Scottish National Party as she accepted what she called political reality. He devoted more and more of his time to promoting Scotland's heritage while adding to it with his own distinctive music.

CATRIONA

The First Minister of the Scottish Government, Catriona McMannan, successfully negotiated a merger of the Scottish Peoples Alliance with the Scottish National Party. The new Party swept the polls with Catriona as leader. She peremptorily took Scotland out of the United Kingdom and gained entry to the European Union as a separate State. She became known as the Ice Queen of Scotland, famed for her steely resolve. Politicians feared her glacial stare: the people loved her.

SIR RAB BRUCE

Sir Rab Bruce, disillusioned with politics, bent his energies to develop a massive industrial development based on alternative power sources. Before his vision was realised he suffered a second massive heart attack and died on the shop floor of a Bruce Engineering factory.

NATASHA BRUCE

Natasha Bruce, with her customary enthusiasm, invested a considerable fortune in a crusade to make birth control in developing countries a reality. Travelling the world, revelling in controversy, she became an internationally admired figure.

THE NECHTAN STONE
THE CALABAR HOARD
THE PICTISH WARRIOR

After protracted negotiations the village of Naughtonwood was chosen as the most appropriate place to display one of the most important finds of Scotland's Pictish heritage. Funds were raised from the Scottish National Lottery, public donations and substantial gifts from Sir Rab Bruce and Murdo McLean McMannan, enabling the creation of a heritage centre at the site of the various finds in The Castle lane.

Nechtans Stone was erected in a protective sheath at the top of the slope. The Calabar Hoard was displayed in a building replacing Kirsty and Dauvit Hunter's house. (The old couple was ensconced in a brand new bungalow on the outskirts of the village) The remains of the Pictish warrior were displayed in Weelum Ramsay's house, converted into a building with a controlled environment to preserve the body.

A thriving tourist industry transformed the village.

John McNaughton was appointed Warden of Naughtonwood Museum and Visitors Centre

The remarkable view to the Ochil Hills so beloved of Weelum, Ruth, Belle and Rangy remained unchanged.

www.ingramcontent.com/pod-product-compliance
Ingram Content Group UK Ltd.
Pitfield, Milton Keynes, MK11 3LW, UK
UKHW051255180426
11947UKWH00020B/1732